KILLING RAIN, KILLING FIRE

by

Joseph Hullett

Answer Publications

San Juan Capistrano, California

Published by Answer Publications
27511 Vantage Circle
San Juan Capistrano, CA 92675, USA

www.answerpub.com

ISBN: 978-0-9844597-1-1

Produced in the United States

To Mr. Spillane for his hero, Mike,
who was always there

CHAPTER ONE

"Hello."
Breathing. Some must choose.
"Hell-o-o? Pinel Investigations."
Nothing.
"I have time if you do, pal," I said.
"This is Dr. Sharfstein. John Sharfstein, I'm — "
"I know who you are."
Breathing. A sigh.
"Veronica is dying, Mr. Pinel. She wants to see you."
I heard a fly buzz and somewhere down the hallway a door slammed.
"Mr. Pinel? Are you there? Mr. Pinel?"
I noticed I was standing with keys in my hand.
"Where is she?"
"Nothing is imminent. Don't — "
"WHERE!"
"University Medical Center, but — "
"Twenty minutes."
"Wait, Mr. Pinel. Wait! Don't go running off — "
I slammed down the phone, stole a second to lock the office door, ignored the balky elevator, and raced down four flights of stairs to the lobby. I darted through a downpour to the lot across Main, fired my Blazer, and aimed it toward the hospital.
Veronica is dying, Mr. Pinel. She wants to see you. Veronica is ... dying.

Raindrops pelted the roof and blurred my windshield. Wipers pulsed with a feverish whoosh-slap-whoosh-slap-whoosh-slap. Hard rain had fallen for three straight days. The gutters were rivers. Some were lakes. And yet November was merely the *beginning* of the rainy season in southern California.

Veronica is dying, Mr. Pinel. Veronica is dying.

The SUV's oversized tires groaned as I seesawed through the tangled San Dismas traffic. I careened left at First and slewed right on Bristol. Glancing at the Timex Veronica had given me ... what? Just two years ago ... I let a trapped breath hiss out through pursed lips.

Three o'clock. And life goes on.

I punched the number for my answering service on the car phone. Waiting through the ring, I mouthed the words etched around the watch-face – words that certainly had cost Veronica more than the watch itself.

ALWAYS THERE.

"Pinel Investigations."

"It's me, Sylvie."

"Welcome back! You have a *stack* of messages."

"I'll swing by later. What's from today?"

"Repeat calls from Fred Lynch and Manny Vasquez wanting you to call them."

"Thanks. I have the numbers. You can start beeping me again."

I made another call.

"Cervantes," barked a voice. Cervantes was ex-FBI, now security boss for Sav-Aide Pharmacies. He had hired me to bust a counterfeit prescription drug operation orchestrated by some of his own people.

"It's Pinel."

"Don't tell me you're blown, man. Don't say it!"

"I won't be there tonight."

"What the – ! What is this?"

"Call Irv Castle. Anaheim."

"Call my *ass!* We've spent a month on this sting. You can't just — "

"I rigged the wire this morning. Irv can take the pictures."

"He'll take your Goddamm mug shot!"

"Just bring him up to speed. I'll still testify."

"Testify to save your *license*! Listen, Pinel — "

"Irv is honest. He'll — "

"Don't you punk out on me!"

"I'll call as soon as I can."

"I'll sue you, Pinel! Hear me? I'll *bury* you! Pinel? PINEL!"

I pushed the disconnect button.

Veronica is dying, Mr. Pinel. She wants to see you. Veronica is dying.

San Dismas Drive was a half mile north. I wheeled left on Memory Lane.

For real. Look it up. Memory Lane.

Great.

Memory Lane.

* * * * *

"Maybe I'm here. Maybe I'm not. Maybe I'm listening right now, but just don't want to answer. You'll never know."

I swallowed half a Sapporo — not my first, but I wasn't counting lately. I *hated* that message. It was *my* message, damn it! My words and Ronnie's Sam Spade impression, our little joke on friends who couldn't believe she had married a private eye.

"And save your breath about how you've never been this route and don't know the ropes. Just do what you gotta do."

Beep!

"Ronnie? ... Ronnie, pick up. C'mon, sweetie. Please! I know you're there, so pick up ... Just talk to me. I need to talk. I want to see you, Ronnie, please. I'm hurting here!"

The receiver was an empty, hollow thing against my ear.

"You know I love you. I know you love me. Dammit, Ronnie, let's *fix* this! ... Ronnie? Pick up. Pick up!"

The recording tape hissed softly like a burning fuse.

Nothing.

"Change your message. It's mine!" I shouted, banging down the phone.

Kicking aside the *Banner* front page plastered with still another round of Clinton/Gore fundraising shenanigans, I bent to retrieve a crumpled *People* page and re-read the society squib I had missed that morning. "John Sharfstein, MD, Newport Beach heart surgeon, seen at a South Coast Repertory fundraiser squiring Veronica Lamb."

Lamb!

Her *maiden* name.

It wasn't final yet. It wasn't over!

I poked the redial button.

"Maybe I'm here. Maybe I'm not ... "

Christ!

I waited.

Beep!

"Squired? Is that what they call it in the family papers. IS IT! Well, how about I go kick this guy's squiring ass! ... No. For...get it. I've tried, Ronnie, but I'm done. Don't bother to call, 'cause I'm not answering either! *Adios*."

I smashed down the phone and knocked it off the table. Simmering for a moment, I wadded the *People* page and threw it at the wall. Upending my beer, I staggered to the fridge for a replacement, then stumbled back to the couch.

I was half drunk.

Half of me was half drunk.

The *other* half wouldn't answer the phone.

I dialed again.

"Maybe I'm here. Maybe I'm not. Maybe I'm listening right now, but just don't want to answer. You'll never know."

I waited.

Beep!

"Oh, Christ, Ronnie. It's the beer talking again."

I glanced at my watch.

"Okay, okay ... it's 3 a.m. Sorry. Honest, I'm sorry! Go back to sleep and forget this crap. But, call me, okay? At least call me."

I stared at the watch and the words engraved on the bezel.

ALWAYS THERE.

CHAPTER TWO

Back in '98 things got sordid fast on Memory Lane. If you went too far, Memory Lane became Garden, a fallen stretch of dives and down-and-outers, peep shows and porn shops. At Harbor, whores trolled the sidewalks. Farther yet in Little Saigon, store signs turned abruptly from English into Vietnamese – a sight that still spooked me if it caught me off guard. But Veronica was a different trip. I turned right on San Dismas Drive just past the engorged River channel.

Cursing snarled traffic, I inched forward in abrupt starts and stops. Crawling past the County facilities on the right – the Branch Jail, Juvenile Hall, the Pound – I heard the baying of caged dogs. Olivewood came next, the county shelter for abused and abandoned children. Veronica worked there. I had met her there.

Veronica is dying, Mr. Pinel. Veronica is dying.

When I opened my eyes to honking horns, a space had cleared ahead. I jerked forward past the Juvenile Justice Center – a seven story juvenile courthouse flanked by offices and a parking structure. The complex was patterned in light pink and aquamarine, anemic pastels that struck me as bizarre shades for weighty things like granite and concrete and justice. Strange, too, was the court tower's glass dome whose thick panes were the murky green of armored car windows. The architect's intent, if any, was baffling, since the peephole cast little light on the Babel below.

Opposite justice sprawled a shopping mall. Spray-painted gang graffiti – *placas* – spread up and around the pedestal of the mall marquee. Scrub off the *placas*, bleach them out, paint over them – they reappeared next day, as impossible to eradicate as parasitic vines.

Beyond the mall, the soaring, lighted cross of the Crystal Cathedral glowed eerily through low clouds. Straight ahead, unlighted and almost invisible, a giant, haloed "A" rose like a steeple beside the stadium where the Angels sometimes played.

I turned onto Medical Center Drive and stalled in more frozen traffic. I remembered when the San Dismas University Medical Center was just a hospital – the Orange County Hospital – a few buildings and plenty of open space. All the space was gone now. I crept past a dozen new buildings, past trailer offices and construction shacks, past gaping holes in the ground and steel skeletons silhouetted against the rainy twilight.

Alongside the main building – the homely, old County Hospital slathered with new makeup – I swerved into an MD ONLY slot and jumped from the car. Bounding up the emergency room ramp through the automatic sliding door, I crowded into a riot of mostly brown poor – waiting poor, bleeding poor, moaning poor, manacled poor in orange, jail jumpsuits; pregnant women wailing on gurneys (*Ai! Ai! Dolor! Dolor!*); giggly children dodging underfoot; silent, ragged men compressing wounds. I barged down a short hallway to the main lobby and interrupted a gray-haired volunteer-lady gabbing across the information counter with an elderly university cop.

"Veronica Pinel."

"*If* you'll wait a moment," the woman began huffily.

"She's dying, you cow! Pinel! Which fucking room!"

The ancient policeman shuffled backwards and gripped his baton. Nervously the volunteer whirled her Rolodex, looked up, and stammered, "There's ... there's no one — "

"Pinel, Goddamm it! P-I-N — " I pressed my fingertips into my temples and ran my hands over my head to squeeze my neck. "Sharfstein. Veronica Sharfstein."

She flipped a few cards.

"Cardiac telemetry unit. Sixth floor."

I lurched at an elevator and dashed between closing doors. The car trembled and rumbled upward.

Toward Veronica.

Who was dying.

* * * * *

"I told you not to come here, Pete."

Veronica stood blocking the threshold of our home in Laguna Beach, a place her father had left her, the house she grew up in.

"Veronica ... ?"

"How much clearer could I be?"

"Veronica! You're acting like — "

"I told you I didn't *want* to see you again. *Ever.* It hurts too much."

"Let me — "

"No! No more talk. No visits. No phone calls. No quick coffees for old times' sake."

"Ronnie ... ?"

"Please, Pete, just leave."

"I *love* you."

She cupped her fists over her ears. "Don't say it. Don't say ANYTHING! I won't play this scene over and over like we did at the hospital."

I felt eyes peering from windows lining the cul-de-sac behind me.

"I can barely walk yet, Ronnie. Don't make me stand out here. Inside we can — "

"NO!" She flung her elbow to shrug away my hand.

"You're nuts! I *live* here."

"Community property? I'll buy you out."

I shook my head sadly. "Christ ... you *are* nuts!"

She lowered her eyes.

"Look at me, Veronica."

She covered her eyes with her hands. Her shoulders trembled.

"I'm *through* looking at you. Night after night I looked at you. I *watched.* A *month* sitting beside your bed in that hospital room. *Watching!* ... Would this be the night you died? Would *this* one?"

"You think it was roses for me?"

"You chose it. I didn't."

"Right! I chose to get shot?"

"You chose to go to that bar knowing it was *likely.* For what? For Jesus Ramirez."

"He's my *friend."*

"A friend? ... A high school buddy you let claim the life of your *wife!* Did you even think about me? Did you?"

"He was in over his head."

"And you saved him."

"Veronica, I told you —"

She grabbed my wrist and shoved the watch in my face. "ALWAYS THERE!"

"No one is *always* there, Ronnie. I couldn't be."

She looked bewildered. "Is *that* what you thought I — ?"

"What?"

She shrugged. "It doesn't matter."

"Be reasonable. *You* have a life. I do, too."

"Of course you do. And I wasn't in it. I don't even *want* to be now. People *died."*

"Who gives a rat's ass?"

"Stop it. They weren't animals."

"No, they were men. And they were *shooting me!* ... Look, Ronnie, I understand the bleeding heart. You're a doctor, you save people. But these weren't good guys, okay? Not patients. Not kids from Olivewood. They were — "

"Stop it. STOP IT! I won't hear all this again."

Her chest shuddered with choked back sobs. Her eyes were swollen and smudged. Black lines of mascara streaked her cheeks.

"What was I supposed to do, Veronica? What?"

"Think of me, that's all. Just think of me. You had your ... your friend. Your duty. You had your job. But where was I, Pete? Was I even there? You had your life. Where was I?"

"Veronica ... ?"

"We've played this out, Pete."

"Veronica, I *love* you."

She hesitated. Some must choose.

"... I *thought* I loved you, too."

CHAPTER THREE

The elevator jolted to a stop. I elbowed through the opening door and followed corridor signs to the Cardiac Telemetry Unit. At the desk sat two chatty nurses, their backs turned to a bank of flickering monitor screens. The monitors bleated now and then with the translated cries of nearby broken hearts.

Next to the chart carousel stood Sharfstein. I recognized him from a photo I had ripped from the *Banner* – a picture taken at his Four Seasons garden wedding. In the photo Sharfstein was nestling Ronnie under one arm while she showed off her ring. The sparkler seemed to offend a columnist covering the reception, Brent Kuntsler, who wrote, "Newport's most eligible heart surgeon can afford whatever he wants." The sarcasm irked me, and I had posted the weaselly little flak's nose on my targets-of-opportunity list.

Looking up, Sharfstein frowned. He tossed a blue binder onto a desk and hurried to block the doorway directly across from the nursing station. At six-plus, he was almost as tall as me, but *way* out of his weight class. Nevertheless, he grabbed my arms before I could bowl past him, and surprisingly packed enough grit behind his thin, white, surgeon's hands to stop me unless I knocked him down.

"We have to talk first, Mr. Pinel."

"Get out of my way."

"She's not conscious now anyway. Comes and goes. Listen to me a moment. Wait. Wait! Listen … no, just listen!"

Snorting, I allowed him to wrangle me away from the closed door.

"Veronica has been frank with me, Mr. Pinel. I know about your marriage, your divorce ... your, uh ... *incident* at the Four-to-Four."

"She told you everything, did she?"

"She told me enough."

He brooded something. I watched the second hand on a wall clock glide past the number two heading toward the three.

So he knew *enough*.

About Veronica and me. About the *incident*.

I let him choose.

* * * * *

"It's a diamond, Pete!

"Sure."

"I tell you, *amigo.*"

"Yag. Paste."

"Paste? *Mierda!*"

The swivel chair squeaked as I propped my heels on the desk and adjusted my shoulder holster where it poked my ribs.

"How does an *hombre* with holes in both shoes cop the Hope diamond, Jesus?" I pronounced it GEE-sus as I had since grade school.

"HAY-sus, you *cabron*," he shot back as *he* had since grade school. "HAY-sus! Not GEE-sus. Okay, look ..." He skittered behind my desk to the office window. He swept the stone across the pane of glass and gouged a long arc.

Scratch test.

"Paste, huh? Paste?"

My feet thudded off the desk, pivoting me upright.

"You've ruined my view, HAY-sus."

"That's San Dismas out there, *amigo*. What's to see? A Goddamm, dry river? Angel Stadium?"

"It's *Edison* Stadium now," I said, holding out my hand.

"Ain't no 'Edisons' play there, man," he grumbled, dropping the marble-sized gem in my cupped palm.

I closed my hand and weighed the diamond in my fist. Funny ... I expected a big diamond to be cold, like metal or ice, but it wasn't, it was warm like wood. I read once diamonds even burn like wood. Funny ... you wouldn't think so. I pinched the gem between my fingers and held it up to the light. I couldn't see through it as much as I saw *into* it ... into its big, pure, perfect, fiery heart. Jesus' yammering dragged my eyes back to him.

" ... so you just gotta help me move this rock, Pete, or I'm dead!"

Jesus was neither black nor white but mixed and re-mixed a long way back. Despite a Spanish accent, his natural born language was Bullshit. He boasted that he was Apache and maybe he was, but when Jesus and I played high-school football, his Dad was just another hard-working gardener. Jesus was a light-foot lad then, a high-stepping half-back you couldn't catch if he got a yard or two on you. I was a muscle-and-heart fullback who punched holes in the line for Jesus to slip through or took handoffs to drive in myself. Some mornings, my knees, like keepsakes, reminded me of those times and how they had marked us.

I positioned the diamond on the green desk blotter in front of me and shook my head. "Sorry, Jesus, you got me spinning here. Whose outhouse did you tip over this time?"

A tic tugged his left cheek and the scarred left eyelid covering the dead glass-eye. He rubbed his face and drew his hands through his black, shoulder-length hair.

"Lemon Tom!" he moaned.

"What! You hi-jacked Lemon Tom?"

He jerked his head. "No way, Pete! I swear on the virgin. Not me. One of Tom's own guys."

"Tom's own guys? Don't you shove a mop at the Four-to-Four?"

"*Que te jodas!* Swamping Tom's bar ain't the same at all, man. Listen, just listen. I'm closing up two nights ago and find Jackson skulking around the dumpsters."

"Jackson? ... Angie's shotgun."

"Right, right! Shaking like a wet dog, eyeballing the alley. He whispers me over and shows me the diamond. Tells me Tom set up a home safe boost for a cash bundle. Tells me the rock was parked in the safe with the dough, and, like, who's to know, huh? But *Tom* knew. Swept the money off his desk like trash and shouts "WHERE'S THE ROCK!" Jackson had to draw down to get out."

I looked at the diamond on the blotter, flicked it with my finger, and watched it flash as it rolled an inch or two.

Jesus had joined the Marines right out of high school, so he beat me to 'Nam. *His* tour was the shorter one, however, unless you counted the hospital time. Mortar frags took one eye, most of his knee, and *other* parts of him ... although, officially, the eye and the knee earned the monthly check. The check bought lots of wine and lots of grass. He said he wasn't in training anymore.

"Jackson gives me a gee to hold the rock 'til he squares it with Tom, only ... *Todo esta jodido*. It's all falling apart, Pete."

He dropped into the client chair and slumped forward.

"The airport stiff with barbequed toes ... " I said. "Jackson?"

"Right! And Angie's scoping my flop this afternoon. I barely got clear out the back."

"So your *amigo* fingered you to Lemon Tom?"

"*Amigo* my ass! *Un hijoputa!* I'm circling the drain, man."

"What do you want *me* to do, Jesus? Ice Lemon Tom?"

"Take his stone back, *amigo*. Tom knows you're straight. You can square me."

"Lemon Tom and I aren't buddies."

"But you're stand-up, Pete. Tom knows. He'll talk. I won't even get a chance to beg! Like the handoff, man. You take it and score."

"Lemon Tom's not some dumb, high school linebacker, Jesus."

"HAY-sus ..." he started from habit, then tailed off. His head dropped. DAMN!

"Grab us a beer," I said to keep his mind occupied.

He shuffled to the compact fridge next to the corner sink, flipped the caps of two Sapporo's, slid mine across the desk, and sank back into the chair. I punched information, then the number the operator gave me.

"Four-to-Four," growled a voice through jukebox noise.

"Lemon Tom," I said.

"Never heard of him."

"Cut the smoke, Maxie. He there yet?"

"Who the — Oh, is this Pinel?"

"Yeah. Pinel."

"Well, since it's you ... Never heard of him," he spluttered, hooting like a monkey.

Dying is easy. Comedy is hard.

"Tom! You here for Pinel?"

The phone clattered and I heard breathing.

"It's me," I said.

Just the blowing of his breath. Some must choose.

"Word's out you lost a diamond."

I heard a grunted aside as Tom covered the mouthpiece.

"I said word's out you lost a diamond, Tom."

"Is that so?" he rasped hoarsely.

Tom was black, and two ambitious skinheads had taken most of his voice when they sneaked into a Chino shower during his only bit and slit his throat. The first skinhead was lucky. He died in the act. Hacks found him with a shank handle protruding from his left eye. Despite running on "E" from the leak in his jugular, Tom had to be billy-clubbed off the back of the second guy who was blowing bubbles face down in a clogged urine trough.

A prison ambulance rushed them both to San Dismas Hospital where the second skinhead recovered well enough to die that night — apparently a suicide since San Dismas police reported no evidence whatsoever of foul play. As for Tom, the incident was clearly a case of self-defense and shysters even eked out a time-served appeal, since, although he had insisted, Tom should never have been housed in the open lock-up. Not for a charge like excessive force under color of authority. Tom had been a cop.

And a good one, too — for a while.

"I find lost things for a living, you know," I said.

Just the breathing.

"You deaf *and* dumb now, Tom?"

"You find something might be mine, bring it by after closing, I'll take a look."

"Wait a min — "

"Alley door. Alone."

"No good."

"Around four. Have a Mescal for old times' sake."

"Sure, Tom. A drink for the trimming you gave me in the station house."

"Be reasonable, man," he hissed. "You broke my nose."

"I paid for it."

I heard a guttural laugh. "Vasquez bargained you a discount, Bro. You walked out."

"Listen, Tom. One hour at the Amtrak station."

"Eating supper, Pinel, then I'm gonna take a nap. 4 a.m. Here."

"Buzz me when you change your mind, Tom."

"Sure, Pinel, another time's probably better for you. By the way, you still pal around with Jesus? You see him before me, say hi."

The receiver seemed to grow colder against my ear.

"I hear he moved to Seattle," I said.

"Yeah, Seattle's nice. I got friends in Seattle. Got friends all over."

Breathing.

Jesus wrung his hands. I downed the rest of my beer.

"Four a.m.," I said.

The phone went dead. I cradled the receiver.

Jesus glanced up, his real eye bright. "What'd he say, Pete, what'd he say?"

"Said to tell you hi."

"*Vaya follon!*" he wailed, shaking his head.

"I'll see him tonight."

"ALL RIGHT!" Jesus jumped up and skipped jerkily back and forth. "It'll work. I know it'll work, Pete."

I flicked the diamond again. It bumped across the green blotter shedding rainbow flares from its facets.

"I better call home," I said, picking up the phone. "Ronnie worries."

The phone rang three times before the machine answered. She wasn't back from her women's meeting yet.

"Maybe I'm here. Maybe I'm not. Maybe I'm listening right now, but just don't want to answer. You'll never know."

I *loved* that message! My words and Ronnie's voice, that false tiger growl from a throat that mewed like a kitten.

"And save your breath about how you've never been this route and don't know the ropes. Just do what you gotta do."

Beep!

"Ronnie, a friend's in trouble. Jesus. You met him that time at the restaurant. I won't be home till morning, so don't worry. Nite, sweetie."

Behind me, tracing the scratch on the office window, Jesus blurted, "*A la chingada!* It's Angie! Tom's guys are here!"

CHAPTER FOUR

Sharfstein chose.

"This ... this tragedy ... " he began.

"Forget the stump speech. What happened?"

"Everything's out of control anymore," he said helplessly. "Like no one's minding the helm. Like — "

"What the hell *happened?*"

He swallowed..

"A tragedy," he said. "A terrible tragedy. Perhaps a greater tragedy with you involved. I ... I chose not to call you until today. I loathed calling you at all. Things will happen. *Bad* things."

I felt a shudder, like the low rumble that surges through a building when the air conditioner kicks on.

"What happened?" I said coldly.

"She was ra... " It caught in his throat. "Assaulted."

The temperature inside me plummeted. I waited, stone silent, frozen.

"Jogging on the River Trail. You *must* have seen the news?" *The River Trail Jogger!*

I *knew* then. I knew the beginning. And more! With those words, whole like a memory, I knew the *end* as well, the end that Sharfstein feared; the bad things that followed from that beginning like the conclusion to a syllogism.

The River Trail Jogger, an Eyewitness News tag seized by the wire services – an unnamed, Newport Beach woman beaten, gang raped and *discarded* beneath the haloed "A" behind Angel Stadium on the San Dismas River Trail.

I remembered the word clearly.

DISCARDED!

LIKE WASTE WATER!

No heart remained inside me. No veins. No blood. Freon pulsed through copper tubes and a compressor pounded midway of my chest.

A bum had found her – dead, he said, until he breathed life back into her and begged help from a passing bicyclist. The ragged bum had wept describing to the TV cameras her broken limbs, battered face, punctured body and the letters smeared across her naked, bleeding chest in excrement. An "F" and an "A", the bum had said, although police asserted it could have been anything, including the bum's imagination. An "F" and an "A", he insisted. For Fallen Angels.

Strained, the compressor forced liquid oxygen through me, immobilizing me until the moment when the end, now written, would *be*!

Fallen Angels.

Sheriff Gangbusters had collared the older ones for questioning. Released the same day, four sixteen or seventeen year old boys, giddy from the swirl of attention, spilled from the Juvenile Courthouse. Egged on by that columnist I remembered for his wedding ring remark, Brent Kuntsler, the Fallen Angels leered, pouted, and scowled for the news crews, then undoubtedly scurried home to watch themselves on TV.

I was watching, too. In the hotel room where I was holed up undercover on the Sav-Aide case. I remembered *one* of the Angels in particular – a gut reaction to the way his eyes burned in the camera lights. He called himself *El Tigre* and, watching him, I had hoped to meet The Tiger some day. His words sprang at the shocked reporters with a calculated ferocity registered in their grimaces.

"I wouldn't dirty my (bleep) in the (bleep)."

Absolute zero.

Inside me *everything* was frozen except the compressor itself — pounding, straining, overheating. Unstable.

"Tiger who?" Sharfstein said.

"What?"

"Tiger. You said Tiger. Just Tiger."

"Let me see her."

"Wait!"

He blocked the doorway again, but backed off when he saw my eyes. I saw them, too, mirrored briefly in his glasses, and I knew what made him look away and shiver.

* * * * *

"*A la chingada!* It's Angie! Tom's guys are here!"

"Stay back," I barked, leaping to the window.

Across Main two men piled from a gray Cadillac parked illegally in front of a boarded-up Savings and Loan. The short one was Angie, Tom's muscle. The other one I didn't know. They rubbernecked the block and then jaywalked.

"They ... they're coming in!" Jesus stammered, good eye wide and flitting. "I'll ... What'll we — Oh, man, they must've tailed me."

"I don't think so," I said, striding to the squat, box safe in the corner. "Four-to-Four's only two blocks away. Tom sent them."

I hauled open the safe door and tossed a taped, plastic-bagged package to Jesus. He caught it against his chest.

"Damn, Pete. I ain't shot nobody since 'Nam, *hombre*."

"Try to keep it that way, but if you do, lose the piece. It won't come home."

Jesus clawed at the plastic, then tore it with his teeth. He extracted the snub-nosed .38, broke the cylinder, checked the rounds, and looked to me for guidance.

"Tom wouldn't try me here. This is just recon, although for both of us, he might risk it, so we split."

I clunked the safe door shut with my hip and nudged Jesus toward the closet.

"In there. You're the hole card. We'll play it the same tonight."

"Play it how?"

I removed my wristwatch, the Ironman Timex Veronica had given me for our first anniversary. Engraved around the face were the words ALWAYS THERE — a less than cryptic reminder, I supposed.

"Show me your watch, Jesus."

"Why? It's the same as yours."

I grabbed his wrist and looked at both displays. Hours and minutes were good, but the seconds were off. I pushed buttons that reset the flashing seconds and synchronized the watches at 8:31:00.

"Okay. In the closet. Best bet is they'll tail me if I go."

The elevator shaft next to my office began to groan.

"They're coming, Pete!"

"Listen up! They're here for *me*. They'll leave with me, so watch the window. If you see them following, get gone. If they're not behind me, I'll double back and we'll try something else."

"Like what?"

"We'll make it up as we go."

"That's what we're doing now, *cabron*."

"We'll try it again then."

"*Mierda!* It ain't gonna work!"

"I got no play book for this, Jesus."

He scowled. "Yeah, yeah, in the closet. Wait here. Get gone if I can."

"Listen at the door," I said. "If this breaks wrong, shoot the gun."

"Through the door?"

"Shoot the gun, Jesus. Through the door, in the air, kill 'em both, whatever — just don't get *me* killed trying to make conversation. Shoot the gun and buy me a second."

"Right through the door?"

"I have to know you're with me on this, Jesus. You're the hole card. Are you with me, Jesus?"

"Yeah, yeah. Shoot the gun."

"Tom's office opens into the alley, right?"

"Last door. The one after the dumpster."

I scooped the diamond from the desk blotter and poked it in Jesus' shirt pocket.

"Okay ... Hold this for insurance. Get clear and stay invisible, but hide in that dumpster before three."

"In the dumpster?"

"Yeah, the dumpster. When I go — "

"Why the damn dumpster, man?"

"Look, Jesus, when I go in Tom's door, it's right fast or it's really, really wrong."

"It'll be right, Pete."

"Fine. Then I'll be out in five minutes to get the stone. If not — "

The elevator stopped.

"If I'm still inside at 4:10, Jesus, I'm making a *big* move, 'cause otherwise I'm not coming out at all. Perfect timing on this. 4:10. EXACTLY. Come through Tom's door *shooting*. Make some Goddamm noise!"

"Pete, I ... " His shirt had wet circles under the arms. Just like mine.

"4:10 to the *second*, Jesus. I come out to get the stone or you come in. Whatever it takes. Shoot the lock, shoot the door, shoot anything but me, just come through the door making noise or I'm dead forever."

"Christ, Pete! I — "

The door to the waiting room chimed. Jesus jumped. I shoved him into the closet and shushed his Spanish curses. A knock sounded. I tugged the .45 from the shoulder rig, jacked the slide to chamber a round, and plopped down in the desk chair. The office door knob jiggled. I held the gun ready in the knee-well and pushed the electric lock button.

The door swung inward slowly. The doorway was empty. I felt a sweat bead trickle down my back. Angie appeared and entered soundlessly, angling to his right. Some kid followed, shuffling left. Both wore red-nylon, Angel jackets. It wasn't that cold.

Angie was medium short with a droopy beer gut over spindly legs. Beneath the jacket, however, the muscles of his arms and shoulders were like sacks of potatoes. He had a cauliflowered ear, a fleshy, crooked nose, and slow, filmy, lizard eyes. Stripes of scalp separated sparse strands of black hair pomaded across the top of his head.

"Zup, Angie," I said. "Who's your skinny pal?"

"'S here's Button," Angie drawled around a soggy cigar stub mired between Mick Jagger lips.

Button was a red-haired, green-eyed, black kid — light brown skin with dark brown freckles. His face twitched and his feet did a little dance. I read him as tanked-on-meth or piss-yourself scared. *Both* were bad news with the kid's jittery hand stuffed inside his jacket.

"Thought you hung with Washington ... Lincoln ... what's his name?"

"Jackson," Angie said. He gestured toward his pants pocket, waited for my nod, then very slowly removed a red, plastic lighter and made a show of firing up his cigar with the long, butane flame.

"Jackson got cold feet." He blew a cloud of smoke my way. "Button's new."

"He hasn't learned his manners yet."

The kid made a mean face, but the tics spoiled it.

"Tom's nephew," Angie said. The black circles of his eyes rolled slowly in an unmoving head. "Been running with some street punks. You know how Tom feels 'bout gangs. I'm s'pposed to straighten him out."

"Like a Big Brother?"

"Whacha gonna do, ya know." The cigar wagged. "I can't refuse Tom nothin'. Who else ever cared about me, 'sides my old man? Take your hand outta your jacket, Button, nice and easy like."

The kid scowled but obeyed.

Angie plucked the cigar from his mouth and squished it between his thumb and forefinger like a sponge. "Lemon Tom says we should look at whacha got. Save ya a trip."

"I wouldn't keep a rock like that here, Angie."

"Ya got a safe there."

"That relic? You could carry it downstairs yourself. Wouldn't even need Mutton to help."

"Button," the kid said, pouting.

"I'll show Tom tonight. Say ... plenty of time. You guys hungry? Let's go get soft tacos."

"Where's Jesus?" Angie said.

"Jesus is a punk," spat the skinny kid. "He can't run from me."

"Ever play football?"

He looked away.

"I thought not. C'mon Angie, let's get tacos. I'll buy the kid an ice cream cone. You like ice cream, right, kid?"

Angie stared. No one moved.

"We could be here all night," I said. "Okay, Angie, look ... you know what's under the desk. I'm dropping the hammer so you can hear it, okay? Now I'm just going to put it away, nice and easy, okay?"

I lifted the gun between my fingers. My eyes never left Angie's eyes. I slipped the .45 back in the shoulder holster and stood.

"I'm hungry," I said. "You guys want to eat, you can join me."

Angie turned and lumbered out the door. The kid minced backwards after him. I followed, glancing behind at the closet door and the scratch test in the window glass.

Button stepped into the elevator. Angie waited.

"I'm taking the stairs," I said.

"I can use some exercise, too. Meet ya in the car, Button." The elevator door slid closed. Angie slapped his belly. "I don't lose a few pounds, I'll end up like my old man."

We took the stairs, side by side.

"I hear he's not doing well," I said.

"I moved him to a better nursing home, but all of 'em are shitholes. Christ, Pinel, I remember when that old bastard could lift a hunnert pound sack in each hand and one in his teeth. Barely lifts a spoon now."

Back when Orange County was mostly farm country, Angie's Dad had owned a bean farm. He lost the land decades ago to unpaid taxes, but even Angie needed bad guys. Bad guys made bad things make sense. Angie blamed a conspiracy of county politicians for some kind of crooked, eminent domain scheme and liked to say that his boyhood home was now a Neiman-Marcus. The mall that got his Dad's land had no Neiman's, but Angie said it anyway. It sounded right to him somehow.

We took a dozen stairs.

"He don't recognize me no more. Asks the nurse, 'who's that man?'"

He mouthed his cigar in silence.

Button was waiting beside the Caddy. I hopped in my Blazer and drove a few miles down Main to Carmel's for soft tacos and Coronas. Angie and Button tailed me, but watched through the window from the lot. When they left, I waved. Afterwards, I meandered toward South Coast Plaza and parked behind Nordstrom's. I called home on the car phone, but Ronnie was still out. I found a jazz station on the radio, set my watch alarm, and fell asleep hoping Jesus could find a hole until three.

Shivering, I woke at 3:30 and rubbed my eyes. A chilly fog had rolled in from the ocean and turned the orange lot lights into fuzzy, glowing jack-o-lanterns. Blasting the defroster, I drove back through San Dismas, pulled over a half block from the Four-to-Four, and checked the .45.

A few cars passed, but no pedestrians. At that hour public sidewalk was the private property of unlucky bums who lay curled on flattened boxes in doorways. One bum — up early or up late — sat braced against a building. Tangled, shoulder-length hair spilled from his black watch cap. Tucked behind his matted, red beard, a blue Navy blanket covered his body and legs, but not his bare feet. His toothless mouth sang "Amazing Grace."

When it was time, I circled the Blazer through the alley behind the Four-to-Four. A faded sign marked the back exit. An unmarked second door stood in a shadowed recess next to a blue dumpster. A cigarette flared in the darkness. Holding a long-barreled revolver *outside* his jacket, Button stepped into the yellow cones of my headlights and flicked his cigarette against my windshield. The butt exploded in a tiny shower of orange sparks.

I doused the lights, but left the engine running. I dropped from the Blazer, sidled over, grabbed the long gun-barrel and levered it backwards with a yank that almost snapped Button's wrist. Spinning him around, I shoved my left forearm into his neck and jammed his cheek against the brick wall. He wriggled and sputtered.

"You're about to screw things up, kid," I spit in his ear. "One goof, and it all unravels, hear me? Mortal stakes, understand? Mortal stakes! No way Angie told you to show a piece or hassle me, so quit improvising. Do it right and *maybe* you'll grow up to be a tough guy, okay?"

I stepped back. He raised his hands away from his sides and froze. I stuffed his rod into my jacket pocket.

"Behave yourself and I'll return this when school's out. Now do what Angie told you and we'll all get home."

I glanced at my watch. 4:02. ALWAYS THERE. I elbowed the kid past the dumpster toward the door.

"You first," I said. "Is it open?"

"'S open."

"Open it."

Button pushed against the metal door spilling a widening triangle of light across the alley. Gripping his waistband from behind, I shouldered him ahead of me and shuffled us both into Lemon Tom's office. Behind us the door eased shut.

Across the room Angie leaned against a green filing cabinet. A cigar stub rolled across his mouth. His slow, black eyes were motionless. In a padded swivel chair behind a paper strewn desk sat Tom.

"Let the boy go, Pinel," Angie droned. "Don't wanna push things too far, ya know. Get outta hand."

"That's straight, Pete," Lemon Tom rasped. "Kid's just trying to show off. Let's all be friends. Hell, I *like* you, man, you know that."

"You're staying right here, Button," I said. "No quick movements. Everything easy and slow."

"Easy, kid, easy and slow like he says," Angie drawled.

Button lurched sideways. I pinned his neck in the crook of my elbow and twisted him as a shield between me and Angie who had flattened against the filing cabinet as we both snatched at our guns. My fingers were on the .45 when Tom, bolting upright, roared a gravelly "JEFFREY!"

The world stopped right at the point where it could still go two ways, but any motion at all makes one inevitable.

"Do like the man says and stand there nice and easy," Tom growled.

The kid stopped struggling, but I kept my arm around his neck. When I saw Angie breathe, I released the air from my own lungs and let go the handle of the .45. Angie dropped his hands to his sides.

"Kid," I said directly into his ear. "Shooting starts, they'll go through you to get me. Don't play it any other way."

"'S my uncle, man!"

I almost felt sorry for him.

Tom sat. He picked up a wedge of fresh lemon from a plate on his desk, bit the pulp lengthwise, and slurped the juice that squirted out. Over the years, lemon acid had etched deep ridges in the enamel of his teeth.

"You do that just to piss people off, don't you?" I said, puckering.

Tom's laugh was a sputtering air hose sound.

"Grew up in the citrus groves used to be here. Orange County black boy ate whatever he could, oranges *or* lemons. I got partial to lemons, but I still eat whatever I can. Where's my diamond, Pinel?"

"Safe. Jesus has it."

The words put a chill in the air. Tom took his time selecting another lemon wedge. He sucked it dry and dropped the yellow peel on the plate. He rested his hand next to a crooked stack of papers. Angie rocked forward on his toes, just enough to swing his jacket open.

"Is that so, Jeffrey?" Tom said.

"'S bullshit! I took his .38 and searched him good, Unc. No diamond. I swear."

Angie's hand was closer to his belt. Tom's hand was nearer the stack of papers. You couldn't see hands moving, but, like clock hands, they *were*. I tightened my left arm around Button's neck. My wristwatch read 4:08.

Tom shook his head. "Jesus didn't make it, Pete."

"I put two in that punk myself," Button boasted. "He's gone!"

"Your *amigo* is still in the dumpster," Tom said. "This isn't going down, man."

Tom's hand *touched* the stack of papers now. Angie's hand was *at* his belt. My watch read 4:09. ALWAYS THERE.

"Give me the stone, Pete," Tom rasped. "We'll work something out."

"Something like what, Tom?" ... *4:09:30 ... 4:09:40 ...* "Something like, maybe ..." *4:09:50 ...* "You won't eat my carcass?" ... *4:10!*

My stomach fell. I squeezed my arm and wrung a choked gasp from Button. Hands were moving fast now.

Behind me I heard the door crash open and the ululated howl of an Apache war cry. Surprised, Angie and Tom dropped a beat. *My* hand streaked straight for the .45. Angie was almost quick enough anyway and, heads up, I would have lost, but it wasn't heads up, it was me and an *amigo*. The .45 roared and Angie slammed into the filing cabinet.

Empty-handed, Jesus staggered in front of me and collapsed. Still holding Button as my shield, I wrenched him to face Tom who had grabbed the piece from the stack of papers and ducked behind the desk. Tom fired, hitting Button high. The kid arched backwards and buckled on me. We tumbled in a heap that left my gun pinned.

Tom reared and fired again. I felt a scorching pain in my chest. He saw me tangled and took his time like someone weighing choices from a dessert cart. The muzzle of his gun circled lazily from my head to my heart to my gut to my groin. A grin bared his teeth.

Mostly dead, but still running the audible he had to call when Button took his gun, Jesus forced out one more gargled whoop. The God-awful noise distracted Tom just enough for me to ram my hand *all* the way under Button, angle the .45, and snap off – BAM-BAM – two Hail Mary shots. The first missed. The second hit Lemon Tom square in the bridge of the nose I had broken. The slug blasted out the back of his skull and bounced him off the wall.

I kicked loose from Button and rolled toward Angie. No need. Leaving a red streak, he had slumped down the filing cabinet to a sitting position. His head hung forward loosely. The mushy cigar drooped in his lips.

The room reeked of gun smoke. Doubled on his side, Jesus lay motionless.

I gripped his shoulder and tugged him over.

"Mother of God!" he moaned. His shirt was blood-soaked front and back. His Apache face was whiter than mine. "Shee-it man ... you could've been a Goddamm four-star *general* in 'Nam. This plan was fucked!"

My left side was turning to wood, making it hard to suck air. I coughed and spat out a mouthful of clotted blood. A cocking hammer jerked my head around. Button had drawn the confiscated .38.

"Punk!" he snarled. Strangely, he wasn't pointing the gun at me. He fired, hitting Jesus in the spine.

I fell across Jesus and brought my fist around just as the .38 barked again. A bullet ripped into my flank, but my .45 bucked twice and knocked Button backwards. Collapsing, I closed my eyes and bled, but I didn't die.

After a while, I coughed again.

"Get off me," Jesus groaned.

I rolled away. "Sorry, man. I keep thinking you're dead."

"You Goddamm generals think too Goddamm much."

I pushed up onto an elbow and dragged Jesus into my lap. His legs were flaccid. I scooted us a foot or so to rest against the open door. I saw blood on the door, the alley pavement, and the side of the dumpster. Through his shirt I felt his pumping heart and a hot oozing against my fingers.

"You're hurt bad," I said.

"Just ... a scratch," he panted.

Scratch test. I held him close since the night was cold.

"Where's the diamond?"

"Figured a frisk and stuck it in my mouth. Button shot me ... I swallowed the sonuvabitch! Coroner will probably put his kids through college."

A wail of sirens grew louder.

"They're coming, man. Hang on," I said.

Nothing.

" ... Jesus?"

"Keep thinking, you fucking Westmoreland. I ain't dead yet."

CHAPTER FIVE

Veronica's room reeked with the commingled odors of flowers and infirmity. I recalled the smell from my own hospital room after the shootout. Sour urine and Sweet Williams, diarrhea and Daffodils, foul breath and Forget-Me-Nots all had fused finally into a singular stench that I carried away with me like cigarette smoke in clothes, and nothing – flowers, cotton candy, fresh air, cinnamon toast – *nothing* had smelled right since.

Rain beat against the window pane. The glass was a mirror. I saw two rooms, two beds, two patients.

"She's alone," I said.

"She's monitored." A green spark traced a jagged line across a tiny screen mounted above the bed. Sharfstein's eyes followed the spark. "The nursing station is just across the hall. Someone checks her every fifteen minutes and the call button is — "

"She wakes alone."

"Everything possible is done," he said brusquely, adjusting the pinch-wheel valve on an intravenous line. "I can't just *wait* here."

I brushed past Sharfstein, opened the door, and shoved it against the wall-mounted, locking mechanism.

"Nurse!" I snapped.

A woman rushed over. "What is it?"

"Get someone in here. Twenty-four hours."

"Excuse me, but ... *who* are you?"

"The guy getting someone in here."

"Dr. Hiatt is Mrs. Sharfstein's attending. Unless he orders a private nurse, I can't — "

"Nurse, aide, whatever. A human being."

"But — "

"DO IT!"

She puckered her face professionally. "It *isn't* medically necessary."

"You've logged a lot of dying time, have you? You *know* how it feels to be dying alone in a stinking room? Waking alone? Falling asleep alone? While you're *dying*? No? ... Well go find out, Cookie. *Then* tell me what's necessary."

"COOKIE! I — "

"It's all right, nurse," Sharfstein interjected. "Hiatt will sign for the special. I'll see to it."

"And this door stays open unless someone is in here with her."

The nurse grimaced. "But, Dr. Sharfstein ... her *sleep?*"

"The sitter will be here. Just when the sitter has to step away," he said.

She whirled and stamped out.

I moved to the bed, looked at Veronica's face, then cataloged all the rest before I dared see her face again.

She lay engulfed in a slurry of sensory overload and deprivation. The light was too bright for sleep, too dim for consciousness – a dreamscape of misperceived shadows. Sound was a deluge of equivocal bubbles, gurgles, beeps and hisses – white noise. Closing my eyes, I was back there again.

Limbo.

I opened my eyes. A sheet covered her body from neck to knees. A cage-like frame surrounded the bed. Anchored to the frame were ropes, pulleys, and weights. On the folded head of the bed, her torso was propped almost vertical. Her thighs angled upwards, supported by weighted traction cords fixed to silver screws that pierced each knee. Her calves dangled downward in sheepskin-covered slings.

Wires, cords, and tubes entangled her like vines. Small tubes – sagging tendrils that coiled around her arms – drooped from bulging, fluid filled, IV bags. Another tube connected nasal prongs to a bubbling, water-filled jar on the wall. A larger tube snaked from beneath the sheet to a two-chambered, clear-plastic, chest-tube box hanging from the foot of her bed. With each staccato puff of her breath, the red liquid in the chest tube box swelled. Every few breaths the liquid shuddered as a loosed bubble rose to the surface.

I clenched my jaws and looked again at her disfigured face, bruised in a gruesome patchwork of purple, green and blue. Her closed eyelids were black and swollen. Her mouth gaped around broken and missing teeth. Her head lolled forward. Above her right ear was a shorn, white oval of stubble-shadowed scalp. An angry red scar looped the oval.

I dragged Sharfstein into the hall.

"Tell it," I said.

Sharfstein retreated to that cold redoubt doctors construct for themselves. His voice was as hard as an autopsy table.

"Blunt head trauma. Probably from a pistol-whipping. Right parietal depressed skull fracture, subdural hematoma and cortical laceration. Left hemiparesis."

"Meaning?"

"Brain damage. She's paralyzed on the left side."

"Is she ... ? I mean, is she still ... ?"

"Is she still Veronica? Yes, Mr. Pinel. Yes. Yes, she is *still* Veronica!" The ice in his voice cracked. "Maybe she was unconscious. I pray that she was unconscious!"

"What else?"

Words escaped like hissing steam.

"They spread her legs wide enough to shatter her hip sockets. They stabbed her *seven* times!"

"Frenzied?"

"No. Deliberate. A pattern."

"Torture? ... What did they want?"

"Her agony, I think. The wounds caused peritonitis."

I winced.

"Worse than what you suffered. The closure was contaminated. The sutures didn't hold."

" ... *Open?*"

He nodded. "Plus two of the stab wounds were directly to her heart."

"But she's still alive. How — ?"

He frowned searching for words. "You wouldn't understand."

"I graduated from San Dismas. *Try* me!"

He took a deep breath. "Surrounding the heart is a kind of sac."

"Pericardium."

"When the heart bleeds, the pericardium sometimes acts like a tourniquet. Tamponade, it's called. Cardiac tamponade. That's what happened with Veronica. She lasted long enough for the best trauma man in Orange County to save her."

"Hiatt?"

"Right. The one who saved you. He repaired the holes in her heart, but the muscle was severely damaged."

"She could still — "

"HER HEART IS GONE, GOD DAMN IT! GONE!"

He glanced toward the startled nurses in the nursing station and lowered his voice.

"Dead heart muscle doesn't regenerate. She's in heart failure. *Terminal* heart failure."

"So *do* something," I said.

"She's failing."

"*You're* failing!"

"Nothing," he said, staring at his hands.

I shoved him. "Goddamm quack. I'll get someone who — "

He shoved back. "Kiss my ass, Pinel! I'm at *least* as good at heart surgery as you are at whatever *you* do. And if that's not enough, *Hiatt* is her doctor. You think she has less than the best? My own team at Hoag evaluated her. San Diego and UCLA transplant teams, too. There's nothing left to build on. I'd save her if I could. I'd operate myself if I could save her. But I can't. I can't and you can't. She's *dying*."

I let it sink in. "Does ... does she hurt?"

"Yes."

"*Why*? If she's dying, give her whatever it takes."

"She gets morphine continuously via the IVAC. That one." He pointed through the open doorway to a blinking, hat-stand-like machine. "But she can barely breathe, and pain medications depress respiration. We *can't* give her enough."

"But ... she's *hurting*!"

Sharfstein paused. I could tell he was choosing his words carefully.

"I'm sure you've seen heroin overdoses," he said. "The pink froth that bubbles from the mouth?"

"I've seen it."

"That's pulmonary edema. With too much heroin, morphine, *any* narcotic – water and blood fill the lungs. Air causes it to froth. You suffocate. Heart failure *also* causes pulmonary edema. Veronica's lungs are already saturated from heart failure. *Any* additional morphine will kill her." His eyes bored into me. "At the point she stops hurting, Pinel, she dies."

A gray haired nurse, stethoscope draped around her neck, scooted past us into the room. She hooked the stethoscope into her ears, then wrapped a blood pressure cuff around Veronica's arm. Pressing the stethoscope bell against Veronica's arm with her thumb, she pumped the squeaky, rubber bulb and suddenly exclaimed, "Dr. Sharfstein, I think she's waking."

"Go on in," he said.

"Aren't you — "

"She asked for you."

Sharfstein gestured to the nurse who removed the cuff and left. I marched to the bedside. Behind me, Sharfstein slowly closed the door.

* * * * *

My mud-spattered Blazer probably offended the parking valet, but he smiled and said nothing. Staff at Dana Point's Ritz Carlton are primed for rich eccentrics who occasionally drop insane tips. When he made no offer to stow the jalopy up front around the circular portico with the Jag's and Bentley's, however, I realized that he was merely showing solidarity with a working stiff like himself, someone too strapped to afford a car wash.

I should have worn my Armani.

If I owned an Armani.

What the hell *was* an Armani?

I took the valet's yellow ticket, whispered in his ear, and nodded toward the rear hatch. He returned the nod knowingly and palmed an offered ten-spot.

An attentive bellman sprang to help Veronica from the passenger seat. The Blazer's big tires made it a long step down for a shorty. Rounding the car, I saw her swiveled in the seat with the pointed toe of one high-heeled shoe just touching the ground. The gaping slit of her slinky, black dress exposed pale thighs above dark stocking tops and a triangle of sheer panties. The bellman was *particularly* attentive.

Maybe they were Armani panties.

I shot him a look and promised myself the ocean would freeze before *he* got a tip.

The Dolphin fountain at the end of the walkway splashed and tinkled while three wind-whipped flags on flagpoles beat a ruffle. Enjoying the fanfare, I marched Veronica up the red carpet runner. Rarely one to snub her reflection, she paused at the glass doors, shook her head to flounce her hair and gave a little shimmy to settle her dress.

"Dinner at the Ritz. Quite a first anniversary celebration, Mr. Pinel."

"Live for the day. That's what I say."

"So did the grasshopper to the ant," she said.

Arm-in-arm we strolled through the lobby arcade. Skirting a Technicolor spray of tropical flowers exploding from a Chinese urn on an antique table, we sashayed down the colonnade toward the library bar and oceanfront lounge. Watching us approach, a tuxedoed pianist broke into a Gershwin tune.

"*The memory of all that. No, no, they can't take that away from me.*"

"I think he's playing for you," I said.

"Of course he is. But what makes *you* think so?"

"I see the way *Piano Man* is looking at you."

She laughed. "Looking or leering. You usually see leers."

She turned toward the Dining Room. I tugged her back.

"Coffee shop?"

"You'll see," I said. "After you gave me your present this morning, I wanted to do something ... fitting."

I held up my wrist. The shiny Timex sparkled in the warm cove-lighting. ALWAYS THERE.

She chuckled.

"I considered a Rolex, Pete. I did. But you're just not a Rolex kind of guy, you know?"

"And you're not a main dining room kind of gal, either."

"Oh, oh," she said. "I'm picking up a lounge vibe. Crackers and beer?"

"Don't forget the free olives. It's easy to make a whole meal out of the olives."

I steered us between long tiers of candlelit tables. The soaring lounge windows overlooked the high palisade of Salt Creek Beach, but on moonless nights the panes were black mirrors. Reflected candles twinkled like stars. I ignored the lounge bar and halted at the elevators.

"What have you done here, Mr. Pinel?"

We boarded an empty car. I pushed Four, the top floor.

"The honeymoon's *not* over!" she said.

I grabbed her around the waist. "It ain't over 'til the — "

She slapped my hand when I reached for the emergency stop button.

"Don't even *think* it!"

"Well ... the beach might be fun. No moon tonight. Remember the time we — "

"Right! You almost *drowned* me." She jostled me through the opening door. "Besides, there's a king-sized bed handy. *That's* where you were today. Here. Getting a room."

"And tipping the piano player," I said, leading her down the hallway. I stopped short and whirled her to face me. I didn't sing it, because I couldn't, but I said it. *"The way you haunt my dreams. No, no, they can't take that away from me."*

"Bittersweet," she said with a knowing smile. "Always a tragic core with you romantics." She raised a hand and brushed her fingertips over my cheeks and lips. "My knight of the sad countenance."

"Your Quixote? I'll take that as a compliment."

"It is, dear. It is. You *are* my hero."

"You can say more about that if you like."

She laughed. "Okay ... that poem you're always quoting ... the world has really neither joy nor love nor light? You *believe* that. I feel the weight of it on you sometimes like ... like a burden. And yet ... you're joyous and loving and bright. That's heroism."

"Down these mean streets a man must go who is not himself mean."

"Mean of you to steal the line from Chandler. But see? That's my point. A Chandler detective is something *I* could never be. I *need* sweetness and light. Mean streets would make *me* mean. I don't know *how* to be part of the nastiness."

"Is *that* all ... schweethaart ... " I said. "Chandler had the fix. Find a detective who keeps you out of it."

I flourished a key card from my pocket and opened a door. Inside the room (which should have come with a mortgage!) sat a tray of chocolate covered strawberries and two bottles of Perrier Jouet in silver ice buckets. Scattered over the bed, the nightstand, the dresser, and the floor were black and white balloons and red roses.

"I blew up the balloons myself."

"How Quixotic," she said with the playful tone of y*ou're it!*

"The chocolate strawberries I ordered."

"*Bittersweet* chocolate, right?"

I grabbed her hand. "Come here, you trained, psychological-observer smarty-pants. I swept her into my arms, kissed her, and whirled us in a circle. "Happy Anniversary."

"Happy Anniversary, Pete. Can we open the bubbly?"

"I thought you'd never ask."

I peeled foil from a champagne cork while Ronnie threw open doors to the oceanfront balcony.

"Later we have jazz in the Hunt Club. Dancing if we're especially quixotic. But first, a 5-star dinner right here in the room."

Planning to make a show of the champagne, I turned back to Veronica who surprised me with a show of her own. Framed contrapposto in the French doors, the full length of one leg thrust through the parted slit of her gown, she twirled her panties like a little lasso.

"No smarty-pants on my end," she said.

"Are those Armani's?"

"Naw. He wears boxers."

Since I had already eased out the champagne cork, a flick of my thumb launched it with a pop – a great trick when it works and no one loses an eye. I let the foamy overflow spill into two ready glasses, filled the glasses, and offered one to Ronnie. We clinked and sipped.

"So. About this 5-star dinner ... when?"

I glanced at my new watch. "Thirty minutes."

"Thirty minutes? However shall we pass the time?" She twirled the panties again.

"Jeopardy might be on," I said.

"Hah! What is *baloney*, Alex? ... Wait a minute. The Hunt Club? How will I repair the damage if you have your way with me? I'll look positively lewd!"

"Aww ... you say the *nicest* things," I said. "But, actually, I sneaked your stuff in the back of the car. The valet is sending the bag up with dinner."

"Always on top of things," she said.

"Not ... *always*." Now *she* was it.

"So I suppose you stashed condoms here, too, when you were blowing up all these balloons."

I winced.

"Damn! In the suitcase."

"For want of a nail," she laughed.

"*C'mon!* I don't carry 'em in my wallet anymore."

"Good answer!"

"Is that jealousy?"

"It's love," she said. She raised my wrist to put the watch in my face. "It demands something in return, Pete Pinel."

I sat our champagne glasses on the table and kissed her – a long kiss, a swaying, slow dance of a kiss that edged toward the bed like a Ouija board planchette gliding toward an answer.

"Thirty minutes *is* a long wait," I whispered. "If I can undo the knot on one of these balloons ... "

"Thanks for the image, Pete. Disneyland will *never* be the same."

"Or … we don't *have* to wait. Maybe it's time we — "

"Don't spoil it."

She let go, walked onto the balcony, and stood looking out. I followed and wrapped my arms around her. To the south Dana Point was a dark mass haloed faintly from behind. To the north lighted slopes twinkled and shimmered. Ahead of us loomed a black unknown.

"You *know* how torn I am about children," she said. "Working with kids, I see what can go wrong. It's the *worst* nastiness and you *do* have to be part of it."

"*Sick* kids, Ronnie. *Sick* families. Not us."

"Who can tell? It's not all poverty and squalor and lack of love. Sometimes it's … it's something inside the child. It's bad luck. Sometimes it feels like … fate."

"Okay, that's sounding *waaay* too much like me."

She turned in the circle of my arms.

"Then you understand?"

"I understand we have to wait for the damn bag!"

She laughed again.

"You're not much of a wait-er, Pete."

"Oh, what the hell. I like Jeopardy. Besides … there's *always* later, right?"

CHAPTER SIX

Confusing Veronica's limbo with a big sleep, nurses had doused the overhead lights with no thought to the countless moments her eyes would open to a world of murky shadows. The walls seemed to waver and sway in the monitor's flickering green glow. The bubbling oxygen jar added to a sensation I couldn't quite name.

When I touched her arm, Ronnie's eyes snapped open. Her mouth gaped as if to scream, but with no breath to scream, she struggled upward silently from the void beneath consciousness. Breaking through, but too weak to lift her chin from her fluttering chest, she raised her eyes. Recognition jogged a brief, involuntary smile. The strange half-smile left one side of her mouth sagging. I squeezed her right hand and felt a frail response. Tears spilled down her cheeks.

"You ... know?" she said, forcing words between shallow gasps.

I was remembering El Tigre's leer on the hotel television screen. I was picturing how his face would darken and swell when I clamped my hands around his throat and crushed his windpipe.

"They're dead, Ronnie. Every one of them. Dead! I'll—"

She floundered to make me see *her*.

"*Me* ... Pete! ... Look at me. *Me*!"

I bent forward to catch the words, tiny puffs almost lost among the wisps of her breathing.

"John told you? ... Dying?"

I held my breath until a pressure inside exploded.

"Yes!"

"Help ... me."

"How?" I begged. "How?"

Her words slurred. Her eyes reeled. She was sinking again. I leaned closer.

"*End it.*"

"No! ... Ronnie, no. You *can't* ask me that."

She coughed. I heard it rattle deep in her chest. Her lips quivered without sound. I placed my ear against her mouth.

"You ... promised."

"What do you mean?"

The words burst wetly against my ear like bubbles.

"I'm ... *drowning*," she breathed.

I watched her eyes flutter shut and clutched her hand as if I could keep her.

* * * * *

Gusts billowed the sheer bedroom curtains of Veronica's oceanfront cottage. Beneath the windows a wave crashed against rocks. I smelled rain coming.

"NO!"

The bedsprings wallowed. I jackknifed in the dark and lunged for my gun. Veronica bolted upright, kicking at the sheet and comforter.

"What? What is it?" I yelled.

"I'm ... I'm drowning!"

"Christ! I almost pissed myself, Ronnie. You're *dreaming*." The adrenalin jolt began to fade. "Everything's fine. Scooch over." I tried to pull her closer, but she batted away my arms.

"The light! Turn on the light."

"I'll stay a while. Just go back to sleep."

"Turn on the light, Pete! Light makes it go away!"

"Scaredy-cat," I teased. But when I switched on the nightstand lamp and saw her shaking, it wasn't funny.

"What is it, Ronnie? What's the matter?"

She didn't answer. She pulled her flannel nightgown over her legs, hugged her knees, and sat rocking.

"You had a bad dream, that's all."

"I ... I drowned again."

"See? Just a dream."

"No! I did drown once. I died. Really, I did."

"You *died?*"

"When I was twelve."

"Died *dead?*"

"SCUBA diving with my friend, John, and his parents. We ... we became separated."

I scrunched her against me. She relented this time.

"So *stupid*," she hissed. "You surface when you lose your partner. I knew that. And my tank was low, too."

She started to tremble.

"I just wanted to see this little kelp forest swaying in the surge. A half-minute, that's all. I swam in and rolled over to look up, but ... something caught my tank!" She stiffened. "Oh, God! Please, God! No!" She was back in the nightmare, back in the sea. After a moment she shuddered and opened her eyes. "Did you ever run out of air, Pete?"

"No."

"The mouthpiece sucks harder when the air starts to go, and ... and you *know*. Two or three breaths, no more. Somehow – it was pure panic, but they drill you on it in class – I ditched my tank and weight belt and remembered to chase the bubbles. I kicked, screaming with my last breath! The compressed air expanded, so the scream bubbled out for the longest time. The longest scream, Pete."

She shook her head.

"Screaming kept my lungs from bursting, but when all the air was gone, I was still kicking, still under water, and finally – I ... I couldn't help myself! I breathed. I breathed *water*. I was coughing ... coughing *water!* Choking water in and out. It hurt. It hurt so much. And ... " She grabbed my hand. "I was *so alone!*"

She started to cry.

"John found me. He and his mother gave me CPR while his father got the boat ashore. The hospital shocked my heart and put me on a respirator. Almost a week of that horrible, *horrible* machine! You fight it. You fight for every breath. Fight to breathe on your own. I was drowning the whole time.

Over and over. On and on. At night it comes back sometimes. Not a dream. Suffocation. I feel water in my lungs. I can't get air and I am ... so ... *afraid*."

I held her while her sobs faded.

"You never told me."

"Some great psychologist, right? Doesn't talk about bad things. Doesn't even want to *think* about them."

"I know guys like that from 'Nam," I said. "Thing is ... it's like breathing. After a while you can't help it."

Whatever she was doing to make it go away was working, because she chuckled faintly and scooted against me. "I'm glad you're here, tough guy." We were quiet for a minute and then she said, "You know, Pete, you *are* a tough guy. I've seen that part of you. It's damn scary, but it's also rock solid, and ... it feels *good* to have a tough guy watching over you."

"You read that in *Ms. Magazine*, did you?"

"Sure. Imagine Gloria Steinem as Emma Peel. In a leather jump suit."

"Oh, I have ... from time to time."

"One might sleep thinking she's awake, no?"

"Not *me*. But, okay, point made. So?"

"So, if anything were to happen to me ... No respirator. Don't let them do that to me. *Stop* them. It would be like drowning again. I ... I can't go through that. Anything but that."

"Are you serious?"

"Promise me, Pete."

I raised three fingers. "Scout's honor."

She reared like a grizzly and shook my shoulders.

"For real! Promise."

"Jesus Christ, Ronnie," I said, wrapping my arms around her. "I promise, okay? I promise I won't let you drown."

She began to cry again, long sobs broken by little saw tooth gasps. I waited for her to catch her breath. When I stirred, I felt her jump.

"I'm just turning off the light," I said, clicking the switch. I settled the comforter over us and snuggled her into the hollow of my shoulder. "I'm here, sweetie. I'm here."

The curtains swayed. The room was cold. Waves boomed outside. Beneath the comforter, her body was warm against mine.

"You're not going home tonight, Pete?"

"Can't," I said. "I'm on call."

"Are you practicing without a license?"

"Don't need one just to be here," I said. "Unless … unless you'd like to make it permanent."

The room was too dark to read her face.

"Be sure, Pete," she said finally.

"You know I love you, Veronica."

"For always?"

"For always."

We made love beneath the thick, satin comforter and afterwards we nestled like spoons. When I was sure she was asleep, I closed my eyes.

"Always there, Ronnie," I whispered.

CHAPTER SEVEN

The walls wavered in the monitor's flickering green glow. The oxygen bottle bubbled. The IV bags drip ... drip ... dripped. Hunched over the bedrail, I clenched Ronnie's hand as if I could keep her, when all I could keep was my promise.

"Don't ask this," I whispered. "*Please.*"

Her battered face was vacant, but *somewhere* she was drowning. The monitor – an implacable accountant – tallied spent heartbeats.

The frozen rage inside me began to crack. "I swear you'll *know* that they paid, Ronnie. Just hold on. You *will* know."

A knock at the door kept the cracks from spreading. The door opened and a doctor stepped into the room.

"Oh! Sorry, Mrs. Sharfstein. Didn't know you had a visitor. Want me to come back?"

White trousers and a short, white jacket branded him an intern.

"Would later be better, Mrs. Sharfstein?" He scrutinized her face, but saw no response and turned to me, "Should I come back?"

I stepped away from the bed. "Do your work."

"Name's Hurley," he said. "I guess I should say *Doctor* Hurley. I'm a surgery intern. I was on duty when E.M.T. brought her in, and ... well, I keep an eye on her." He retrieved a clipboard hanging at the foot of the bed and scanned the graphed dots and numbers. "Was she awake?"

"A minute or so. Right before you came."

He bent to examine the plastic chest-tube box.

"That drains the fluid from her lungs, right?"

"In a way," he said.

"A lot?"

Hurley was just an intern. *His* cold safe-hold was still under construction.

"Yes," he said sadly. "Yes. A lot."

Standing to interpret the monitor squiggles, he gnawed his lip and shook his head. The screen cast a greenish pall over his face. He noted the lighted red numbers on the IV machine, counted drops from the second IV bag, and adjusted a plastic, pinch-wheel valve attached to the IV tubing. Squatting to check an empty urine bag hanging from the bed rail, he ran his hand back along the clear tubing as if hoping to find fluid collected in the sagging loop. He scribbled notations on the clipboard.

"I need to examine you, Mrs. Sharfstein? Is that all right?"

Once again he gave her a chance to answer as if the chance were important. When she didn't, he asked me to step outside."

"I'm not in your way."

"It's a bad idea. I'm being straight with you. You don't want to see this."

"You know that, do you?"

"I know *I* don't want to see it."

"Do your work, Doc."

"Are you a relative?"

"She's my wife," I said.

His eyes narrowed.

"*Was* my wife."

"You're Pinel."

I wondered how he knew my name.

"Trust me, Mr. Pinel. *No one* should see this, least of all you."

He waited for me to change my mind. When I didn't, he took a deep breath and peeled back the bed sheet halfway.

Beneath the sheet Veronica lay naked. Bruises like an abstract, multi-colored tattoo covered her body. A railroad track of puckered sutures slashed downward from her throat. Unbandaged stab wounds pocked her chest like rat bites. Hurley examined the sutures and wounds, then peeked beneath a yellow, grease-coated dressing that acted like a gasket where the chest tube pierced her ribcage. Repacking the dressing around the tube, he drew the bed sheet lower.

From Sharfstein's description of her injuries, I knew what I would see. Hurley was right about seeing it, however. *Absolutely* right. I jerked my eyes away the instant I glimpsed the depression in Veronica's abdomen and the coils outlined beneath a covering layer of wet gauze. I didn't need the lesson twice.

After the Four-to-Four – when I was able to visit him – Jesus had schooled me well about contaminated belly-wounds. How, sometimes, the surgeon leaves the wound open for several days to prevent infection; or how, sometimes, as happened with Jesus, the stitches just pop-pop-pop without warning, like ripping pants, Jesus said.

You think you'll die, but you don't. A doctor re-stuffs you right in your bed. He jams wet packing around the edges of the wound to hold things in, covers the hole with layers of gauze, and douses the gauze with saline – *Holy Water*, Jesus called it. Usually they can sew you back together in a few weeks, after the infection clears, but every day in the meantime some resolute doctor changes the packing and the gauze and sprinkles you like a priest.

You try to look away, but you can't. You're paralyzed by the secret unseeable things inside, the snake-like coils that turn something in you to stone. Jesus taught me all about it. He did! You try to look away, but your eyes always return to the terrible prophecy revealed in your belly. You lay there – split open like a sacrificed augury – and the thing is, you don't die.

You *watch.*

But you *don't die.*

CHAPTER EIGHT

"Are you all right, Mr. Pinel?" Hurley said.

I shook my head to scatter the images. When I looked up, Hurley had replaced the sheet. Veronica remained ... where?

A knock sounded and the door swung open. A large black woman bustled in. She wore a gray sweater over a crisp white uniform and carried an enormous straw tote bag embroidered *Puerto Vallarta*.

"I'm the LPN," she announced. "You Dr. Hiatt?"

Hurley looked perplexed. "I don't believe I've seen an order for a special duty — "

"It's covered," I interrupted, glancing at the woman's name tag. "This is Veronica Sharfstein, Ms. Holden. Keep her company."

The nurse waddled to the bed, sized up the IV's, the tubes, the monitor, then patted the back of Veronica's hand.

"Poor thing. You scared, huh? No good waking alone, when you're sick. But don't you worry *now*, honey. Leticia will watch over you." She turned back to me. "If I do have to step out for a bit, I'll just prop the door open so this girl can see the ladies cross the hall."

"Why aren't you in charge of the hospital, Ms. Holden?"

She smiled. "It's Miss, honey, but you just call me Leticia, hear?"

I drew a business card from my shirt pocket.

"If she wakes, call. Service will beep me." I reminded myself to dig my beeper from the console and change the batteries.

"Yes, Dr. Hiatt."

Hurley chuckled.

I handed the nurse the card. "I'm not Hiatt, but he'll be okay with calling. Ask him."

She eyed the card suspiciously. "I'll *do* that."

The only seat in the room was a low, cushioned chair next to the head of the bed. Leticia ensconced herself in the chair, rummaged in her embroidered tote, and removed a Danielle Steel novel and a jumbo bag of midget Tootsie Rolls.

I crowded beside her and leaned over the bed rail.

"Ronnie?" I said. "Can you hear me, Ronnie?"

No change in her face. No change in her breathing. I took her hand.

"You won't be alone anymore, okay? Leticia will be here, and when she has to leave, someone else will come. I'll be back as soon as I can." I craned to whisper in her ear. "To keep *both* my promises."

I stood and turned to Hurley.

"Got a minute, Doc?"

We stepped outside.

"I ... I don't think I should be talking to you, Mr. Pinel."

"A cup of coffee? You drink coffee, don't you?"

"Well ... " He glanced at his watch. "Oh, what the hell. I need a God-damned donut."

The cafeteria was busy enough for privacy. Nurses, lab-coated employees, and visitors sat eating and chattering. I tapped a silver urn for two cups of coffee while Hurley selected a chocolate-covered donut, dropped it on the tray, and paired it with a humongous cinnamon roll.

"How about I buy you dinner, Doc? They *do* have real food."

"I just ate," he said, blushing. "Cripes! I used to be in good shape. Tennis. Running. *Now* look at me!" He pinched his stomach and shook his head. "Exercise? I don't have time to *sleep.* And sweets? I can't stop. Fifteen pounds since medical school. I think I have an ulcer."

I slid the tray past steam tables to the register, paid the cashier, and parked near a window. Outside – holding a jacket draped over an upraised arm to protect her hair from the rain – a woman in surgical greens dashed toward a doorway. I sipped my coffee and toyed with crumbs on the table top.

"How'd you know my name, Doc?"

"The trauma team keeps a bulletin board in the call room covered with your clippings. Hiatt turned your bar shootout into a legend around here. Told your story to the interns in July and repeats it to the students who rotate through. Tale gets bigger with each telling. Last I heard, you were Mike Hammer in the flesh and Hiatt personally wrestled the Angel of Death to win back your life. Your buddy's, too."

"That sounds like Hiatt, all right, but I'll vouch for any story he tells. I owe him."

"A lot of people do," Hurley said. "Every day lately a drug shoot-out or drive-by. Bullet wounds are a snap for me already. Soon I'll qualify as a battlefield surgeon." He shook his head. "Some war."

I picked at a dry noodle stuck to the tabletop.

"So that's how you knew Veronica and I had been married?"

"Hospitals are gossip mills, Mr. Pinel. Hot topic lately has been the lack of carnage. Most people figured you were off the grid somehow."

"I'm back."

He stared at me. Not a pleasant stare.

"Would it help to say I'm one of the *good* soldiers?"

He shrugged.

I leaned forward, weight on my elbows.

"Listen, Doc, is Veronica dying?"

He sat back. "I'm ... I'm just an intern."

"You'd know. Looks like you keep a pretty close watch. Sharfstein says for certain. True?"

"I can't say, Mr. Pinel ... I, uh ..."

"*Any* chance?"

A heaviness settled in his face. He jerked his head sharply from side to side. I watched him poke half a donut into his mouth and wash it down with a slurp of coffee.

"Soon?"

"Hiatt says a few days."

I pounded the table, jostling coffee from both cups.

"Why can't you do something?"

"I ... I try. I try!"

"No, c'mon, Doc. I didn't mean you *personally*."

He wasn't looking at me. I think he was seeing pictures in his head. He kept shaking his head as if to erase the pictures.

"She was *so badly hurt!* ... Accidents are one thing. Wrecks, falls, burns. I've seen it all. But this was ... God help her, this was *deliberate*. I remember saying to myself *she needs a Doctor!* And it hit me. For the first time it *really hit me*. I'm it. Until Hiatt could take over, I was all the Doctor she had. Just me."

He scowled. I think he was replaying the scene, watching himself do his work. Muttering something like *Hiatt caught the distention,* he shook his head again.

"I did what I could," he sighed.

All things considered, it was probably good enough. But what did I know and what did it matter. People built to make choices walk alone through the consequences.

"She said she's drowning," I said.

He blinked. "Sorry?"

"Drowning. When she woke she said she's drowning."

He thought about it. "Well ... she's in heart failure. Blood and water seep into the lungs. I suppose it *feels* the same."

"Will you put her on a respirator?"

He shook his head. "DNR ... Do not resuscitate. As soon as she could, she signed a directive."

I massaged my neck.

"So … so she just *waits*? Why keep her alive at all?"

"That's Hiatt's first lesson," he said sternly. "Because she *is* alive."

"You call that life?"

"It's the life she has. We promised to preserve it."

"She didn't ask for your promise. What if she doesn't want it?"

"Then … I don't know. Bad luck, I guess. Wrong door, wrong day, wrong emergency room. Bad luck."

"Sharfstein said pain drugs were out," I said.

"No. She gets Morphine through the IVAC."

"Enough?"

He hesitated, "As much as possible."

I stood. "Thanks, Doc. Keep an eye on her."

"Sure," he said, wiping his face with his palms. "Sure, I'll do what I can."

"Are *you* okay?" I said.

"I'm … tired. Haven't slept for almost two days. Sometimes when I get this tired, I wonder."

"Why you do it?"

"No. Just *why*?"

He gazed into the black window and watched the rain.

"Two people died last night."

"It's a hospital, Doc."

"A middle aged mother with half a box of chocolate covered cherries on her nightstand and an old man whose granddaughter is expecting next month. I was on call, and sure, sure … the art is long and all that. I did what I could. But why did it happen? Why were they sick? Why does Mrs. Sharfstein have to suffer? Isn't God on call?"

He glanced at me and looked away.

"Sorry. I'm not some religious nut. I'm *just … so … tired!*" He wiped his face and rubbed his eyes again. "Do you ever go to church, Mr. Pinel?"

"I'd rather believe it's just us. It's less scary."

"I used to. Go to church, I mean. When I was little. My

Mom made me go." He stared at my scarred knuckles. "An eye for an eye. That's what they say."

I said nothing.

"I wouldn't stop you."

"No?" I found myself studying *his* hands – wide palms with long fingers, a grip that never let go. "*Maybe* not, Doc, but afterwards you'd try to keep them breathing, right?" I squeezed his shoulder. "If I wind up here again, I hope it's *you* on call."

He cupped his palms over his mouth and nose like an oxygen mask, and gave a hollow sigh. I left him sitting with his coffee and half the cinnamon roll. I knew from his face that – rounds, spare moments, days off, if he had days off – he'd do what he could. For Ronnie, for all of them. His *patients*. I glanced back from the doorway and saw his sad countenance reflected in the black window pane. The cinnamon roll was gone.

* * * * *

Relinquishing city lights, Ronnie and I crested a sea cliff and faced a black expanse of ocean. A hot, offshore wind – a Santa Ana – beat against our backs, whipped our hair, fluttered our clothes. Ronnie stopped to knot her baggy, tropical blouse beneath her breasts. Impatiently I scuffed my running shoe against a tuft of dry grass and coaxed her forward. Single file, we picked our way down a rock-strewn path toward a vague crescent of sand fifty feet below.

"Ouch," she cried.

"What is it?"

"My toe! I stubbed my toe!"

"I told you sandals were a bad idea."

"This whole thing is a bad idea! It's dark. I can't even see the ocean."

"If your shorts get wet, you've gone too far. Here ... give me your pail."

"We could fall! We could — "

"Hold my hand. We're almost there."

"If this is your anniversary celebration of a first *date,* what would you do for the real thing?"

I stooped to retrieve her pail and nudged her down the path.

"Is that a hint, *Miss* Lamb?"

"Right now, Pete? *No.*"

I laughed.

"This is silly," she said. "Californians don't hunt grunion."

"Sure they do. I saw it when I was a kid. New moons in March and April, schools of grunion wriggle onto the beach to spawn."

"Sounds like Spring Break."

"People grab them. Toss 'em in a bucket before they beat it back to the water."

"*Coitus interruptus.*"

"Well, it's gentlemanly to let them finish. Anyway one character was called Moon Downer ... Moon Dogger ... something like that. Fred MacMurray was the Dad."

She pressed between two scrub laurels blocking our way.

"So you saw it in a movie? Did you personally, in real-life, ever do this? You didn't did you?"

"Well ... you had to go at night and all."

"None of your friends did this either, did they? I grew up on the beach and I wouldn't know a grunion if I saw one."

"They're small and long, I think ... silver-ish. Like little silver bananas only with eyes."

"Bananas with eyes. Great! *Tourists* do this, Pete. Californians do not."

"Sally Fields did," I said. "Annette Funicello did."

"And Fred MacMurray, I suppose."

"No. He stayed home."

We clambered over a small boulder and scrambled down a mound of talus at the base of a tiny cove carved in the sea cliff by tide and time. Ronnie halted when her feet hit sand.

"Pete, I hate to burst your bubble, but Sally and Annette probably grew up someplace like Pittsburgh or Nebraska. Honest."

"Look, Ronnie, you can put on Eastern airs if —"

"Eastern airs? I'm a native."

"So you say. Yet you scorn the Grunion hunt? Shame! Time out of mind Californians have braved the Pacific ..."

I swept my hand emphatically and grazed her with the empty bucket.

"Oww!"

She pursed her lips, balled her fist, and slugged me in the arm.

"Hey! It was an accident."

"That was, too," she said. "I was aiming for your nose!"

"Where was I?" I said, massaging my shoulder.

"Braved the Pacific, I think."

"Braved the brooding Pacific in search of Grunion."

"Oh, much more expressive," she said. "Brooding. Yes, I like that better."

"The dark of March's moon. Primal stirrings —"

"*Your* primal stirrings."

"Primal stirrings impel star-crossed grunion onto this lonely strand where we await, bucket in hand. The convergence of the twain."

"You've been reading on those stakeouts again, haven't you?"

"Henry Miller."

"Coals to Newcastle ... Look, Pete. What if there are millions of them? Billions? What if the beach is teeming with shiny, sex-crazed, silver bananas. Eyes bulging! Razor-teeth clacking like castanets!"

I dropped the bucket and shrugged a gym bag from my shoulder.

"Here. Far enough. It is not good for a man to go out too far."

She chuckled. "Wise move, Santiago. Now how about some light? It's scary here at night."

"I'm here."

"'Nuff said!"

I knelt to remove a blanket and a Coleman lantern from the bag. Veronica spread the blanket and sat cross-legged while I pumped the lantern plunger to pressurize the fuel tank.

"Should I rub two sticks together to impress you?" I said.

"Technology impresses me," she replied, removing a pack of matches from the gym bag. "Here. Close the cover first."

A scratched match sizzled, flared, and ignited the hissing lantern. Bathed in blue flame, the delicate mantles glowed red then stark white. I planted the lantern in the sand and rummaged through the gym bag for a bottle of wine and a box of cheese crackers.

"Open the crackers," I said. "You have nails."

"Which I'd like to keep," she grumbled.

I unscrewed the cap of the wine bottle, filled two plastic tumblers, and raised a cup in a toast.

"Here's to a year behind and time ahead."

A wave hurled itself against the strand.

"Listen to that surf!" I said. "Boom!"

"... And then a sigh," Ronnie added. "The wave's *regret*. We're very close, aren't we?"

I hoisted the lantern. Ancient sedimentary cliffs reflected the circle of light in oblique bars of black and gray. A thirty-foot high sea-tunnel pierced the south wall forming a black oval. Unseen waves crashed against rocks beyond the tunnel. A hot, changeable wind blew in then out like breath.

"Rocks to rollers about a dozen yards," I said. "Caught between the devil and the deep blue sea."

She hugged her knees.

"How do you talk me into these things?"

"What things?"

"Things! ... A dance in the park that turns into *Clockwork Orange*."

"Those punks were just bad luck."

"You're awfully lucky at finding bad luck, Pete."

I tossed back my wine and poured another. "If you're still carping on that Knott's parachute ride, I —"

"THAT! Don't even mention the parachute fiasco. I can't believe I went out with you again."

"It rarely gets stuck like that."

"An hour. An HOUR we were up there."

"They didn't charge us extra."

"An hour listening to you recount the D.B. Cooper hijacking – how they never found his body after he jumped."

"I was trying to distract you. Weren't you distracted?"

"*Quite* distracted." She sipped her wine and chuckled. "Remember that huge pillow they dragged beneath us?"

"The air-bag?"

"It had a bull's-eye on it."

"A coincidental, circular pattern."

"A bull's-eye! Comforting or what?"

"Fear of flying," I intoned.

"Flying is fine. *Falling's* a bitch." She shook her head. "How *do* you do it?"

"Animal magnetism."

"Really? You should get together with John. He's chock full of ideas about attraction."

"Who's John?" I said suspiciously.

"I'm sure I've mentioned John before."

"No. Don't think so. Seems like old *John* slipped your mind."

"Oh, Pete! We were childhood friends."

"I bet you played Doctor."

She giggled. "Well ... he is a doctor."

I sat up. "Great!"

She laughed. "You're not at all alike, but you *do* remind me of him."

Wordlessly we drank wine and listened to the suspiration of the sea.

"So where's Annette?" she said after a while.

"See the fires? Probably up the coast with everyone else."

"Uh ... Pete? Why is everyone *there* while we're *here?*"

"They don't know."

"Oh, I see," she said. " ... Know what?"

"That *this* is where the big ones come."

"The *big* silver bananas with eyes. Someone up there likes me."

"Stay alert. I think they sneak up on you."

"Well, let me know."

"Oh, you'll know," I said.

She lay back on the blanket and gazed at the stars. The Santa Ana wind had blown away a marine layer and left the sky twinkling.

"There's Pisces," she said pointing.

"Pisces?" I scooted closer.

"And Andromeda. Over there."

"Andromeda you say!"

"The sky is a calendar. The sky is a clock. The stars, the moon ... how *else* would the Grunion know that it's time?"

"Doctors," I muttered, trailing my fingertips over her stomach, bare between the knotted, yellow blouse and the top of her shorts.

She wriggled. "Stop it! That tickles!"

"Very sexy that hard, flat stomach. No stretch marks. Not bad for thirty-five."

"NOT until TUESDAY! And don't remind me then."

"What? You want to live forever?"

She turned her back and began to scratch in the sand with her finger. "Maybe. Do you know the secret?"

"No secret. Run an extra mile each day. What's-his-name – that jogging writer – he said no one ever died running."

"*He* died running!" She frowned. "My God! … How can life be so *unfair*."

"Time and chance, right? The race is not always to the swiftest."

"That thought doesn't give you the willies?"

"An occasional shiver maybe, but … I suppose I find it comforting to think that things aren't rigged. That what we do matters." I inched closer. "What are you drawing?"

She exaggerated her hand strokes. "'P.P.' plus 'V.L.' and a —"

"Heart with an arrow through it? Awwww."

She glanced uneasily at the cliff face. The rock seemed to writhe in the flickering lantern light. She turned toward the hard, black ocean. Catalina was a dark mass on the new moon dark horizon. A single point of light winked at the tip of the island.

"Have you brought many women here, Pete?"

"Told you, only been here once myself. Jogging along the cliffs and stumbled on that hidden path. I made my way down and found this little strip of beach. Lucky timing. High tide, I would have missed it."

She continued to doodle in the sand.

"Do you want children, Pete?"

"Whoa!"

"Relax, relax," she said. "I'm not proposing. I'm just … wondering."

"I'm not … *against* the idea, I guess." I gave it some thought. "Okay … Sure, one day."

"I *want* a child, but I don't think I'm brave enough. At the shelter you see how much can go wrong."

"Go for what you want and be ready for what you get. That's my philosophy."

"Be ready how? A child can be unpredictable."

"*Anything can* be unpredictable. But usually it isn't."

"Usually." She was silent for a moment. "Okay … what are they waiting for?"

"Who?"

"Who? The grunion, that's who! What's the hold up?"

"You're the Ph.D."

"And apparently you're a *philosopher*."

I chuckled. "Okay. Here's my take. They're waiting because they're ambivalent."

"Hey! That's one of my words. Stick to words like gat and shiv."

"They wait until fate aligns the moon and stars and tide just right and ... splash!"

"They master their ambivalence?"

"The brave ones *go* for it!"

"Right into the bucket."

"We..ll, they don't know about the bucket," I said. "And most of them make it. The ones that stay in the water — "

"Are smart."

"They die out. That's dumb."

"You think? Ask the ones in the bucket."

A breaker boomed. Veronica flinched as a tongue of foam and whitewater lapped the blanket.

I laughed. "There go the initials."

"The tide is coming!"

"Probably."

She sat abruptly and wheeled toward the high surrounding palisade. Lantern light etched her frown.

"We have to go back, Pete."

"We have time yet."

"No! Look. The line on the rocks."

"We have time yet."

"No. No, this cove floods."

"I bet you're right. Like that rock bench in *Toilers of the Sea*. He who sleeps must die. What's the French? *Qui* —"

"Damn it, Pete! The tide is coming. I'm scared!"

I rose to my knees and straddled her legs. Leaning forward, I forced her down onto the blanket. My weight pressed her hips into the sand.

"Pe..te? Not now! ... The tide!"

Deliberately I began to undo the knot of her blouse.

"I said we have time yet."

* * * * *

Rain stung my cheeks as I strode down the emergency room ramp. I yanked a ticket from beneath my windshield wiper, looked back, and saw Sharfstein peering from a second floor window. When our eyes met, he withdrew.

How carefully he had phrased it. At the point she doesn't hurt, she dies. How very carefully the son-of-a-bitch had phrased it.

I climbed in, keyed the Blazer, and aimed it toward San Dismas.

To do my work.

CHAPTER NINE

I expected to find Jesus at our regular haunt, Blake's on Main, an easy walk from my office, depending on whether I was coming or going. I parked the Blazer behind the old San Dismas Courthouse, clipped my beeper to my belt, and slogged around the corner to a green door beneath a red neon sign. Inside, I shook water from my trench coat and nodded to Blake tending bar.

Most San Dismas taverns were dives, but Blake saw to it that his was clean and well lighted. It was a boisterous joint, loud in a good way with men bullshitting, pool balls clicking, a juke box warbling, gabby ex-jocks pontificating on the tube. The place had a homey, rec-room feel, probably because it *was* Blake's home. He lived in two back rooms that violated a half-dozen city and liquor control ordinances that the judges and councilmen and lawyers who lined the bar made sure were overlooked for an old friend. That's the way you felt at Blake's, like an old friend dropping by an old friend's place. Blake was glad to see you. He called you by the nickname you preferred, knew your brew. You could park in front of his big TV to watch the game. Or you could shoot pool, listen to music, get happy-drunk and argue amicably and endlessly with the jolly-good fellow on the next stool. And if you thought the air was too smoky, the AC low, the channel wrong, you kept it to yourself, because it was *Blake's* place, not yours. And when, now and then, a newcomer ignored that fact, a few of Blake's *old* friends escorted him out the rear door and suggested Los Arcos or the Four-to-Four as healthier choices. Half of Blake's friends were cops of some sort, and half the rest carried guns, too. It made for good manners.

Eleven years back, two gangbangers named Luis Leija and Robby Banning hid in the store room until closing and tried to squeeze Blake for his safe combination. Despite their guns, he got *gung ho*. He landed a few, but the punks had twice the fists and feet and half Blake's years. Although they broke a few fingers and put a blood clot on his brain, they never got the combo. They made off instead with the 400 some-odd dollars in the till.

This happened before Lemon Tom owned the Four to Four, before Chino, back when he was still watch commander. After a sixteen hour day, Tom liked to share his loneliness with other Blake regulars who only had home waiting. He liked the noise. He liked watching Johnny Carson, especially the Amazing Carnac who knew answers to the questions written before. He liked the warm mescal and the lemon wedges Blake set out for him. He liked Blake.

About a week after the robbery – still recuperating in Orange County Hospital from the hole docs drilled in his skull to suck out the clot – Blake woke to find a shoe box on his bedside table. Inside was $418 in bills, $23.74 in coins, and two little lemon seeds hammered flat. Luis and Robby were never caught, never seen again, actually, and Blake hadn't been robbed since.

"Semper Fi, Pete!" Blake bellowed as I elbowed up to the bar.

He reached into a cooler and withdrew a dripping Sapporo. He flipped the bottle cap and shoved the beer across the bar. Beneath a mat of red hair, Blake's arms were a story-board of fading tattoos including an eagle-globe-and-anchor. Somewhere among the bottles on the back bar sat his framed Silver Star paid for at Hue.

I hooked the neck of the Sapporo, saluted, and swallowed. Water beads, spilling down the side of the brown bottle, etched jagged paths in the condensation like the squiggles on a monitor screen.

"What's up, man? You look ragged."

"Ronnie's in the hospital. It's ... it's bad."

"No! What?"

I shook my head. "I'll tell you later."

He gripped my arm with a big paw. "Anything you need man, you know that, right?"

I knew.

"Seen Jesus?" I said.

"Usual table ..." He glanced over his shoulder, squinted, and shrugged. "That's his ditty bag. Must be in the head."

I laid a five on the bar, wedged through the throng, and dropped into a chair. A notebook covered with scribbled figures lay atop a racing form spread open on the table. A fresh cigarette smoldered on an ashtray lip.

I waited patiently since Jesus took longer to pee than most folks. After a few minutes, I saw him making his way down the back hallway. A lawyer type, apparently in great need, lurched into the hallway, stepped and sidestepped, then backed out with a mumbled apology. No room to squeeze past Jesus' wheelchair.

Jesus rolled up to the table on autopilot. His face was slack and his good eye so far away I didn't register on him immediately, but after a few seconds the half of his face that still worked smiled.

"Saaayyy ... Peeettte ..."

"Say, Gee-sus," I said flatly.

"HAY-sus, you cabron. HAY-sus ... not GEE ..." but even familiar words demanded a focus he couldn't hold. His half-smile faded and Jesus was somewhere else.

Midnight black Apache hair still spilled over his shoulders, but the dark, Apache complexion had yellowed in the last year and the tic that jerked his scarred left cheek and eyelid had worsened. He stared at nothing, his good eye as glazed as the dead glass eye.

Somewhere inside, though, the heart still beat. The heart that hides, but never changes. The fiery, perfect heart I saw proved at the Four-to-Four when Jesus honored his contract and took his wages – the useless legs, the rolling chair.

"Jesus," I said, shaking his shoulder. "Jesus."

His good eye focused a bit. "Saaaayyy, Peeettttee."

Jesus had been hooked on pain pills since Nam, but the Four-to-Four turned the monkey on his back into a gorilla.

"You're bleeding, man."

He looked blearily at the red bead on his left forearm. A strap mark was still visible on the skin above his elbow.

"Jus' a scratch."

Ambling over with my change, Blake saw Jesus on the nod, grabbed a handful of his hair and jerked his head upright.

"Goddammit, Jesus! You're killing yourself!"

Despite the anger in his face, Blake released the hair and clasped Jesus' shoulders in something like a hug.

"What do I do with this asshole, Pete?" He looked around the room. "What do I do with any of these assholes?"

The question was a knotty one since Blake framed it as a family affair. Jesus was his brother. So was I. So was Gonzales, mumbling to himself in the corner – Peterson, blowing his last dollar on a pool game – Freiberg, just released again from the Long Beach VA psych ward. All of us were children of a mother called The Corps and Blake felt duty bound to be there for every sad shadow in a tattered field jacket who blundered in still searching for something lost an age and a world away.

"Jesus has to choose, Blake. He's a man."

"He's a god-damned doper!"

"Still a man."

Jesus squinted through his good eye.

"Caballeros! A drink!"

"Bullshit," barked Blake, stamping back to the bar. "You come down first."

"Grouchy bastard!" Jesus drawled. "Ain't been happy since they drilled that hole in his skull."

I drank my beer and waited for him to get right, or at least get better. His cigarette, long gray ash drooping, burned down to the filter and started to stink. I crushed it out.

Jesus rubbed his hands over his face a few times, then tapped the scratch sheet.

"Come to pay what you owe, *cabron*?"

I dug a wad of ones from my pocket, peeled off the only twenty, and slapped it onto the paper. Jesus smiled crookedly.

"Bad judge of horseflesh, *amigo*. Who you like today?"

I craned across the table.

"I need a favor, Jesus."

My lowered voice brought him closer. Our heads almost touched.

"Make a buy for me."

His face asked why.

"Better you don't know."

He nodded slightly as he stitched pieces together. He dropped to a whisper.

"I can score fresh Mexican. Wholesale tar, man. I mean *hard*. One spoon and it's OD number whatsis, no film at eleven."

I shook my head. "Morphine. Factory box. Sealed."

"You're off base, Pete. Ain't nobody doing morphine, 'cept the docs and nurses boosting it from the med locker."

"Can you *get* it?"

"Damn straight, but ... " He sighed. "Okay. I guess you know what you're doing. I'll need to dig around though. What time is it?"

"Seven." To be on the safe side, I added, "At night."

"Will tomorrow work?"

I tugged out my wallet. "What's the ticket?"

"A deuce maybe. You need it now, I can't shop."

I fingered two C-notes from the billfold reserve and dropped them on the racing form.

"Just get it."

He pocketed the bills and sat back in his wheel chair. His good eye tried to read my face.

"Fallen Angels," I said. "What's the skinny?"

He shrugged. "Heard the name. Gangs come and go these days. Kids mule some drugs, buy a gun, and start shooting neighbors. Nobody's in charge, 'cept maybe Twelfth Street and *they're* barely off the block."

"Know where these Fallen Angels hang?"

"Near the stadium. Orange, maybe. Important?"

"The honcho in particular. *El Tigre.*"

"Tiger? Hmm ... I heard a Tiger called bad-fucking news once. Can't say he's your guy, but it's not a common handle. Takes balls to call yourself a tiger. I'll recon."

I stood to leave. "Need anything?"

He waved his arm. "Got it all, man."

"Hang in there, GEE-sus."

"HAY-sus, you *cabron.* HAY-sus."

He smiled, but it faded fast.

* * * * *

Shoulders hunched against a stiff Santa Ana wind, men and women trudged past the restaurant window. Shielded by the glass, I slurped my after-dinner coffee, grimaced, and clinked the porcelain cup back onto the saucer.

"Ouch! Hot!" I spluttered.

Ronnie rat-ta-tat-tatted her fingers against the white table cloth.

"Men!" she huffed.

"What? ... What is it?"

"I expected one of your little surprise scenes, Pete, but no! I think you *have* forgotten."

I glanced at my watch for the date.

"Oh, Christ, Ronnie, I must've ... Wait a minute. Your birthday is half a year away. Forgot what?"

"Six months since our first date. Six months today. I dropped hints all week."

"Women! ... You know, I think these anniversaries are like performance reviews to you."

"The past is important."

"Sure. It's prologue. How long till I'm a keeper?"

" *Twelve* months."

I laughed.

"Well, Pete, a girl's has to have standards."

A tuxedo-clad waiter appeared holding a small cake with a single burning candle.

"To the future," I said. "Happy Anniversary, Ronnie."

The waiter placed the cake on the table and withdrew.

"You're off the hook *this* time, Mister," Ronnie said smiling. I liked the way her face beamed when she smiled. I liked the way her eyes sparkled in the candle light.

"You think men don't remember. I took you to see Hedda Gabler. Then for Mexican. You wore that shiny, red dress."

"You *do* remember."

"How could I forget? Risky business, a cop-type dating a psychologist. Figured you for a mind reader."

"Male minds read like Dick and Jane books."

"Sexist insults from a woman who scarfed down four – count 'em – *four* enchiladas. I'd boned up on Ibsen and you had guacamole on your nose!"

"I like to eat."

"No *problemo*. I like to watch you eat."

"You like to *watch*. Period!"

"Don't talk nasty!" I said, eying nearby tables, adding a chuckled, "In public."

Laughter disturbed the angled line of her bob. She brushed at the under-curl with an inconsequential flick of her fingers.

Through the doorway limped a man in a bedraggled Marine Corps field jacket. Black, unkempt hair spilled over his shoulders. The waiter rushed to block his way.

"Wrong door, Pancho," the waiter whispered.

"'S my *amigo*," the man bellowed, waving. "Say *Pete!* Saw you through the window! *Que paso?*"

I waved back eagerly.

"Vamoose!" the waiter growled.

Despite a crippled leg, the man feinted right, pivoted left, and scrambled to the table with the waiter in pursuit.

"Same old moves GEE-sus!" I said with a big grin.

"HAY-sus, you cabron. HAY-sus, not GEE-sus."

"I've called him that since first grade," I said to Ronnie. "We played — "

"C'mon, let's go," the waiter said, grabbing an arm.

Jesus jerked away.

"It's okay," I said to the waiter. "It's okay. He's my friend."

"Your *friend* is disturbing other patrons."

I stood.

"I said he's my friend. I'll take care of him."

"A jacket is required," the waiter persisted.

I pinched a faded, green sleeve. "Field *jacket*. Military nomenclature, pal. You don't want to argue with the Marines."

"And a tie ... sir."

"Well, maybe he left his tie somewhere. Maybe in the 'Nam along with his eye and half his hip."

I yanked off my own tie and draped it around Jesus' neck.

"Happy? He has a tie."

"And now, sir, *you* do not," the waiter intoned.

I couched my voice in a register he would feel as much as hear. "I could wear ... *your* tie."

The waiter opened his mouth to object, but some primeval instinct silenced him. He turned and retreated.

"Pete!" Ronnie said curtly. "You're not in the jungle."

"There's a world of things you might not know, Ronnie." I dragged over an unused chair. "Huddle up, buddy. *Cerveza*? Something stronger?"

Ronnie sat stone faced.

"Strong as I need, *cabron*, they don't have!"

"When did you get back?" I said.

"Yesterday."

"C'mon, sit down. You make me dizzy wobbling like that."

Jesus looked wistfully at the chair, then at Ronnie. He shrugged.

"Naah ... I'm no tent peg, man. Just eyeballed you through the window and figured, 's been a while." He offered his hand to Ronnie. "Jesus Ramirez, ma'am."

"GEE-sus. Call him GEE-sus."

"Veronica Lamb," she said, pinching his hand with her fingertips.

"Careful what you say, GEE-sus. Ronnie's a shrink."

"Get out, man! With you?"

"Show him your license, Ronnie." I patted the chair again. "So ... what happened at Bethesda? How's the leg?"

"Six months older. Shee-it, place was just another stinkin' V.A."

"Sorry, man. I know you had your hopes up. Hey, at least Uncle Sam's still got your back, right?"

"In this economy? Barely get high on that check anymore. I'm shovin' a mop at the Four-to-Four. Start tonight."

"Watch your step, " I said.

"It's only a mop. Tom pays me under the table."

"Watch your step."

He glanced again at Ronnie. "Look, I'm gonna blow, man. Buttin' in here was bogus."

"Stay a minute, Gee-sus!"

"HAY-sus, you cabron. HAY-sus, not GEE-sus!" He bowed toward Ronnie. "Nice meeting you, Doctor Lamb."

"A pleasure, Mr. Ramirez ... HAY-sus."

He smiled.

I stood, crushed Jesus against my chest, and pounded his back. He broke free and staggered out the door.

"Pete. Your tie."

"He'll get it back to me," I said, dropping into my chair.

Through the window we watched Jesus halt at the curb as if trying to choose a direction. The harsh wind whipped at his black hair. He tugged up the collar of his field jacket and, favoring his balky, left leg, dodged traffic to cross the street.

"Who is that man?" Ronnie said.

"Jesus Ramirez. He told you."

"Not his name ... Who *is* he?"

Her tone made me bristle.

"He's a friend."

"He looked drunk and ... and homeless."

"He isn't homeless. He *is* drunk. So?"

"I'm ... *astonished*, I suppose. What could you possibly have in common?"

I counted my breaths for a moment.

"Call it twelve months, Ronnie." I nodded toward the cake and still-burning candle. "First grade. First beer. First date. We had football in common ... Goddamm, he used to fly! We had our first win and our first — " I took a deep breath. "We had the Nam together, Ronnie, but he left more behind than me, so he doesn't run like he used to, and they nail him now every time."

"So it's a *'man'* thing."

I chose my words precisely. A final, unmistakable explanation.

"He's a friend," I said.

"I understand, dear."

I turned away. She waited.

"Are we not talking now?" she said.

"I'm talking."

"Then talk."

Melting wax formed tiny beads on one side of the candle. I licked my thumb and quenched the candle flame between my fingers.

"Sometimes, Ronnie ... not often, but sometimes ... we speak different languages."

CHAPTER TEN

Spiteful hit-and-run showers alternately blurred my windshield or left wipers squealing against dry glass. Wet asphalt reflected a mosaic of white headlights, red taillights, orange streetlights. I drove north along Main past empty San Dismas sidewalks and dark, gated storefronts.

Everywhere I looked – scrawled on walls, signs, bus benches, lamp poles, parked vans – I saw spray-painted street gang symbols: *placas*. Goddamm weeds! Given an inch, the *placas* seized miles. I scanned the scrawls searching for something that might represent Fallen Angles – *FA or FxAx*, perhaps, since small x's stood for periods.

12th Street OxC was most common. The few *Dog Troop SD* still visible were all overwritten. 12th Street had won that particular bleeding contest. One *placa* read *14 Varrio Boys Mr. Joker* – a jab left by someone nicknamed Joker, just passing through, since 14 meant the Varrio Boys were out of Northern California. Southern California gangs used a 13. "Mr." made Joker a honcho with the Varrio Boys. "*Don*" was the Spanish equivalent. *Don Wacky* had puta'd *Mr. Joker* – slashed a red 'X' and his own nickname over the Joker moniker, along with 187, the penal code for murder. A death threat.

I passed the Main Street Station House and noticed

the *placa* covered cornerstone. A few years back *placas*
were barrio markers – rare in middle-class neighborhoods
and unheard of on police stations. I saw no *placas* the
night Lemon Tom, as watch commander, had me hauled
in on parking warrants to persuade me to drop a client
suing the city for police brutality. Tom advanced a
number of painfully cogent arguments, but I knew a little
rhetoric myself, and – a beer or two over the line – I broke
his nose. The next hour lasted about a week, but it could
have been longer, or terminally shorter, if not for Manny
Vasquez, a Sergeant at the time who happened in and
risked his own hide to hold Tom back.

Soft on parking crime, I guess.

In the end, Tom let me walk, since — as he said the night I
killed him — he liked me. But Tom was not soft on any crime
except his own, and no one ever puta'd Mr. Lemon Tom with a
placa on his station house, not even when he ran things from
the other side of the law.

Now the station house was pocked with insults. Something
was missing. No ... no what? A phrase from college tickled my
memory.

Sovereign?

Is that what Lemon Tom had been? Sovereign?

I remembered a lecture about monarchy and monotheism;
the war of all against all; nature – red in tooth and claw –
subdued by a single set of rules.

All against all. Who said that?

Hobbes?

I turned in at the *Orange County Banner*.

The lobby – bustling during the day – was quiet. Business
hours were over and, as a morning paper, the *Banner's* first-
run deadline was six p.m. Reporters had filed their stories
and adjourned to Blake's. The action had moved out back to
the pressroom and loading dock.

I signed the lobby-cop's visitor log and got a go-ahead to
see Fred Lynch, the Night Editor. Fred and I had spent a good

part of ten years arguing politics and pugilists over beers at Blake's. We were friends.

The elevator opened on the third floor newsroom. Three long rows of reporters' desks always conjured an image of advancing rabble stalled halfway down the room by a barricade – the opposing desks of the News Editor, City Editor, and Assistant Editor. At night with the rabble dispersed, Fred manned the barricade alone. Behind him, two men and a woman – copy-editors – sat hunkered around the semi-circular copy-desk like defenders of a goal.

Listen to old news hawks gab and you imagine newsrooms raucous with clattering teletypes, banging typewriters, ringing phones, and constant jabber. Words moved noisily back in the day. Scurrying copyboys ripped scrolling newswire from teletypes and nabbed pages of literature-in-a-hurry fluttered aloft to shouts of COPY. They slapped words-on-paper onto editors' spikes and rolled the blue-penciled words into pneumatic tubes that whooshed KA-THUNK to the composing room to be cast in lead. Modern words moved electronically, so the newsroom, particularly at night, was surprisingly quiet. Unlike nostalgic old news hawks, however, I was okay with quiet. The jubilant cacophony was nothing I knew enough to miss.

Grunting into a telephone receiver pinched between his shoulder and ear, Fred sat clicking a computer keyboard. Two furious fingers easily did the work of ten. I dropped into a chair and waited.

Fred was at least seventy, but legend had him doctoring his records to avoid retirement. He was black – or as *he* liked to say, as black as darkest Africa. Despite a wall-full of regional and national awards from panels ignorant of his color, he called himself the *Banner's* sop to affirmative action. Fred was a *rara avis* – a black Libertarian – so he hated affirmative action. He also hated most Libertarians.

Fred was shiny bald and big – John Wayne tall with a James Earl Jones bulk that promised a mellifluous baritone voice. Instead you got a cigarette-scarred contralto. As they say, all writers are liars.

"Got it," Fred said into the receiver. "Indictments tomorrow. Right, right ... right. Get there by eight and I'll make sure the photog ... What?"

I spied a *Bartlett's Quotations* buried in the paper drifts on Fred's desk, picked up the book, and thumbed through the index.

"No fucking kidding!"

I looked up. Fred's eyes were wide. Listening intently, he pawed through a cluttered desk drawer, found a bubble pack of nicotine gum, worked a piece out of its plastic dome, and popped it into his mouth.

"Sanchez *and* Warren? I'm peeing my pants. I am peeing my pants!" He pecked a dozen keys excitedly then stopped. "No, Reed. Not this time you don't. No. No! I said *no*, damn it. Only if it's ... I said no. Only if ... No! Only if it's in the indictment."

His jaws pounded the gum.

"Listen you little ferret! Listen to me. Listen! I'll save four inches from the final until eleven. Get a quote or a ... Bullshit! Tape, Reed. No, no, no, no ... on *tape*. None of your deep throat crap on this one. Nail it by eleven and ... I mean it, Reed. Nailed! No, no, damn it! Nailed by eleven. *Tonight* it's a scoop. Tomorrow it's rehash."

He hung up and typed another hundred strokes, talking at the same time.

"The San Dismas Sheriff stink. Grand Jury brings it all to a head tomorrow. And guess who was getting what from whom?"

"I heard."

He hit the save button with a finger flourish.

"Barring a meltdown, that Reed is Pulitzer bound. He's a Goddamm bullshit-seeking missile. He'd fly right up their bungholes for the story." He smacked his lips a few times, grimaced, and spat the nicotine gum into his palm.

"Christ, you ever try this crap, Pete?"

"I quit years ago, Fred. They didn't make it then."

"Shouldn't make it now," he groused. "Nothing in it. Maybe I should smoke it." He dropped the gum in a wastebasket and waved his hand. "Can you feature it? A smoke-free newsroom? Not a nursing home. Not a fucking hospital. *Newsroom*! You see oxygen in here? You see rocket fuel?"

"Smoke anyway, Fred. Who's here to stop you?"

"You don't know this new breed, Pete. *Sneaky* bastards. Stamped out in some Goddamm politically correct Stepford factory. You don't think I tried it? I tried it. Goddamm empty room, for Christ's sake, and Publisher gets a petition citing the new ordinance."

He swiveled his chair toward the copy editors.

"That was you, Barnes!" he shouted. "Save your lungs? Why? You got a rain forest inside? You got whales? I hope you get fucking cancer anyway. Cancer of that tight asshole of yours!"

One of the men shot Fred a finger without missing a beat on his keyboard. The woman laughed.

Fred turned back to me.

"Close that Bartlett's," he said. "I know what everybody said about everything."

"War of all against all?"

"You taking adult education classes? I thought all you read was Spillane."

"No one better, Fred."

"Spencer. Social Contract. And it's 'war of everyone against everyone.'"

"Thought it was Hobbes."

"Hobbes, my ass." His voice grew somber. "So ... how's Veronica?"

I was quiet. Fred looked at the floor.

"I just found out. Tonight."

He exhaled sharply. "Oh, Christ, Pete! ... I haven't seen you in weeks. I figured you knew."

"I've been undercover on a counterfeit drug case."

He smelled a juicy story – I saw it in his eyes – but he was too good a friend to birddog it just then. I tossed the Bartlett's back onto the desk.

"I followed the news, but, of course, she wasn't named. Fill me in."

He hesitated.

"Listen, Pete. The ones who did it? Beat 'em to death with a wrench, I won't lose a wink. But I can't see you being objective here. Your judgment *has* to be haywire."

"You're saying there's reasonable doubt and I'm unreasonable?"

"About this? Yeah, that's what I'm saying. It was probably a gang, but which one?"

"The bum saw a Fallen Angels *placa*."

"See what I mean? He *thought* he saw *something*. No one else saw it."

"What does Ronnie say?"

"Retrograde amnesia, they call it. Head injury erases part of the tape. Last memory she had was going jogging."

His phone made a quiet, warbling sound.

"Get that, Barnes," Fred said. Barnes made an okay sign. "The lab has evidence galore; blood types — " He cut himself short, shrugged, and continued. "Semen, secretor-non-secretor stuff. But no matches in the data base. Arrest someone and they'll run DNA, but ... " He spread his hands. "Nothing anchors an arraignment."

"What *wasn't* in the paper, Fred?"

"Four Fallen Angels ditched school that day, but they had solid alibis with some 12th Street goons."

"12th Street? That's middle management. These punks are street labor."

"The *Jefe* – calls himself *El Tigre* – he's a comer."

"With 12th Street?"

"If they covered his ass, it means something."

I smacked a fist into my palm. "It means Frankie Mendez

was involved."

"I said *if*. Besides, this was random. Once upon a time, sure, but nowadays? Too senseless. Mendez has zero tolerance for needless heat."

"Bullshit!" I snapped. "You think he and his crew suddenly found religion?"

"See? See what I mean? You just want to whack something. *Anything*! … Frankie's boys stay busy gobbling up Tom's pie. They're past sport crime."

I forced myself to drop Mendez for the moment. "Okay. Four Angels alibied out. What's with *them*."

Fred grabbed the nicotine gum, but stopped and flicked the card back onto the desk.

"I *gotta* have a smoke." We stood and headed for the stairs. "Watch the phones, Barnes. I'm taking a whiz."

"Pinel gonna hold it for you?" said Barnes.

The woman, Rita, hee-hawed. "Once you go black, Pete … "

"What's it to you, you politically correct, Stepford sons-of-bitches?" Fred sneered. "You'd give me a medal."

"Wrap those rascals," Barnes snickered.

Puffing down the stairs, Fred led me outside. Under the loading dock roof, he shook a Camel from a fresh pack and tore off the filter.

"See that Chrysler?" he groused, pointing to a beige car with fogged windows parked in the employee lot. "A pressman. Union steward so he's untouchable. Sells grass by the key, but I can't buy Camels without filters. What's the world coming to?"

"Go ask him. Maybe he's holding."

"Shee-it!"

He lit the cigarette, breathed deeply, coughed a half-dozen times, and smiled.

"Doesn't get much better, Pete."

Step vans backed into the dock. A buzzer blared. The conveyors clattered to life. Wire-bound bundles of newspapers began to wobble down the line. Circulation jumpers sprang to stack bundles in the trucks.

"Quit stalling, Fred. What's the dope on these Angels."

"Cut me some slack, Pete." He took another deep drag on the smoke. "Okay. Here's something you'd get anyway. It's a new gang and still pretty young. Mostly middle-schoolers for Christ's sake! The older ones go to Taft."

"Near the stadium? That's a good high school."

"For now."

"Who's this *El Tigre*."

"He and three chums got booted from a little league team. The *Angels*. They formed their own team."

"*Fallen* Angels," I said.

"Maybe they read Milton."

"Priors?"

"Juvies. Damn hard to get rap sheets."

"Any street cred?"

"Talk that the Tiger moniker fits. He's clearly the shot-caller. His three pals sound evil but brainless. The rest? I'm sure they're *all* shitheads, but most of them are still just kids and *only* the four were out of school at the time. That's solid."

He sucked on his cigarette and eyed me sharply.

"*Solid*," he repeated.

"Who are the other three?"

"Go by Boo, Ratboy, and Chaka."

"And they were just hanging with 12th Street that day?"

"Skipped school to help a 12th Street *Don* move furniture. The move was legit. Sworn citizens and rental truck receipts."

"Were they really there?"

"Only 12th Street could swear to it, but they did."

"C'mon, Fred. Real names? Addresses?"

He took a deep puff, coughed, and flipped the cigarette butt into a puddle.

"We can pull the clips."

"No detail and you know it."

"Got to buff the juvie pieces. Wouldn't want to stigmatize the little fucks."

"That columnist. Kuntsler. He's turned this into some kind of oppressed masses campaign. He'll have background notes."

Fred spit out a piece of tobacco. "Sure. Locked in his desk."

"I can get in if you can't. Let's look."

"You *Goddamm* know me better than that, Pete."

"Well excuuuse me! I didn't mean to *insult* you."

"But you *did*. And it shows how wrong-headed you are right now. I'll give you Kuntsler's home number. Best I can do."

Climbing the stairs, Fred mulled something.

"So you've read Kuntsler's stuff?"

"What I can stomach. The *Banner* is a right-wing rag. Where'd you find this asshole?"

"An import. Boston."

"The *Globe*?"

He nodded.

"Cats and dogs together," I said. "Makes no sense."

When the stairwell door opened, Barnes looked up from the copy desk, glanced at his watch, and sniggered, "Minute men!"

"Like my ex," chimed Rita.

"Was your ex a *man?*" said Fred.

"Before our little spat ... By the way, check FIRE. The lead reads like *Mein Kampf*."

Fred plopped at his computer and pecked a few keys. A story slugged FIRE appeared. He scribbled an address and phone number on a card as he scanned the story. I read over his shoulder.

"Reckless vagrants occupying the City Hall courtyard squandered taxpayer dollars and endangered innocent lives when illegal cooking fires ... "

"How'd this get by Thomas, Rita?" he said, sour-faced.

"How? He re-wrote it."

"Wasn't his Jag keyed at City Hall a few days ago?"

"Probably by a reckless vagrant," Rita offered.

"Squandering taxpayer dollars," added Barnes.

"Power corrupts," Fred muttered. "Okay, Rita, scratch the vagrants."

"Yuck!"

"Kill the squandered dollars and, of course, no lives are truly innocent, are they? Try 'Sheriff deputies routed homeless poor occupying City Hall Courtyard when blah, blah, blah.'"

"Poor homeless poor," said Rita.

"They wuz routed!" chuckled Barnes.

Typing gleefully, Rita said, "Are you sure you want to do this, Fred? Thomas will soil himself."

"Let the Nazi bastard work nights, too, if he wants to slant every word. When I work, *I* slant the words. Besides, I know where he parks."

Fred handed me the note card.

"Kuntsler won't help you, Pete."

"Oh, he might," I said.

"Prick or not, he's still *Banner*. That means he's *family*."

"Those columns of his are — "

"Pete! Sit down. Sit down. I hear you. Kuntsler's one of those stick-it-to-the-man kids pissed that he missed the sixties. If he were any farther left, he'd be beside himself. But he's *Banner*."

"Well, I still don't get *why* he's *Banner*."

Fred shrugged.

"Join the club. You never know what the guys upstairs are thinking. Or even if they *are* thinking. Why do they shuffle the comics around all the time and alienate half the circulation? Why do they change the fonts and screw with the horoscope? Publishers just *do* things, that's all. Because they're publishers. Because they can."

He sighed.

"Expect the worst with Kuntsler, Pete. I'd hate to see you tanked for taking a poke at him. He's not worth it. And he's not worth a *friendship*."

He was drawing a line, or more accurately, posting a familiar line as a reminder and a precaution. I said nothing, pocketed the note card, and stood.

"Go easy, Pete," he warned as I waited for the elevator.

I stepped into the car, turned, and nodded through closing doors.

CHAPTER ELEVEN

Outside the rain was resting, gathering strength for the next round. The world looked sloppy-wet and arm-weary. It was hard to feature the bout going the distance, but it always did. And – save for that one exhibition match back in Genesis – the world always won.

On my way to Kuntsler's, I called the hospital, checked on Ronnie, and paged Sharfstein.

"She told me what you wanted me to hear," I said, adding over his sputtered reply, "Some things you don't discuss on car phones, Sharfstein. Some things you don't discuss at all."

I disconnected.

Kuntsler lived north of Main in a neighborhood of small homes. The Palms. A *real* neighborhood, one with roots. The people were mostly older folks, life-long residents of that part of San Dismas. That's why, despite dated, incandescent street-lighting, I knew that lawns were mowed, hedges trimmed, and sidewalks edged. I knew that all the chrome-laden, made-in-Detroit, land yachts I saw were routinely washed and regularly serviced. I knew because n*eighborhoods* were places where pride and preservation mattered. The Palms was still that way.

Except for Kuntsler's part. *His* lawn was brown, the shrubs overgrown. Weeds sprouted through cracks in an oil stained driveway where a grungy VW bug sat parked in front of an open garbage can.

I pulled into a vacant stretch of curb, walked up the driveway, and squeezed past the VW. The trash can brimmed with take-out chicken buckets and wine bottles. I stepped onto a small slab porch, rang the bell, and waited. Raindrops peppered the aluminum awning.

Kuntsler's rants in the *Banner* made clear his radical bent regarding crime and law enforcement. His garbage, however, showed an indifference to communitarianism, recycling, and animal rights. I could only wonder about his take on abortion, war, education, federal spending and the like, but when he opened his door, I detected a *strongly* positive, if wobbly, stance on cannabis legalization.

"What?" he snapped.

Kuntsler was tall but skinny. Not runner skinny, but sickly skinny. He had a mop of greasy, long hair and a thin, patchy goatee. He wore sandals, torn bell-bottomed jeans and a baggy, short-sleeved, tie-dyed shirt.

"Far out! It's Shaggy," I chuckled, flashing a peace sign. "Where's Scooby-Doo?"

He eyed the yard to see if I had company.

"Lighten up, man. I'm just goofing on you. You're Brent Kuntsler. That little picture atop your column rats you out."

I gave him a business card. He glanced at the card and flicked it toward the garbage can. He missed.

"More wrist, less finger action," I said, demonstrating with a swish of my hand. "Watch as many people toss your card as I have, and you learn the tricks."

He tried to slam the door, but my boot was in the way.

"You're writing stories on the River Trail Jogger."

"Jingoism," he pouted. "A name obfuscates crime's social dialectic."

"Since *neither* of us knows what the hell you just said, why say it?"

"A *name* makes crime seem personal."

It was impossible to keep the anger out of my voice. "Well, me? I'm *waay* into personal. But I *dig* your objectivity. Like … it's no skin off *your* nose if I break it. It's just a dialectic."

Kuntsler stepped back and crooked his arm so I could see

the nickel-plated .32 he was hiding behind his leg.

"You don't scare me," he said.

I let a silent moment tick by, shouted BOO! and cracked up when he almost jumped out of his Birkenstocks. I waited while he pounded the door against my boot some more.

When I could keep a straight face, I said, "Nice little lady's gun you have, Brent. Shiny. Fits in your man-purse. Why am I not amazed that the *anti*-gun nut is armed?"

A page of text glowed on the desktop computer monitor behind him. The screen-saver hadn't kicked in yet.

"The People have a right — no, a *duty* to resist oppression."

"By any means necessary," I said.

His blank face told me he didn't get it.

"I did my research, Pinel. You're the ex-husband. Big macho Marine Man. Vietnam." He paused to throw his trump card. "*Baby Killer!*"

"Baby killer? ... Like wow! Ba..ad trip, man. You read a lot about those times, did you?"

"I didn't have to be there to know what this country did."

"And you don't need a weatherman to know the wind is blowing."

"What is that supposed to mean?"

"Pearls before swine," I muttered. "Look, Kuntsler, *good* research would have shown I was military police, not a grunt."

"And *intelligence*, Pinel. Hiding the spook work?"

"Yes ... Yes I was." I shook my head sadly and reached for my gun. "Too bad."

Kuntsler reeled backwards. I howled with laughter.

"God, Kuntsler, you are *funny*. I wish we could have a sleepover and just be silly all night, but I think I've interrupted your work on the story."

He whirled to look behind him.

"Oh, you'd love the story to go away, wouldn't you? Youths tortured by an oppressive culture."

"Tortured? Why, that's horrible! You mean like ... like a savage beating? Stabbings? Gang rape? Murder?"

My hands had become fists. I had to watch myself.

"Don't blame the children. Blame the society that raises them."

I flashed on children I had known in Nam – children raised in Hell. Some chose to be Devils, but some chose to be Angels, and most simply tried to stay alive without hurting anyone.

"Right ... " I drawled. "Southern Cal is the pits."

His eyes narrowed. I wondered what I had said.

"Nothing against your, uh ... writing, Kuntsler, but I think I need to meet *El Tigre* personally. You know ... feel his pain?"

"I won't help you. Ramon may be another Che."

A first name! What else would the piñata drop?

"By Che you mean another murdering terrorist?"

"You belong here behind the Orange Curtain."

"Rape is *not* politics, asshole."

"No? Isn't politics the use of power?"

I ached to erase his smirk and crammed my erasers into my pockets as a precaution.

"How about the Marx brothers – Boo, Ratboy, and Chaka. Little Che's fellow travelers."

I wanted to rattle him with the names and succeeded. He glared at me. I felt the piñata cracking.

"Do you know what Ratboy means?"

"Sure," I said. "A kid pushers use to test drugs."

"Exactly. A worthless lab rat. Well, I happen to know a Ratboy. His *father* gave him the name for services rendered. Imagine living across from your white-bread, high school in a *crack house!*"

There it was! I could try for another goodie or two, but I knew I'd clock him first.

"Every damn one of us gets to choose *something*," I said. "What is it you want to pretend *you* couldn't help?"

He banged the door against my boot some more.

"Okay, Kuntsler, I tried to take the high road, but screw it. A little of you goes a long, *long* way." I glanced at my watch.

"I'm jake with a guy at the *Banner*. Come shift-change, I'll get what I need from your desk."

I strode down the drive. Kuntsler slammed the door, but I knew he was watching from a window, so I made of show of banging the lid back onto the garbage can while I retrieved my business card. Climbing in the Blazer, I counted six houses to the street corner, zigzagged for a few minutes, and circled back with my lights off. Sure enough, the VW was gone.

It was time to do my work.

In the older parts of San Dismas, back-alleys separated the rows of houses. I turned right at the corner and parked. I stashed my beeper and pocket contents in the front console and dragged a Navy pea jacket from the back. I pulled a black watch cap over my hair and changed into a brand-new pair of cheap, super-market sneakers. Choosing a few tools, I made my way down the alley.

Counting off six gates in the tall rear fences, I scaled a stucco wall and plopped onto muddy grass. My footprints were sharp and deep, perfect for plaster casts. Footprints were the reason I bought my disposable shoes three sizes too large. Crouching, I listened for the *chichink* of a shotgun slide or the growl of a Doberman. I heard muffled voices, but none sounded excited. A few doors down, a poodle yipped.

I tugged on a pair of latex gloves and cracked the back gate in case I had to leave quickly. I peeked around the house, saw the tell-tale garbage can, and made sure the drive was still empty. Examining a window to rule out an alarm system, I knelt on the dark back porch and jimmied the door keyset with my picks until it turned. And since Kuntsler had probably chosen Elm Street to avoid the demoralized lumpenproletariat that he championed, he had no bar latch. I pushed open the door and scurried inside.

Even with plenty of time, it never paid to dawdle. The mission was seizure not search, and I knew exactly what I wanted. I crossed the kitchen – a sink overflowing with dirty dishes; what a slob! – and went directly to the living room desk.

I drew a screwdriver from my coat and broke the drawer locks. I ignored a baggie of grass, found nothing that mattered among papers and files, but pocketed a stack of diskettes. Yanking free the power, monitor, mouse, and printer cables, I hoisted the computer tower under my arm, scanned the crime scene to make sure I hadn't dropped anything to ID me, and skedaddled back down the alley. I stashed the computer on the back floorboard and covered it with the pea jacket. Stowing the sneakers and latex gloves in a paper bag before I put the bag in the car, I drove with my lights off for a block. I doffed the watch cap, combed a hand over my hair, and looked in the rear view mirror.

By any means necessary, I said to the face in the mirror. The face did not smile.

CHAPTER TWELVE

I cut through a Main Street supermarket lot to ditch the sneakers in a Goodwill bin and continued to what passed as a downtown in San Dismas – a few blocks of old, three- and four-story buildings near my office. The first floor storefronts were all gated save for a few open liquor stores and bars. I turned onto Fourth Street and parked across from Positively Fourth Street Electronic Repair. I was in luck. A shadow crossed a drawn shade in an upstairs apartment. I punched a number on my car phone.

"Zup!" chirped a voice through a haze of heavy metal. Ricky was eighteen, but his ears had to be nearer a hundred.

"Ricky, it's Pete. I'm downstairs and I — "

"Zup?"

"Turn down the Goddamm *VOLUME!*"

"Dag the box!" he yelled.

Silence.

"Ricky, it's Pete — "

"Zup, you boogerhead!"

Boogerhead as a term of endearment. The world had passed me by.

"I'm downstairs. Can you open up? I need a favor."

"For real, dude? C'mon! 'Bout to do the do."

"Tell her to hang."

"*Not*! I got gear up here, man!"

"Close friend, huh?"

"Some hose bag from Los Arcos."

"Who you callin' a hose bag, zit-face?" piped a female voice.

"You're going to get cancer or something, Ricky," I said.

"What can I do? I got needs, but no social skills. That's what the school counselor told me. No social skills. Hold on."

I heard the shouted conversation.

"Suit-up and book, sweetcakes. Sumpin's come up."

"*Nothin's* come up. No refunds for cummin' in your jeans, little boy."

"Nice mouth. Listen, Medusa, bail! I'm getting a bad feeling maybe you got a trouser trout."

"One of us needs one," said the lady.

The phone went dead. I was still laughing when a woman backed through the stairway door shouting obscenities. Whirling, she flipped her hair with all the attitude of an upraised middle finger. She stashed a few bills in a tiny purse, hitched up her panty hose and wobbled toward Los Arcos on six-inch heels.

Scratching his crew-cut head with a key ring, Ricky peeked out, spied my Blazer, and darted in his boxer shorts to the shop door. He removed a padlock from the *placa* scarred accordion gate, unlocked the front door, and snapped a light switch. I crowded into the store behind him, carrying the computer in my arms.

"Law, law, dude!" Ricky said, latching the door. "Finally catchin' the techno wave? But listen, they got laptops now, man."

Cackling at his joke, he brushed through a curtain and marched into the back room where he cleared a space for the computer on a tool-strewn repair bench.

"Zup?" he said.

"I need to see the files."

"Sure. You snake this, man?"

I was still wearing the latex gloves.

"Yep."

"Goin' home?"

"Yeah ... yeah, I suppose."

"Then best put some rubbers on these," he said, wiggling

his fingers.

He rummaged through a drawer for his own surgical gloves, plugged a knot of cords from the work bench into the back of the computer, and pushed the power button. Silently we waited for the machine to boot.

Ricky was a bronze-skinned, sun-bleached, California kid. It was hard to see the little squirt as a computer geek, much less as a *Bobby Fischer* of computer geeks. A Grand Master.

According to his Mom, Ricky first got into trouble when he figured out a rad way to make free long-distance phone calls. He shared the secret with friends who told their friends who told their friends, all of whom reached out to touch Ma Bell for about 30 million dollars before men in suits paid Ricky's Dad a visit.

Dad was the perfect suspect – a sixties IBM egghead who tuned in, dropped out, and fell from corporate heaven through Woodstock and Altamont to splash down in what he called his Walden Pond – San Dismas. He opened Positively Fourth Street as an experiment in simple living and self-sufficiency. Radio and TV repair offered a primitive routine that provided for his family's needs but left time to think his own thoughts.

The suits quickly lost interest in Dad, however. He disliked phones and rarely made or accepted calls. They discovered, too, that Ricky – constantly at his father's workbench – had learned oscilloscope calibration and assembler language before he started kindergarten. When they buttonholed the kid, he readily explained his electronic wizardry and showed the suits he could do *international* calls, too. According to Mom, he called the Kremlin, something I took as an exaggeration.

At first.

Ricky agreed to reams of conditions, but, in fact, Ma Bell had few options with a perp who was 1001 years old.

Or in decimal notation – *nine*.

At eleven, a budding interest in biology led Ricky to modify his subscription-TV decoder box to capture anonymously, and thus keep off his parents' monthly bill, a raft of nudie channels he was using as a self-study course. While tidying his room one afternoon, Ricky's mom switched on his TV to watch her soaps and inadvertently audited his class. Dad was happy to let things slide, but Mom insisted on blasting the broadcaster to the FCC. An investigator confiscated the box, knocked off 50,000 units and scooted to Costa Rica.

Although Ricky agreed that selling the boxes was wrong, he had no qualms about hacking the content. Content, he said, was like the ocean and no one owns the ocean. They own the land *around* the ocean and build fences to keep you off the beach. But find a way to the water without getting arrested? Surf's up, Dude!

Ricky spent his life finding chinks in those firewall-fences so he could play. *Play* best described it, because the motivation was pure fun, never malice or greed. His take on malevolent hackers and pointless destruction was basic. "You *don't crap* in the water, dude!" He sometimes tracked down and potty trained hackers who needed a refresher lesson. As for selling what he accessed? The idea bored him, so he didn't, although scoring things for free and sharing with friends was simply "Who wouldn't?"

The kid was so passionate about his games, I readily got caught up in his enthusiasm. After all, I loved my work, too. It *was* work, however. I got *paid* for it. It was a *living*. A part of me wondered how Ricky could squander his life with no return. I asked him about it once.

"Why do I do it?" He mulled it over, his head cocked as if he were listening to something. Judging by his face, it was the music of the spheres. "I can't *not* do it, man," he said finally. "It's sooo awesome!"

I got it then. At least I got it as close as, say, some chess potzer gets Bobby Fischer. The nature of Ricky's genes – the hard-wired intelligence and aptitudes that give some people a leg-up with certain skills –nurtured by a lucky environment – his Dad's tutelage, his Mom's doting – in combination created a gift so elemental as to seem instinctive, like birdsong.

An idiot savant, however, is still an idiot. No *instinct* turns birdsong into opera. While Ricky's *gift* was innate, its value to him was a free choice, and its transformation into genius the action of a Philosopher's Stone.

Will.

A bird sings to communicate. But Ricky's music was in an alien mode, an unearthly key, a preternatural scale. Its harmony was resolvable only to his singular ear. Thus, unlike a bird, he sang to himself. The ever-perfection of his melody was its own end of pure pleasure.

Play.

But since he chose the pursuit above all else, it was play for mortal stakes.

And that made it *love.*

As with any mad love, the courtship and consummation often flirted with disaster. When Ricky was fifteen, the NSA detected penetration of Defense Department computers. Since the Agency kept young geniuses like Ricky on the payroll (in lieu of a rock-pile), it linked him to "signatures" in the data trail. Buying 72 hours to scope the damage and patch firewalls, a task force of FBI, State Police and local cops swooped Ricky and his skateboard into a black van and parked him incognito in a Federal lock-up. When a benevolent guard gave him an old transistor radio to catch Angel games, however, Ricky jerry-rigged the circuit board to transmit Morse code. A nearby ham operator relayed Ricky's location to his Dad. The press made Ricky's plight national news.

Nevertheless, a judge, declaring Ricky a clear and present danger, pegged bail somewhere near the national debt. Dad's lawyer hired me to help him spring the kid. Poking around, I discovered things the Feds had not yet *imagined* and was about to drop the case when three gold-badges tried to muscle it away. The fullback in me took defensive holding as sufficient reason to score. I dug up evidence to show that the *particular* charges against Ricky were a last resort frame to prevent things the Feds *couldn't* prove.

While pre-trial hearings wore on, however, Ricky's Dad died. A gangbanger, for no discernable reason, emptied a Glock into him on the sidewalk in front of his shop. Citing security, the Feds refused to let Ricky attend the funeral. Now, several times a month, some initialed government agency comes hat-in-hand asking Ricky to consult.

He *doesn't*.

When the judge finally tossed the case, I drove Ricky's Mom to pick him up. She baked a delicious apple-raisin cake that we shared on the way home. Ricky was quite a character. We became pals in a little-brother big-boogerhead sort of way.

The following month, my car phone bill was only six bucks. Apparently, I had made no calls. I spoke with Ricky who said free minutes for life was his way of saying thanks. I told him thanks, but no thanks, so he removed something that looked like a camera battery from the phone. I'm sure PacCell was glad to see me back.

"Okay, man, let's shred it!" Ricky said when the Windows logo appeared on a nearby screen. He jostled a mouse, clicked the cursor here and there, and got a password message.

"Wha's the word, mockin'bird?"

"Search me. Owner's an asshole. Try asshole."

He typed a few characters.

"Nope."

"Is it a problem?"

"Don't be joanin' me, Pete. I got access to missile silos in North Dakota. This is a spud!"

The back of my neck prickled.

"Uh, Ricky ... you can't *launch* anything, can you?" His chuckle made me feel gullible. "Okay, okay ... Password's a spud. Can you do it here?"

Ricky had high-tech hardware and untraceable accesses at locations no one had found.

"This thing? Fer sure."

How long?"

"If asshole is a digithead who improvises, 10 or 15 minutes. If he uses commercial software, an hour maybe."

I looked at my watch and wondered if Jesus had found the morphine.

ALWAYS THERE.

"Get it working, Ricky. I'll be back."

He jiggled the mouse and stroked the keyboard. The colored screen changed to black-and-white. A flashing *c: \ > prompt* widened his pupils like a dirty picture.

"I'll snap the gate lock as I go, okay?"

He wasn't listening. I doubted that he even heard me. Ricky was *thinking*.

Watch pros run, jump, throw, swing, and you see them do things *anyone* can do in ways almost *no one* can. I conceived of Ricky's concentration that way – a *thought* counterpart to that *zone* top athletes are said to enter, a place where, outside their focus —

The words in my head were "the world disappears" and suddenly my heart flip-flopped because Ricky had finessed my question about the missiles.

"Ricky ... RICKY!"

I had to shake his shoulder. He looked surprised and a little disappointed to see me, the look of a person waking from a perfect dream to slapdash reality.

"Listen, Ricky, about those silos."

"What silos?"

"Missile silos. You said you had codes or doors or keys or something."

"Oh, that." He waved his hand dismissively. "Back doors, not codes. Forget about it."

"I wish I could! Now listen to me. Straight up, man. You can't launch anything, right? I mean *really!*"

"Well ... " He considered it. "I *really* don't know. I mean, it's like the codes are a *rad* problem. Max encryption. Bell-LaPadulla multi-level security. Covert channel control and multifactor authentication."

He was in his zone again, talking to himself since *I* couldn't understand him. What scared me was how familiar he seemed with the monologue.

"It would take some honking big crunchers, but that's no sweat. I have tunnels into a half-dozen mainframes. I'd just cloak chunks of free space and run undetected. I'd have to keep exporting the throughput to stay invisible, of course, but ... I dunno. Maybe."

"Goddamm it, Ricky! You can't — "

"Chill! You want an answer, don't you? ... So, let's say I'm all amped solving the problem when I overwrite some little subroutine and somewhere a million dads and moms and kids are smoke. Or say, like with my TV box, some dude hacks *me*, some asshat who *likes* to crap in the water. Or say I eat it big-time and scramble things so *no one* can launch? Like how good would that be, dude? I mean ... as much as I wish gangbangers didn't have guns, they do, and if, say, *you* had been around that day, well maybe ... "

He paused. "So like, here's the thing. It's a mondo puzzle that would be bitchin' to solve just for the *fun* of it. But I remember my Dad talking about why he bailed from Big Blue – how it hit him one morning that for *some* problems, *all* the answers are bogus. I didn't get it, not for a long time. Then, one day, when I asked him again, he spouted this line from a play or a poem or something, and damn, it hit me, too! He said, '*Though boys throw stones at frogs in sport, the frogs do not die in sport, but in earnest.*'"

Ricky's face looked faraway for a moment. "Is that outrageous, or what?" he said. Shaking his head sharply, he smiled again.

"Tell you what stoked me a few weeks ago. You know Deep Blue, the chess computer that beat Kasparov. IBM said they dismantled it, right? Lies and bullshit! They serial linked it with this gnarlatious mainframe that I tunneled a while back." He started to giggle."I had it play itself. All draws, dude! *Sooo rad!* I wanted to see if it would give up, but I had to bail. Maybe next time."

"Your Dad was a good teacher, Ricky."

"Fer sure," he said, returning to the keyboard.

Outside, I glanced at the sidewalk where some boy had shot Ricky's father in sport. Against the shop lay a single flower – nothing special, some weed Ricky had picked. During the day the flower got kicked around, stepped on, swept away, but each morning as he opened the gate, Ricky dropped a new one.

CHAPTER THIRTEEN

Kuntsler had let slip that Ratboy lived in a crack house across from his school, which Fred had ID'd as Taft. A crack house at night would be as hard to spot as a McDonald's at lunchtime. I drove toward Orange through a slow, steady shower. Crossing the roiling San Dismas River channel on the Main Street overpass, I realized that the River Trail was just below me. Less than a mile away, dark but visible, stood the giant haloed "A." Railroad tracks jarred my attention back to the road.

Taft was a typical, southern California high school – a core building, mostly stucco, connected by roofed walkways to rows of trailer classrooms. Surrounding the complex was a tall, shiny-new, chain-link fence – uncommon, but not rare. Despite the fence, the school walls were a quilt of beige squares – cover-up paint hiding *placas*.

Circling the school, I spotted a dark house with barred windows and cars idling out front. I parked and watched runners – kids not yet in their teens – dart back and forth like car hops. Patrons preferring more of a sit-down, fine-dining experience spoke with two grown-up maitre d's who manned the front door. I jacked the .45 to chamber a round, flicked on the thumb safety, and stashed the gun loosely back in the shoulder rig.

Stepping from the Blazer, I ambled up the driveway. The little ones skittered away like startled bunnies. The two goons at the door held fast. Both wore black Raiders hoodies over white tee-shirts. The taller one – buzz-cut with a bushy black

mustache – was short. His even shorter buddy was a long-hair
– Indian style with a braided-rawhide headband. Both of
them were fat. Buzz-cut stepped forward.

"Wha' can I do you for, man," he said.

"Produce Ratboy."

Long-hair rapped at the door – two, a pause, then a third.

"Ratboy?" said crew-cut. "Don't know no Ratboy. Maybe
you got the wrong house, man. Maybe you should try the
Boy's Club."

Melodramatically, long-hair slipped his hands into the
pouch-pocket of his hoodie. I laughed. It annoyed him.

"Chu gotta problem, man," he said.

"I don't see one."

"Chu lookin' at me, like chu gotta problem. If I can help chu
with chu problem, chu lemme know."

"Chu got it, man," I said.

He pushed away from the door and moved closer, waggling
whatever he had in the pocket.

"You look like you're playing with yourself, and it's not
flattering, pal. Ratboy lives right here. That's his school."

"Chu the truant officer?"

I stooped to stick my chin in his face, close enough to smell
onions on his breath.

"No, I'm the dog catcher. I put sons-of-bitches like you to
sleep. Now why don't you two Chihuahuas just do your little
knock-knock trick again so I can see the big dog."

Long-hair was a hard-case or perhaps he had forgotten the
secret knock. Either way, he got mouthy, so I whipped out the
.45, and jammed the muzzle against his ear.

"*Chu* gotta problem now, man," I said. "Chu gotta big, *big*
problem."

He froze. Crew-cut hesitated, then stepped back to knock
twice and twice again. The door opened on a tee-shirted hulk
whose log-sized arms were covered with crude tattoos. The
jail ink implied a *lot* of time in the joint, but probably not
enough.

"You want Ratboy, man?" he said. "Take a number. Little fuck and that *Tigre* made me for ten gees. You see him, tell him I'm puttin' him down."

"You must be his Dad."

"You cops! You dance around. Do your dance, man. You wanna dance inside? Well, you got no fuckin' warrant, man."

"I have a *habeas corpus* instead."

He frowned. "What's that supposed to mean?"

I shoved long-hair aside and leveled the .45 at Dad.

"It's Latin for *you can be a body*."

He roared with laughter. "Good one, man, good one! *Habeas corpus.*"

I must have looked shocked.

"Hey, I get it. Last bit, I got me a paralegal ticket."

"Shame you couldn't stay longer. Go for the J.D."

He frowned again.

"Big cannon. Big dance. You want entrapment, man? You want illegal search? Excessive force, man? You want it, I got it for you. I know the *law*. I say, go fuck yourself. You hear that *amigos*? I told him, no warrant, go fuck himself. You're witnesses."

I asked myself how Lemon Tom would have handled this new breed of educated thug.

"Move," I explained.

Dad stepped aside. "Compulsion by threat. Unlawful constraint. Nothing sticks. Nothing!"

Inside bare bulbs provided light. Black-out tarps sealed every window. The air reeked of ether and grass and whiskey and body odor and morning mouth and vaginosis and piss and shit and vomit. Bodies spilled over stained furniture or lay sprawled on floors. Among the open-eyed bodies were some who looked cop-behind-you scared, a few weaselly-faced ones probably weighing a grab for my wallet, and a majority with slack, thousand-yard stares. Holding the .45 ready, I picked my way through two rooms. My boots crunched broken glass littering the carpet.

"Where does Ratboy sleep?"

"Take four quick lefts and go straight up your ass!" said Dad, stamping away. "You are *done*, man. You are so fucking done."

The kitchen was teeming with four- and six-legged creatures scuttling over mounds of garbage. A trash-filled hallway was deserted. Whatever occupied the fetid, unlighted bathroom was probably not Ratboy and *certainly* not worth identifying. Upstairs a bedroom festooned with sports posters looked promising, and since the trio gyrating on the bed paid me no mind, I poked around. A desk held a book bag and – unbelievably – *books*. I stooped in the closet to paw through a pile of dirty clothes and found an abandoned baseball glove.

The squeaking bedsprings screened long-hair's tiptoe footsteps. Creeping up behind me, he swung a stubby bat, but misjudged the tight quarters. The bat foul-tipped the closet door-frame and glanced off my left shoulder. I rolled, saw him aiming for the cheap-seats, and fired at anything.

Blasting through his left knee, the slug bowled the leg from under him. The bat flew from his hands and smashed the window beneath a tarp. Arms flailing, he broke his fall with his face, clutched his leg and yelped.

Stampeding out the doorway, the screwing trio, actually a foursome, collided with buzz-cut who was trying to raise a shotgun.

"Drop it!" I shouted, my .45 straight out, dead bang on his chest.

I winced when, taking me literally, he let the sawed-off clatter onto the wooden floor. Otherwise, however, he knew the etiquette of such affairs and spread-eagled himself, face down.

I wobbled to my feet. My ears were ringing from the gunshot, but not enough to spoil my enjoyment of long-hair's wails. Bending over to retrieve my spent shell casing, I yelled, "Chu gotta problem, man?"

Laughing, I stuck the shotgun under my arm, gave crew-cut a wide berth on the side, and came up behind him. He probably expected a head shot, but, to be fair, the guy was just doing his job and I *was* armed. Still, the 12-gauge would have cut me two, so I gritted my teeth and tried to kick his balls through the broken window. Lungs emptying in a single, explosive whoosh, he jackknifed clean off the deck, grabbed his crotch, and collapsed, contorted and frozen, like a kid playing statue tag.

Downstairs the good times were over. Through the front door, I saw forms lurching across the lawn, piling into cars, stumbling down the street. Ratboy's Dad sat smoking a cigarette.

"I been making a list of your infractions," he said.

"Tell me about Boo. Where does he live?"

"Ratboy ain't there. None of 'em. I checked. You should worry about *you*."

"Where?"

"Wetback house. Jimino off Main. First one past the alley. You find him, tell him what I said. He better run."

"Physician heal thyself."

"Talk plain, cop."

"You better run, too."

"You got nothing!"

"I have the fact you're ten grand short. Frankie Mendez will think that's plenty."

The cigarette dangling from Dad's lips slipped onto his lap. He wriggled to brush it off.

"I been straight with 12th Street. Straight up."

"Frankie will hear you've been holding out."

"It was Ratboy and those other little fuckers. They — "

"Tell it to Frankie. Explain the law to him, Dad."

Hearing sirens, I ran to the Blazer. Pain shot from my shoulder into my neck with each step. I hid the shotgun under the rear seat and saw Dad burst from the crack-house. He tossed a briefcase into a ten-year old Ford, scrambled under the wheel, backed wildly down the driveway, and swung wide into the street. Crunching gears finding first, he roared away.

Dad was a bad guy, probably a *very* bad guy. But he *had* laughed at my joke, and for that I felt a twinge of pity. I doubted he would get far.

CHAPTER FOURTEEN

Shoulder cramping from long-hair's batting practice, I groped in the front seat console and found a small bottle of aspirin. I shook three tablets into my mouth, but couldn't work up saliva to ease them down, and had to chew.

I punched Ricky's number on the car phone.

"Zup?"

"Any luck?"

"Luck is for twinks, dude. Besides, this was no heavy. A standard windows lock and the lame hidden-files trick five-year-olds use."

"Stuff readable?"

"And lookable if you're into ropes and gags. Asshole subscribes to RichBitch.com. I cracked the site and jacked his VISA number if you need it."

"You're a force of nature, Ricky. One stop and I'll be there."

Although Ratboy's Dad had checked the place, Boo might have returned home or sent news. Wincing as I lifted my arm, I turned left off Main onto Jimino.

This area – neighborhood no longer applied – was another facet of San Dismas. Dead, unpruned, fronds draped the trunks of palm trees like fuzzy, brown skirts. Sun-faded 'For Sale' signs leaned drunkenly in front of abandoned houses. Paint peeled. Awnings sagged.

Among the occupied houses were squatter flops whose

windows flickered with candlelight or the glare of camp lanterns. Most places, however, were management company rentals. *Easy* rentals. Cash by the week or month. No paperwork. No questions. No *headcount.*

Steady lights and television glimmer said that the first house past the alley, Boo's place, was a rental. A proud row of tended flowerpots and a makeshift latch for the sprung gate said more. The house was a *homestead* – a stake planted in a new frontier where wits, guts, luck, and calloused hands earned a *chance* at a chance.

I opened the gate and sloshed up a walkway. From inside I heard *Sabado Gigante* and the unmistakable braying of Don Francisco. I flipped my wallet to flash the P.I. badge and rapped the door.

Silence was instant and absolute. No good came from nighttime knocks in those houses. I tried again. At length a mustachioed man wearing a sleeveless undershirt and grass stained khaki pants opened the door. His face was a stone wall. Behind him, frozen before a muted television, sat six others. I smelled meat sizzling. Onions. Cilantro.

"I'm not with immigration," I said. The man ignored my stinking badge, so I put it away. "I'm looking for a boy who lives here."

"*No hablo Ingles,*" said the man, rubbing his stubbly chin with a stained, calloused palm. Only five-ten or so, he nevertheless seemed to look me straight in the eye. I often experienced that optical illusion with proud, working men. He reminded me of Jesus' father.

Women's faces appeared and disappeared from other rooms.

Whispers.

Women's whispers. Children's whispers.

"*Muchacho,*" I said, making a 'so-high' gesture with my hand. "*Amigos* with Ratboy. Chaka."

"*No hablo —* "

"And *El Tigre*."

His eyes narrowed.

"*El Tigre?*" He spit. "*El Diablo*. Maria!" he barked over his shoulder.

Wiping her hands on a striped dish towel, a squat woman shuffled from the kitchen. She wore a voluminous brown blouse and a long print skirt beneath which poked cheap blue sneakers. The man stepped back.

"*Es Paco?*" she said.

The expressionless men gathered around the muted television pretended to watch Don Francisco make big faces and wide gestures.

"*Perdon*," I said. "*Hablas* English?"

"*Un poco*," she said, staring at the floor.

She smelled of onions, ammonia, furniture polish, and sweat. She looked tired, probably from a full-day of hard work and long walks between bus rides.

Little faces peeked from the kitchen. Bigger kids pushed the little ones into the room. The little ones giggled and scampered back. More faces appeared, cautious but curious faces, faces of kids who had not yet learned to fear a knock. A whispering, tittering mass crept forward – barefoot toddlers in hand-me-downs and cast-offs, snot-nosed kids licking upper lips with long tongues. A grim-faced woman bustled from the kitchen and shooed the children back.

"Paco calls himself Boo?" I said.

"*Si*. Boo."

"He's your son?"

Her resignation said the question had been asked many times. The response had become automatic.

"*Si*. He is *muerto?*"

She knew that day was coming. A knock on the door. News that her son was dead.

What could I say?

Soon?

Very soon?

"No," I said. "Where is he?"

She shrugged. "With *El Tigre.* He no come home ... " She held up three fingers.

"Three days?"

"*Si.*"

As we talked, a tiny, brown, shirtless girl in stained polka-dot panties inched from the kitchen. Close enough, she grasped the woman's skirt with one small hand. The other hand clutched a naked, blonde doll.

"*Mama? ... Mama?*" Frowning, the little one rubbed the naked doll against her bare belly.

Hungry.

"How many?" I said to the woman. "*Cuantos ninos.*"

"*Tres ninos.*"

The little one had huge eyes. She looked up at me, smiled, and buried her face in her mother's skirt.

I stooped.

She peeked and smiled again. The game of peek-a-boo had blunted her hunger.

"*Hola,*" I said.

"Hi," she giggled, hiding her face.

I didn't know what else to do, so I stood. I felt bad. Bad about ... I don't know, lots of things, hunger maybe, just bad. Ignoring all the reasons *not* to do it, I pulled bills from my pocket, whatever little I had, lifted the woman's hand, and pressed the money into her palm.

"For food," I said. "*Por los ninos.*"

"I am not beggar woman. I have job. I have — "

I closed her hand around the money and barged down the flowerpot-bordered walkway amid a new downpour. Someone who lived there – probably one of the women, maybe even Boo's mom – had borrowed from necessary drudgery time to invest in white flowers, because, in the world we wish for, beauty is also food. Grateful for the shelter of the car, I turned the key, but realized I had forgotten my manners. Ducking my head against the rain, I climbed out, stood the sagging gate straight, and re-hitched the make-shift latch.

CHAPTER FIFTEEN

"No security on this thing at all, Pete," Ricky said, sitting at his workbench. "The OS is two updates behind."

"OS?" I glanced at Kuntsler's computer as if I expected to see something.

"Operating system ... *Windows*, man."

"Oh, right. Sure." I felt a few updates behind myself.

"See the little file cabinet picture?"

"No need to get cute, Ricky. It's an *icon*."

He grinned. "That *icon* is the file manager link."

"I have a computer at the office. I can turn it on and everything."

"Click the file manager and you open ... ?"

"Kuntsler's programs and files."

"You're shreddin', Dude!"

A two sided window appeared on a workbench monitor. Ricky moved the cursor to the Word Perfect program and clicked again. An alphabetical list of file names ran off the screen.

"I can't wade through all that. Try sorting by date."

"Gel, man! Scope the list."

"I'm watching."

"I figure, if you're snaking this thing, it must be for files someone wants to *hide*."

He moved the mouse to VIEW on the menu bar, and clicked SHOW FILES on the drop down list. A new window of check boxes appeared.

"When you save a file, you can choose properties. Hidden is one property. Hidden files don't show up on the file index unless you put a checkmark *here*." He moved the cursor to an empty box that read *Show hidden/system files.*

"Okay. Show hidden, I get it. Now what?"

He checked the box and deleted checks from other boxes.

"Now when we list files we'll see the *hidden* files and nothing else. Dig?"

He clicked the mouse a few more times. The new list also ran off the screen, but most of the files ended in *.gif.*

"Gif?" I said. "Pictures?"

"The sicko stuff. But you just want the documents, right?"

He clicked to sort the list for Word Perfect files. The most recent was SHERIFF3.WPD. Toward the bottom – dated the day after the assault – FLNANGL.WPD.

"Got him!" I crowed, tapping the screen, but I caught myself. "Let's work backwards so we don't miss anything. Show me this SHERIFF3."

He maneuvered into the Word Perfect program and opened SHERIFF3. I read enough to see that it was juicy dope on the Grand Jury investigation of campaign financing that Fred had mentioned. Among a list of contributors were the usual Republican suspects along with a raft of Clinton/Gore backers, Lemon Tom shell companies, and newer names I associated with Frankie Mendez. Local politics made for strange bedfellows

"No help," I said. "Try the next."

We plowed through seven more files, all background notes on current events, and then opened FLNANGL. While Ricky printed the pages, I read from the monitor and etched one paragraph into my brain.

Ramon (El Tigre) Guiterrez. 17. Telephone (714) 555-
1212. Address 9 Pacifica Vista, Lemon Ridge.

Lemon Ridge was an old hillside orchard terraced into million dollar estates. Technically it was San Dismas in the same way Bel Air was technically L.A.

Mother: Anna. Father: Hector.

That explained Lemon Ridge. Hector Guiterrez was a face in *Banner* ads and TV pitches for dozens of Guiterrez Nurseries scattered across southern California. In one respect *El Tigre was* another Che – a poor, little rich kid.

I continued down the list, but the files, all dated before the assault, contained info on older, unrelated stories, nothing useful. I folded the FLNANGL printout and slipped it into my coat pocket to study later. Reaching for my wallet, I remembered that I had given Jesus the reserve.

"I'm tapped right now, Ricky. I'll catch you tomorrow."

"Whack that, man. This was jank. You and me's *homies*."

"Homies have to eat. Not to mention I interrupted — "

I mulled it for a moment and decided.

"How about I ask Tawny to come over?"

"Squash that!" he sputtered, blushing. "I'm just a woofie to Tawny!"

"She likes you, Ricky. She told me."

"You're talking out the side of your neck, man!"

I squeezed his shoulder. "No, really. She says you treat her like a real person – like a person you could *like*. Plus she thinks you're cute."

He rubbed his hand over his crew cut.

"Get out! Fer sure, man?"

"For real, Ricky. You can ask her."

CHAPTER SIXTEEN

I rang Blake's from the Blazer.

"It's Pete, Blake. Jesus there?"

"Lemme look ... Naw. He left a little after you. Haven't seen him back."

"How about Tawny?"

"Yeah. I'll get her." He paused. "Say, Pete. You okay, man?"

"It's not that, Blake. Put her on."

"Okay. Just a sec."

Tawny was a good kid with bad breaks that had nudged her into a lousy job. Off the clock and wanting decent company, she frequented Blake's. Often we teamed for eight-ball and usually won. Sometimes I sprang for a champagne cocktail or she treated me to a Sapporo and we talked. Occasionally, if I was undercover, I hired her as a decoy or arm candy. When necessary I schooled guys who mistook her private enterprise for a public conveyance, and I shooed away creeps who wanted to tax her revenue.

"Hello?"

Her voice was a warm, breathy whisper.

"Hi, Emily, it's Pete." Emily was her real name. Not many people knew that. "I've never asked you for this, but ... are you available?"

"Oooooo," she said with a playful little squeal. "All things come to she who waits."

"C'mon, kiddo, I'm old enough to be your father."

The dead air made me cringe.

"Emily, I ... Listen, that was a dumb remark. I'm sorry."

"If this is business, Pete, call me Tawny." Her voice had turned wintery. "Emily is personal. *No* one calls me Emily."

"Just your friends."

"Sure. All my friends."

"Look, *Emily* ... I can't afford to lose my eight-ball partner, so we'll skip this, okay? Tell Blake I'm buying you a drink."

She took a deep breath. "Just hold on, Pete." Another couple of breaths. "Okay, okay ... I'm over it. So ... who, where, and when?"

"I wouldn't even do this, but — "

"*I* chose my profession, Pete. I choose it again every day."

"Well ... look, I think you like the guy anyway and I *know* he's gaga over you. Ricky. The computer kid."

"He's a sweetheart," she said, warming. "Blushes when I catch him peeking up my skirt."

"Feelings will do that to a guy," I said. "Can you make a house call? He has a flat on Fourth."

"Over the TV place, right?"

"That's the one. He'll be waiting for you."

"I'm on my way then."

"Great, but listen. I'm busy now. Am I good till tomorrow?"

"I trust you, Pete. Sure. You're good." She said it a little wistfully.

Ricky scooted from the shop, locked the accordion gate, and shot me a hang loose gesture. Waving the phone, I made an okay sign. He pumped a fist and darted upstairs.

Before I could drive away, I noticed a muffled, message-waiting tone from my beeper and cursed myself for forgetting it in the console. Grimly I called my service.

"We beeped and beeped, Mr. Pinel!"

"The hospital?"

"No. Several calls from the same irate, uh ... gentleman. Fred Lynch of the *Banner*? He said you used to be friends. He insisted I deliver his message word for word. It's quite graphic. Should I?"

"I can take it if you can, Sylvie."

"Don't worry. In this job I get an earful."

"Then say it."

"He said ... these are *his* words, Mr. Pinel ... he said you crossed the fucking line. The police have your name and he'll do what he can to put your nuts in a wringer. The *Banner* guards have orders to escort you off the property *with prejudice* ... he said to emphasize that last part. He said for you to look up *damnatio memoriae* and hung up. Did I pronounce that correctly?"

"Razor perfect."

I disconnected and sat stewing. I punched myself in the leg and cursed. Kuntsler was a dumb play. Dumb! I should've tried harder to work it through Fred somehow. I should have trusted him or ... or something. I should have thought of *something*.

I shook my head and phoned the hospital. Leticia was pulling a double. She said Ronnie woke for a few minutes, but was out again by the time Sharfstein got there.

I disconnected and made the other call.

"*Banner*. Lynch."

"I got your message, Fred."

A long, long silence.

Some must choose.

"I know it's Veronica, Pete. I know you just found out and I know you're bat-shit crazy right now."

I listened to another silence, that peculiar echo-y silence of car phones, a sound that always brought to mind the bottom of a deep hole.

"So ... I've cooled some. But I can't just strike through the fact that you fucked me, man. I was a friend, and you fucked me."

"Fred, this Kuntsler is a stone prick. And I ... I never thought it would link back to you. I wasn't thinking."

"You're *never* thinking. You scratch whatever itches!"

"I'll return it, Fred. All of it."

"You don't get it, do you? You're so gone, you don't even get it! Can you return the security of his sources? Can you return the standing of the paper? And how do you return the certainty I had that you wouldn't fuck me?"

"Fred, when this is over, I'll explain."

"Sure, Pete. At Blake's. A few weeks, you'll buy me a beer and tell the tale. Maybe throw in some dope on that counterfeit drug case. Hell, man, you're always good for copy, and I guess I have my uses, too."

"Fred ... ?"

"I hope it was worth it, Pete."

For the first time since I'd known him he sounded as old as people claimed. I heard a deep sigh and the connection ended.

I sat for a while more. The storm had waned and the sound of rain brushing against the roof and windshield was like a quiet whisper inside my head. I thought about Hurley stuffing his mouth with cinnamon roll and realized I was hungry. I drove back to Carmel's, but kept going when I saw two patrol cars sitting outside.

With nothing yet to connect me to the crack house and only accusations regarding Kuntsler's computer, I doubted that the Blazer had made a stop sheet. Before my luck ran out, however, I turned into an all night drugstore, parked inconspicuously between two cars near the door, and climbed into the rear seat to take advantage of the tinted windows. Donning latex gloves again, I disassembled and wiped prints from the shotgun, then field-stripped the automatic. Since I had retrieved my spent shell casing, I left the firing pin and extractor in place, but reassembled the gun minus the telltale barrel. Until I could fetch a spare barrel from my safe, I traded for a clean .45 I kept in an under-the-dash lockbox that routine searches had missed for years. Even if the car were impounded and fine-combed before I got back to the office, a suspiciously incomplete .45 was still merely suspicious.

I zigzagged several miles to drop shotgun pieces in widely separate trash bins. Since I didn't want some dumpster-diving kid using the shotgun rounds for firecrackers, I deep sixed those, the shell casing, and the barrel from the .45 down a rushing storm drain.

Breathing easier, I stopped at an ATM for cash and made my way to Denny's. I tucked the Blazer out of sight behind the restaurant and slogged through the rain to the entrance.

"Why you poor thing!" a skinny, brunette waitress fluttered. "Out without an umbrella on a night like this."

"I'm a tough guy," I said.

"Tough guys get wet, honey, just like the rest of us." She escorted me to a rear booth. "I'll bring you some toweling paper. Coffee?"

"You're an angel," I said, blotting my face with the napkin from the placemat. "Sheez! Think this rain will *ever* stop? We may need an ark."

"Fire next time," she said sweetly. "And you tough guys best believe in the *only* umbrella for that."

Preachy Christians, like grumbly Republicans, were part of the Orange County landscape. I was used to both.

She brought the coffee along with a stack of toweling. I ordered the steak special, blotted my face, neck, and hair, then overflowed the coffee cup with four plastic thimbles of cream. I took a sip, felt better, and began to read FLNANGL.

CHAPTER SEVENTEEN

The pages contained black and white background facts buried in purple prose slathered red with commentary that the *Globe* would have blue-penciled, much less the *Banner*. Perhaps Kuntsler was writing a book. Mao had. Hitler, too. I memorized the addresses I needed and kept reading.

Ronnie's history was there along with a bit about me and a *lot* about Sharfstein's money, including a tirade about Ronnie's wedding ring. Ratboy and Dad were there – how Ratboy had spent years in foster homes while Dad was serially rehabilitated. Boo's mother was there – not much about working two jobs after her husband disappeared, but plenty about how her "identification with their oppressors had stunted the children." Thank God for *El Tigre*. "Ramon's revolutionary fire kindled Boo's class consciousness and illuminated his road to freedom." Apparently the road had way stations – charges of truancy, possession, burglary, assault, and finally declaration as an Incorrigible Youth.

Chaka was different. *Very* different. Real name Frank Stebbins, he sprang from an intact, hard-working, middle class family. Nevertheless, by kindergarten, setting fires had become his passion and mutilating neighborhood pets a special calling. Often he combined his interests. And since Frank was already six feet tall in grade school, he spent most of his childhood in locked mental hospitals where – immersed in rules with consistent consequences and steeped in medication – he was *sometimes* good. But when he was bad!

He was *especially* bad when he stopped taking his medication.

Turned out, he *hated* medication.

During an outpatient stint, Frank's psychiatrist suggested Little League baseball as recreational therapy. Good idea or not, the team was bum luck, because the Angels introduced Frank to Ramon. According to Kuntsler, "Ramon saw in this pitiful, yet fearless beast, a tool as necessary to the struggle as was Beria for Stalin." Soon Frank heard Ramon's voice even louder than the ones in his head. Wondering about voices in Kuntsler's head, I sipped my coffee and continued to read.

As the only person who neither feared, despised, nor rejected Frank, Ramon became his absolute master and jokingly bestowed the boy a new name, Chaka. In a sacramental test of obedience, he ordered Chaka to break the arm of a handy subject who happened to be the team coach. Chaka – unsuitable for Juvenile Hall – cycled through another mental hospital. Kuntsler saw a mark of greatness in the fact that "Ramon's *genuine* fondness for the coach had not deterred his experiment." He also railed against the "class injustice done" when "on the flimsiest of pretexts" Ramon, Boo, and Ratboy were bounced from the team, as well.

I read the last paragraph.

> "With fascist vacuity, the police trust to muscle
> and manpower while class blindness obscures
> intersections of oppressor and oppressed. The
> masses quaff random violence as an opiate.
> Asleep, they miss the obvious statement."

STATEMENT! I clutched the papers as if I could squeeze life from them.

"You spilled your coffee, honey."

I looked up and found the waitress holding my steak and

potato in one hand and a coffee pot in the other.

I lifted my arms so she could put down the platter. She wiped the table with a rag from her apron pocket and refilled my coffee cup. I struggled with the cream thimbles again and ate mechanically, reminding myself that, anger-blinded or not, I needed fuel since I might —

Blind to what intersections?

I re-read Kuntsler's pages.

Chaka was mentally unfit for Juvenile Hall. In Orange County, that meant Olivewood as a first stop before placement. Ratboy spent time in foster homes for which Olivewood was also the prelim. Boo had been deemed incorrigible, a pronouncement the Court made *after* an Olivewood evaluation. Rich kids ended up there, too. Rich kids like Ramon, anyway.

I saw a far uglier picture.

Veronica had stumbled into a web of spiders she *knew*.

I clenched my eyes and fists and tried to breathe. When I succeeded, I covered my check with a ten, went outside, and huddled momentarily under the entrance overhang while a fresh deluge strafed the lot.

I had plenty to convict Ramon and the others in *my* court, but I seemed to hear Fred insisting that I was bat-shit crazy. To shut him up, I considered how I could move from preponderance of the evidence to beyond reasonable doubt.

Medical records, especially mental health records, are hard to tap. Even if cops had dug up as much detail as Kuntsler, enough to link Ronnie to the Fallen Angels, her case files might still be intact. Proof could be sitting in her office at Olivewood.

As I broke for the Blazer, something about FLNANGL flitted through my head. Standing with my key in the door lock, I waited for the thing to circle back. Cold rain streamed from my hair, down my forehead, over my cheeks, but the date that exploded in my mind's eye burned unquenchably – like white phosphorous, like brimstone.

I raised my face against the rain and brayed. Hurrying toward his car, a man toting a Denny's doggie bag saw me laughing and halted. Looking scared, he turned and ran.

As if he had just seen the devil.

CHAPTER EIGHTEEN

Inside the car, I wiped my face with my hands, started the engine, and buzzed Ricky.

"Zup?"

No music this time.

"It's Pete."

"Are you wasted? This is *harsh*. Emily's here!"

Tawny had made a new friend.

"I'll square it so she stays the night if this pans out, okay?"

"What?"

"The date on a file is the date it was saved, right?"

"Yep."

"And anything added later changes the date?"

"Fer sure."

"Then Kuntsler wrote FLNANGL *one day* after the crime. *Way* too much detail. He knew the subjects *before* the crime."

"Like an accomplice or something!"

"I'll turn you into a private eye yet. But what I'm hoping, Ricky, is that there's more. Earlier stuff."

"Nothing, Pete."

"How about the diskettes?"

"Checked."

I pounded my fist against the steering wheel. "Damn! He must've deleted it."

Ricky chuckled. "Is that all?"

"All? If he deleted everything — "

"Chill, man! Even digitheads sometimes forget that

deleting a file doesn't *erase* it."

"Meaning?"

"It's probably still on the hard drive. Some of it, anyway. Finding what's left is no biggie."

"How?"

"When you delete a file all you do is clear its name and address from the index."

"Okay. *And?*"

"The computer forgets that it still remembers. It treats the address as free space and overwrites it with new stuff. But if the space hasn't been used yet, the file is still there. Plus, new stuff might fill only part of the space, so pieces are left."

"You can find the pieces?"

"Eat chain, man! I can do that right here. I mirror the hard drive and dump any indexed bytes. What's left is the free space. Any code in the free space is part of a deleted file. I gather the pieces that convert to text and filter them using key words from FLNANGL."

"How long?"

"Couple hours. Maybe less. A few more and I can do the same for slack space in indexed files. If it's honkin' critical, I can dig beneath the overwriting, but I'd have to find hardware I don't have."

"Go the quick route. Can you jump on it?"

"Well ... *pretty* soon."

"Let me speak to Emily."

She came on.

"Sounds like you two are getting along," I said.

"I told you. He's a sweetheart."

"I need him to do something. Can you stay while he does? Stay the night?"

She spoke away from the mouthpiece. "You want me to stay, Ricky? You want to watch over me?"

I heard Ricky say, "I won't close an eye all night, Emily!"

"See? A sweetheart. Sure, Pete, I'll stay."

"But let him do my work first, okay? Put him on."

"Here Ricky," she chuckled. "Pete wants to say he comes first."

Ricky took the phone. "I'll call when I — "

His voice broke and I knew that he was dealing with a growing distraction. I probably had less than a minute before all the blood was out of his brain.

"Listen, Ricky. Whatever you find, fax it to my office ASAP. Can do?"

"Yeah ... I got the number. Couple hours."

"If I have questions, I'll buzz you."

Breathing.

"Try ... *not to* ... Pete."

Disconnecting, I decided that a couple of hours was optimistic. Considering how long refractory periods had lasted when *I* was Ricky's age, morning was more likely. I had rarely finished a smoke.

CHAPTER NINETEEN

As a Child Psychologist at Olivewood, the county children's shelter, Veronica saw things that broke faith, dashed hope, and destroyed charity. Abandoned kids. Abused kids. Kids plucked from homes to save their lives. Insane kids. Defiant kids. Kids just short of serious crime. Kids who had crossed that line.

Usually the kids were drowning and Olivewood was a last, desperate life ring before a raging current of events swept them on to the Juvenile Hall next door and the Branch Jail after that or – in the other direction – the hospital and the morgue.

But evil washed through there, too. Not just chosen, but choosers. Malevolent souls who would yank the life ring, hoping to drown their rescuer. Although Veronica had always squirmed when I put it that way, a part of her knew how true it was – the part afraid to have children.

Olivewood came up on my right. Since the administration building was closed and dorm visiting hours over, the rain-swept lot sat mostly empty. I buried the car among other parked cars, climbed in the back seat, and made my burglar transformation again. Jotting a mental note to buy more throwaway sneakers, I waited for my eyes to adapt to the dark before I scurried to a side entrance.

I knew the layout from two weeks I had spent at Olivewood undercover, back when I first met Ronnie, back when —

No.

I couldn't look at that yet.

I shook my head to dislodge the memory and shouldered my thoughts toward the *soluble* problem of the door.

Admissions went directly to dorm buildings after eight. A cleanup crew finished with the offices around nine. That left only a watchman who made —

I caught the glow of an approaching light, stepped backward, and squatted in the giant, arching spread of a wet philodendron. Heavy raindrops pattered the elephant-ear leaves. Waggling a flash, a watchman rounded the corner.

The beam swept by me as the guard meandered up to the door and jiggled the handle. He was close enough for me to smell his after-shave, one reason we burglar types avoid the stuff. Probably he shined his light through the glass panel to peer inside, but I kept my face down and my latex gloves tucked into my armpits until he moved on. When I heard his footsteps disappear, I tried again.

At the end of the undercover job, I had recommended that Olivewood uproot the Philodendron. Judging by the absence of door and window trips, the County had ignored my alarm recommendation, too. I had a jimmy-bar hooked in my belt, just in case, but a break-in would have drawn attention to Ronnie's office, so I spent ten minutes picking the lock. Inside I stood listening for sounds other than rain against windows, decided I was alone, and felt my way down a dark corridor.

A warbling phone jolted me. I froze through two rings, then remembered that calls were forwarded to the dorms at night. I continued to the last office and tried the locked door knob. Kneeling, I used the picks again, stepped inside, and closed the door behind me.

It was possible that Ronnie had moved since I was last there. The County might have surrendered finally the window-office she longed for. Despite total darkness, however, I knew the room was hers, because ... well, because she *lingered* in it. The feeling was so strong I reminded myself that feelings can distort perception and bend judgment. I knew that any *physical* basis for the sensation was, at best, some molecular residue of her shampoo or a persistent pheromone that the reptilian part of my brain recognized. Still ... all experience, even false experience, is real, and the *experience* was of a presence.

Sure enough, when I switched on my pocket flash, I saw Ronnie's pictures on the wall. One was an astonishing likeness of her painted by an older kid she had treated, a prodigy whose parents had died in a car crash. As always, the brilliant eyes made a catch in my breath, although, to be honest, the kid had not quite captured them.

Since I was strictly a stick-figure doodler dumbfounded by *real* drawing, my observation was curiosity not criticism. I imagined a painter having to talk his way through his subject, feature by feature, having to explain each feature to himself, and then somehow translate his words into brush strokes. In that scenario, eyes easier to explain would be easier to paint. I pictured the green-eyes of that Afghan girl on the *National Geographic* cover: eyes that stun with color and contrast. And Faye Dunaway's eyes in her smoke-framed afterglow in *Chinatown*: eyes that astound with shape and form. Even *I* could paint eyes like those. Well, *almost.*

But Ronnie's eyes? How *could* the kid have rendered their unforgettable quality when I myself struggled to explain it? Not color. Her eyes were almost black. And while certainly they were large, arched and sparkling – I called them cathedral window eyes – I suspected something more ethereal than shape stirred *that* comparison.

The kid had *nailed*, however, Ronnie's devouring gaze.

I studied the painting a moment and shook my head no.

The look was there, but the *name* I had always used for it was wrong. Ronnie's stare *enveloped* you, but not to swallow. Not with teeth. Penetrating? No, she never saw through you. If anything, her stare reflected you, more like an ultrasound than an x-ray. You saw your reflection in Ronnie's gaze, and the reflection you saw reflected her. Share that gaze long enough, and I suspected that you'd actually come to know each other – not everything, but *enough*.

I stood looking until a ringing phone broke the spell. Glancing at my watch, I realized how late it was and forced my attention back to my work. I tipped the file cabinet to get at the locking mechanism. I freed the bar, lowered the cabinet, and opened the 'G' drawer. Between files labeled *Guiterrez, Paul* and *Guiterrez, Tomas* hung *Guiterrez, Ramon*. I glanced inside. *El Tigre.*

He knew her.

And still he did this thing!

I stashed the file contents in my shirt, replaced the empty folder, and glanced to confirm files on the chums. Securing the office, I crept back to the side door, made sure the door locked behind me, and darted to the Blazer.

Although the signal at the end of the driveway was green, I stopped. To my right was a waiting hospital room. To my left was a fax machine. I sat wrapped in the patter of rain and the hush of my breathing.

I *needed* to finish it.

I had to *tell* her I had finished it.

I *had* to.

Ricky's fax might be key.

Some must choose.

I turned left, rushed back to my office, and ditched the Blazer in the lot opposite the building. As I bolted across the street, a cannonballing bus splashed a flooded pothole over me. Cursing and brushing slop from my coat, I pounded the lobby-door for the night guard to buzz me in. Ignoring his wave, I barreled straight onto the elevator. When the door rattled open, however, I realized that his wave had been more than a greeting.

Cross-legged on the hallway floor outside my office, quietly enjoying his cigar, sat Lt. Manny Vasquez.

CHAPTER TWENTY

"Why didn't you let yourself in, Manny," I said, twisting my key in the lock. Manny stood, brushed off his pants, and followed me inside. I flipped on a light.

"Tom's gone," he said. "We have rules now."

"Beer?"

"Sure," he said.

Ignoring the chair, he poked around the familiar office as if it were a fresh crime scene. I hooked two Sapporos from the fridge, pried off the caps, and watched him snoop.

Manny was scarcely taller than average, about as tall as Mike Tyson. But he was built like Tyson, too, every inch thick and solid. In a ring with Manny, Queensberry rules, I'd rate myself an odds on favorite based on reach and weight. But *real* fights have no rules, and I'd seen Manny in action enough to know that reach and weight alone wouldn't do it. Some people would take the odds. *Particularly* Manny.

I sniffed. Manny always smelled like a barber shop. His black hair – combed straight back and shellacked in place with some fragrant, bottled tonic – looked slick and shiny. His thin moustache was finely etched, and his cheeks were forever baby-butt smooth from twice daily shaves. He dressed well, too – not expensively, but correctly. I asked him once if he used those hangers that kept the creases in your pants. He did. Shoe trees, too. *Shoe trees*, for Christ's sake! A fastidious, punctilious gent was Manny with an air that asshats might construe as gigolo. All others read the unambiguous *Not For Sale* sign in his eyes and saved themselves the lesson that went with asking.

Fed up with his snooping, I said, "Chu gotta problem, man? Chu look like chu gotta problem."

He blew a smoke ring at me. "Funny, Pete. You're really into funny now that your brain is turning to mush."

He dropped into a chair. I handed him a beer and cold glass. Manny considered drinking from a bottle uncouth. And since we spent a lot of Saturdays in my office watching Angel games or whatever, I kept glasses chilling for him in the fridge. I plopped into my own chair, raised my bottle and chugged. Leisurely Manny inspected his glass for grime and poured – just the right angle and flow for a proper head. He lifted the glass, observed his handiwork and sipped.

"You're over the line, Pete," he said finally.

"Write me a ticket."

"See your mouth? I'm here to talk."

"You want to talk to me?"

"Damn few people *ever* want to talk to you, 'cause you're as full of crap as a Christmas turkey! You burgled Kuntsler's house and stole his computer. That's not like you."

"No?"

"Shortcuts are like you. Bending and breaking the law when you think you're right is like you. Screwing your friends is *not* like you."

I studied the label on my Sapporo bottle. There wasn't much to see.

"That's right," he said. "Fred talked to me. Now *you* talk to me."

"Up yours, Manny."

"Sure, Pete. Up mine. And then which friend do you screw? Blake? Jesus? You don't have many, you know. You're over the line."

He looked around for an ashtray, found none, and stood to douse his cigar in the corner sink. He rinsed the ashes from

the sink bowl, then dropped the quenched stub in a
wastebasket.

"Over the line ..." I mused. "That's what you called Tom
the night you pulled him off me at the station house."

Manny ambled to the window and looked out. On a good
night he could have watched Disneyland fireworks through
the gap between buildings across Main, but it wasn't a good
night. Rain beaded the window pane and trickled down. The
long, arched, scratch-test Jesus had gouged in the glass
contrasted sharply with the fickle, natural patterns of the
raindrops.

"You remind me of Tom sometimes," Manny said. "He was
a lot like you."

"I was taller. And whiter."

He ignored me.

"Like you, he was flawed. *Visibly* flawed. But he was a
diamond among good-*looking* zircons and crumbly yag. He
was a damn good cop, a damn good guy. For a long time he
was. San Dismas was a straighter place when he was in
charge. The dope was pretty much corralled and it wasn't
crack. He made sure the whores and the bums *had* a place
and kept them to it. Because of Tom, old folks could stroll the
streets at night, kids could play in the parks. But – like you –
Tom often skimped on the thinking. If it felt right, he did it.
But what feels right, often *isn't* right. Not in the long run.
Tom crossed the line. Before he knew it, he couldn't get back."

"Verily, verily, let he who has ears ... C'mon, Manny, cut
me a huss with the parables! Some cop-hating flack whines I
violated his rights, and suddenly I'm Lemon Tom's evil twin?"

"I said you were *like* him, not the same. Tom had to be a
big shot while you go your own way. That's a real difference.
Tom *needed* people. Needed them like those lemons of his. He
needed people to boss, people to help, people to punish. He
needed ... *awe*."

"He should've run for President."

Manny snorted. "Sure! Like *Patton* as President. I said he

was a *diamond*, Pete, not a politician. Christ ... can you see Lemon Tom making himself that common – chatting up old ladies, kissing babies, glad-handing a crowd, *asking* rather than telling? ... You know, I think that's what broke him in the end."

"What?"

"Asking. The knowledge that beyond a certain point he would always have to *ask*. Get permission from lesser men. I think asking was a worm that gnawed at his heart. And to rid the pain, Tom finally just crossed the line and *took* what he wanted, mostly power. *That's* the part that's you. Not the taking or the power, but that you act your own mind, and the rest of us be damned. *That* part, that's Tom."

The FAX machine started to clatter. We turned our heads. Print side down, a page ratcheted onto the output tray.

"What you came for?" Manny said.

I raised my beer. "*This* is what I came for, Manny. I'm sticking around in case the hospital calls."

Trying to look indifferent, I stood and curled the sheet for a peek. No source stamp and Ricky would have used hacker tricks to cover his tracks. Nevertheless, Kuntsler's name plastered the page. It was enough for Manny to run me in if he took liberties with his report. Enough to hold me for arraignment if he thought a little cell time would build my character.

"A collection job," I said.

"Skip tracing is off your beat. You're bottom feeding, Pete."

"We all have to pay our debts," I said.

Manny watched a second page creep from the FAX. He was mulling a grab; I knew I would have. I noted the position of his feet, his hands, the snapped retaining strap on his belt holster.

Over the line. Screwing your friends. The words buzzed in my head like gadflies, but I shooed them away to focus on how I would do it if I had to – how I would take Manny down if he moved toward the machine.

"I couldn't reach you, Pete. I tried. Believe me, I thought you knew about Veronica."

"I've been off the grid on a case," I said. "But let's get real. You know me well enough to *know* I didn't know."

"Meaning that I hadn't seen what would follow from you knowing? Maybe. But I'm not such a bastard that I'd keep it from you either. You choose between the two."

I said nothing.

"Let it be, Pete. Let me take care of it. I *will* take care of it."

"I have a client," I lied, betting Sharfstein would cover it. "I have a license. I have rights."

"This one's different, Pete. Time was, you had the *Banner* to carry water for you. And friends on the force. Even Tom looked the other way for you. And when he ran the rackets, you could move in that world, too, because he liked you."

"That's what he *said*."

"Because he *did*. But it's a different world now."

"That reminds me." I pulled a book from the bookshelf and riffled the pages.

"What's so important?"

"I was right!" I gloated. "Hobbes ... war of everyone against everyone."

"Go ahead. Ignore me. The fact remains, you can't go toe to toe with these punks like you did Tom. Tom led an army. Now it's rabble and riot. You see the news this morning? Some Dog Troop survivors sprayed a packed church to ice a 12 year old who sent someone's girl a birthday card. Eight wounded. A baby and the twelve year-old on slabs."

"Kids against grown-ups are a dead fall, Manny. Adults put the kids down, that's that."

"You calling an audible, Pete?"

He leaned forward, muscles taut, arms dangling between his legs. He looked a little like an offensive lineman about to spring. I primed myself, but I saw him stand down.

"Look, Pete ... I can't keep you off Veronica's case without jailing you, probably without killing you, and I'm not ready to do that. Not *yet*." He rose. "Fred says you're bat-shit crazy, but I'm betting you're still too good a cop, too good a *man,* to drop *major*-hurt on someone who hasn't earned it. As for Kuntsler? Nobody on the force gives a damn *what* happens to that crap-spouting weasel. The *Banner* juice buys a lab crew to dust. A few uniforms asking around. But minus some bonehead error on your part, you skate."

"Are *you* crossing the line, Manny?"

"*Not* so I'm stuck. You skate until you slip and break your dumb neck." He glanced at the FAX again, moved to the door, and looked back. "Your balance is zero, man. No one's covering your bad checks anymore."

I took a long drink from the beer bottle and contemplated the label again.

"It's cold out there alone," Manny said.

"I've been," I said.

"No, you haven't, Pete. You just like to think so."

CHAPTER TWENTY ONE

Standing at the window, I scanned the half-dozen, curled
FAX pages – a jumble of words, letters, numbers, symbols.
When I saw Manny cross the street and drive away, I scooted
downstairs to use the lobby pay phone. Ricky answered on the
tenth ring without a "Zup."

"It's Pete," I said.

"No, duh! ... Pete, I love ya, but you gotta cut me loose
tonight!"

"The FAX is gibberish, Ricky. Explain what I'm looking at."

"Translated unaddressed hexadecimal."

"English!"

"Gel, dude! Hey, I dunno, I guess sometimes ... sometimes
I figure you're like my Dad, you know? That you know most
everything, like he did, you know? ... Okay, look. Remember
what I said about a hard drive and forgotten memories? I read
the drive front to back as a single string of ones and zeros.
Each digit has an address. I subtract from the string any
addresses listed in the drive index. That gets rid of all the
current programs and files and leaves the free space. A lot of
the free space – spoiled and unused sectors, overwritten
stuff – won't translate. I subtract that part, too. What *does*
translate is deleted code and text. I weeded out as much as I
could of the formatting, graphics and op code, but text can

have numbers and hexadecimal notation includes letters so the result can be messy."

"Okay, I get it. The words and syllables are from deleted text files. The rest is noise. But why so jumbled?"

"Deleted files get overwritten with new stuff, right? The new stuff is indexed, so it's subtracted."

"Punching holes in the deleted files."

"Get up, man! Plus, computers don't always store things in a line. The disk gets fragmented. The beginning of a file might be near the end of the drive, the end at the beginning. Dig?"

"So bring me home here. What I'm looking at is like shuffled picture-puzzle pieces laid end to end with a lot of pieces missing?"

"Fer sure. Move 'em around. Fit 'em together. If you're lucky, you find *enough* pieces to guess the picture."

I glanced at the pages again and began to see sentences and sentence fragments peeking through the camouflage.

"You sorted using key words from the FLNANGL file."

"You're a brainiac, dude."

"So there's more."

"You said quick and dirty."

"Okay, hold on a sec. Let me see what I have."

I heard Emily sigh in the background.

"C'mon, Pete," Ricky said, "I — "

"Just hold on!"

He held, but the silence was frosty.

Skipping around, I saw that dates *definitely* preceded the assault. I weaved some of the words into notes about Boo, Chaka, and Ratboy, but Ramon was the star.

> "... Ramon is a born leader who transcends
> Hector's bourgeois ... Ramon lulled 12th Street
> into ... "

Some of the pieces referred to a hideout near the stadium.

> "... The Pit is Ramon's secure ... despite the Pit's
> proximity to the Angel "A" ... Ramon always
> falls back to the safety of the Pit ... "

That's where they were, but *where*? I slapped at the pages.

" … Ramon threatened me! … my connection to
Ramon jeopardizes … must delete my notes as
soon as … "

Several complete sentences referred to a Fallen Angels hangout – the Mini-Mart on Main in Orange. I had my next stop.

"Pete? … You there man?"

"You hit a homer, Ricky. When you can, sort for one more term and see if anything pops up. Pit – P .. I .. T. That's what I'll be looking for."

"You got it. First thing in the morning?"

"Good enough. Did you break anything?"

"Naw. Still cherry."

"Hide it."

"No sweat."

"I mean *hide*, Ricky. Someone may look."

"Get real, Pete! I've got Feds up my chute non-stop. Those knobs keep me in business repairing TV's just so they can plant bugs and follow me around."

"I'll call you Monday at the latest. If you don't hear … well, you know Manny, right?"

"The cop? Sure."

"If you don't hear, shoot the works to Lt. Manual Vasquez, SDPD. Add a note from me saying … oh, I don't know, say… 'Adios, Manny. Put these guys down for me.'"

A long silence.

"Nothing … like, nothing's gonna happen to you, is it, Pete?"

"No. Of course not."

"I mean … if you need help, I can come now."

"You've done your part. Plenty."

"No, really, I'm stronger than I look. And I can fight. I had to fight dudes in the lock-up that time. I could — "

"The rest is *my* work, Ricky. I'm good at it."

"Yeah, but, I mean, like … if something happened, I'd hate

to, uh ... not *be* there, you know?"

"Everything's jake! I'll see you soon, okay? Come spring we'll take in an Angel's game. The opener, how's that?"

"Fer sure, man?"

"Absolutely."

Another silence.

"Just be careful, Pete. Cause sometimes, like, you don't know, dig? I mean, like you see somebody and its all cool, but, like, you never, ever see 'em again."

"That's a downer, Ricky. Enjoy your company. I'll see you soon."

"Yeah?"

"Yeah, soon."

"... Okay, man. See ya."

The lobby guard, accustomed to my use of the pay phone, sat absorbed in a crossword puzzle. I stood staring at the FAX pages. I stirred the fragments in my mind and watched them bump and stick or bounce apart.

Suddenly two colliding pieces fused violently into a nucleus whose gravity captured another piece and another, the mass altogether becoming a *critical* mass, becoming the end written when Sharfstein called.

The end that now would be!

My shaking hands blurred the words, but I didn't need to see them again.

> "... Ramon reviled her haughty ... told Ramon
> that I, too, knew those spoiled ... Ramon took my
> term 'rich bitch' concretely ... Fallen Angels'
> stunt was useful theatre ... Ramon's only
> blunder was that the psych ..."

The final letters were either buried somewhere in the gibberish or lost as one of the holes, but I *knew* what the sentence had read.

*Ramon's only blunder was that the psychologist **lived**.*

My hands steadied. My breathing quieted. My heart slowed. I felt that finally-above-the-weather serenity I had always felt forward-spotting in Nam when I at-last found the target and spoke into a handset words that summoned F4s swooping like archangels.

And down rained hellfire.

CHAPTER TWENTY TWO

I had Ramon, guilty beyond doubt. I had Kuntsler, equally guilty playing Charlie Manson to ignite a Helter Skelter Gotterdammerung to settle scores with some "rich bitch" from his past. I had a gathering spot I knew and a hideout called the Pit that I would find.

I took Ramon's file from my coat pocket and skimmed the pages. Psychological tests, answer sheets of filled in circles, wordy reports, and Veronica's handwritten session notes dated a year back. The word *tiger* appeared repeatedly in the notes. Ramon seemed to have some nutty fixation with the zoo.

The River Trail Jogger was an accident that *wasn't* an accident. Maybe somewhere in the words was a reason. But I didn't need a reason. I didn't even *want* a reason. I glanced at my watch.

ALWAYS THERE.

Ronnie was waiting, but — No, not *yet*. I *had* to finish it. Kuntsler, Ramon and the others. *After* I had finished it, I would find Jesus and ... keep my promise.

I slammed my fist against the phone. The lobby cop jumped. I fished more coins from my pocket, checked my address book, and dialed.

"Put Mendez on," I ordered the flunky who answered. "Tell him it's Pinel. Tell him I'm the one who crashed his house near Taft tonight."

I heard mumbling through a hand smothering the

mouthpiece.

"I diss you somehow?" said a new voice.

"Frankie, your breathing disses me. I wish I'd done more that night in the park than clean your clock."

He laughed. "That ass-kicking was my wake-up call, man. Put me on the road to success. You're like a Big Brother."

"Well, tonight had nothing to do with you or 12th Street. Strictly business. I want Tiger. Your house was a lead."

"Who's Tiger?"

"Save your breath, Frankie. You don't have that many left. I'm thinking you know *why* I want him, so you know *what* I'll do to get him."

He considered it for a moment.

"Where's my man from the house?"

"Two hours gone in a white, three year old Ford. He's running from *you*, Frankie, not me."

"Why?"

"Because he's ten large short. Took your money to set up shop with Tiger."

"Yeah? Fredo says a cop busted in and made him for the ten large."

Dad hadn't got very far at all.

"You're not nearly as stupid as everyone says, Frankie. Not stupid enough to think I knock over crack houses for chump change. And Tiger was buying, right? Ask your man where Tiger got the dough."

Silence.

"Ask him how I knew about the deal. How I knew to find his house. Ask him how I know about the Pit."

"I been looking for this Pit."

I was stitching it together on the fly, but I had to keep sewing.

"I have it all, Frankie. From Kuntsler, that reporter Tiger is cozy with. The Grand Jury tomorrow? Supposed to indict the Sheriff perps? A *cover-story*. The Jury is finally going to nail 12th Street. Tiger gave Kuntsler your ass. And tomorrow

Kuntsler sings like the fat lady and then it's over, Frankie. For *you*."

"Maybe he needs to go away."

"Sure," I scoffed. "Like you're going to fuck with the *Banner*."

"I'd fuck with God if he provoked me, Pinel. Maybe *you* need to go away, too."

"Frankie, I'd rather shoot you than look at you. And if it comes to that, remember I'm the *good* guy. I got cops on my side, and newspapers, and friends all over. You're as low as whale shit."

"You think you scare me?"

"Yes, Frankie, I do. Because you know if *anything* goes down, I'm skipping the middlemen and coming straight for you."

"I'll be waiting."

"Sure. You'll try me *then*. When I'm just about to get up your ass, when you *have* to, when you're blind with shame like that night in Laguna. But it's hard to aim when you've pissed yourself. Remember?"

The phone went dead.

I must have been shouting, because the lobby guard was standing bolt upright, ready to run. I flashed him a big smile and an okay sign, but it didn't seem to help.

I imagined the scene at Frankie's. Dad would change his story to *Tiger* stole the money.

But Frankie was a simple man.

He disliked too many stories.

And Grand Jury witnesses.

It was almost midnight, the hour when devils gather. I crossed the street, started the Blazer, and shot from the parking lot toward the Mini-Mart on Main, not far from Olivewood, not far from the stadium where the Angles sometimes played.

CHAPTER TWENTY THREE

I found the Fallen Angels at the hangout named in Kuntsler's notes – a side lot of the Mini-Mart on Main Street in middle-class Orange. Approaching from the cross-street, I doused my headlights and coasted into the curb. Twenty yards ahead, shielded from the rain by an overhanging roof, convened six cholos. I recognized the species by their baggy, cut-off pants, flannel shirts, white socks. Particular packs identified themselves with tattoos, team logos, colored kerchiefs. The Fallen Angels' insignia appeared to be a knotted, yellow bandanna worn as a headband – a low-riding halo, perhaps. Scrawled repeatedly across the Mini-Mart brick-o-block wall was *Don Tigre* along with other black names and elaborate FxAx's. I didn't see the *Don* himself, however, nor his pals from the news footage.

I cracked my window to hear the voices.

"*Me costo un huevo!*"

"*Vaya puneta!*"

"But not at the end, man. He cried like a *culicagado*."

"*Se cago de miedo!*"

A smaller boy said, "I'll ride this time. C'mon. Me, too."

Laughing, two of the bigger boys jostled the small one off the sheltered sidewalk into the rain.

"*Hace falta tener cojones.*"

"*Chinga tu madre!* I got balls."

They scuffled for the sidewalk.

"Stay off. Stay off, *caguetas*."

"I'm no kid, man!"

"Fuck you, *caguetas*!"

Schoolyard boasts.

Schoolyard games.

Just kids.

Until a tricked-out Ford turned into the side drive. *As one,* the Fallen Angels locked eyes on the car. Their heads swiveled in eerie synchrony as the car sped past to the well-lighted, front lot. I imagined their widened pupils, cocked ears, flared nostrils.

Wearing a roomy, hand-me-down blazer and a skinny, black tie, the teenage driver of the Ford sprang to open the passenger door for his date, a young girl dolled up in a poufy, black dress. Fixed and silent, eyes unwavering, the Fallen Angels stood poised. When the girl swiveled her legs, they yipped and bayed. At the boyfriend's gutsy *"go fuck yourselves,"* the gang surged forward like an opening claw. Shoving his girl back into her seat, the poor kid scurried behind the wheel and squealed away.

The Fallen Angels howled.

* * * * *

Large and orange, a full-moon rose above Saddleback. Long, dark shadows of a jungle gym fell across two concrete picnic tables. A warm breeze rustled nearby pines.

" *This* is the big surprise?" said Veronica. "Top of the World park? At night? All alone?"

"I'm unpredictable."

She rolled her eyes. "*Au contraire!*"

The small, hilltop set-aside overlooked Laguna Canyon. In the notch between the canyon slopes, the lights of Laguna Beach ended abruptly at the ocean. Inland, beyond the dark ridge line, Orange County was a twinkling carpet that faded into a shimmery, faraway haze.

"Scope that view! Your property tax at work. I bet you've never been here at night."

"You win."

"Actually ... " I wrapped my arms around her. "*No one* comes here at night."

She wiggled free.

"*You* aren't coming here tonight either."

"We'll see." I removed a portable radio from my pocket. "Music hath charms to sooth the savage breast."

"These breasts will remain wroth until I get them home, thank you."

I tuned to the local jazz station and propped the radio on a table. A bossa nova sax was playing.

"I believe this is my dance," I said.

"You bring me to Top of the World Park in the middle of the night to dance?"

"Consider it foreplay."

"Consider it *endgame*."

I took her in my arms and began to move.

She chuckled. "I didn't know you could square dance."

"It's a *samba*."

"Really! ... Okay, Pete. One, er ... samba. But let me lead before we do-si-do off the edge."

"Hey! I haven't had much practice," I said. " *Tough* guys don't dance."

"Nor do you."

Before I could retort, three rowdy teens appeared atop the small rise separating the park from the parking meters. Spotting us, they galumphed noisily down the slope. All wore flannel shirts, baggy pants, and baseball caps turned backwards. The biggest one, eyes wide and wild, bumped chests with me.

"Gimme a dollar!"

"Beat it, you fucking crack-head." I shoved him backwards.

Veronica gripped my arm.

"PETE!"

"Hey, Pete. S'at ya mamma, Petie?" said one of the sidekicks.

"Twelfth Street's table, man," said the other, pointing to marker scribbles on the concrete bench.

As far as I knew, Laguna was one of the few places left with no gangs. Twelfth Street was a San Dismas bunch and the three *amigos* were probably just killing a day at the beach. As much as I hated Lemon Tom beating hell out of me that night at the station house, the streets were safer before the city cashiered him. And while he still kept things from unraveling completely, more and more the edges were fraying.

"Look, punks. Haul your asses back to San Dismas while you can."

"Use our table, gotta pay," mouthed the big one.

"If you're a table troll, you should sit *under* the table."

He didn't get it. "Gimme the dollar."

"You should wait for my brother to use the table. He's much richer than poor ol' me."

He *still* didn't get it.

"It's a fable, *guey!*" smirked the pudgy back-up. *The other back-up laughed.*

P.O.'d, the tall one grumbled, "Gimme the dollar, Grandpa, or the bitch pays."

I stepped forward. All three held their ground – a ballsy choice, but a bad one, since my step was strategic. When the tall one opened his mouth, I snapped it shut with a bell-ringer uppercut. He stumbled backwards into his two pals and plopped onto his ass. The pudgy one raised a beer bottle, but couldn't quite decide if it was a club or a shield. I wrenched his arm backwards, breaking the glass against his forehead. Yelping, he let go the bottle neck to wipe at his eyes. I thudded a right into his soft gut and dropped him to his hands and knees. I swiped up the jagged bottle neck, but the last of the Three Mouseketeers was already scrambling over the slope to the street.

I ambled to a trash can and discarded the bottle neck. Veronica stood with her hands to her face. I gave her a big grin.

"You boys have to clean up this glass," I said turning back. "Other little kids play here, too."

Spitting blood and pieces of teeth, the tall one looked up dizzily. He lurched to his feet and charged. I shifted my body in an acceptable *pase* and pounded a left cross to his ear as he shot past. He splayed forward and smacked face-first into the picnic table.

I grabbed the shirt-back of the pudgy one and jerked him to his feet. While tempted to stuff him in the trash can as a lesson in humility, I was bored with the grabass and wanted to get back to my dance.

"What's your name?" I said, shouldering him over to his moaning homie.

"Frankie Mendez," he grunted.

"You look a dollop smarter than most, Frankie, so pay attention. This is *my* table now. *MINE,* got it! Don't ever come back."

I punched him in the kidney. He screeched.

"Never! I'll be checking. I see you jokers near my table, you get worse."

I hit him again. He twisted and squealed and grabbed at his back.

"Couple more like that and you'll piss blood for a week. Now take this other clown and get away from my table."

About to let him go, I said, "Wait a minute. Gimme a dollar."

He clawed in his pocket, dropped a bill on the ground, and hoisted his buddy to his feet. Together they staggered over the hill. When I heard a car door slam and saw the glow of headlights, I laughed, picked up the dollar, and turned to Veronica.

"I got you a souvenir," I chuckled.

She shook her head sharply. I shrugged and pocketed the bill.

The radio – knocked over as Veronica scrambled aside – was spewing heavy-metal caterwaul. I found the jazz station again.

"Now ... where were we?"

Veronica gripped my arms. "Are you insane? We're out of here!"

"No way."

"You *are* insane! Can't you see my face? This is *spoiled!* Take me home."

"I won't let little punks run me off."

"You ... YOU! What about ME!"

I wrapped her in my arms. "I'm here."

"Ohh ... you're as scary as they are, damn it."

"Worse, I hope. But, thing is, I'm on *your* side."

I kissed her forehead and felt her relax a bit, but caught a glint of moonlight on metal at the top of the rise. I wrenched us both to the ground behind the table and covered her with my body.

Crack-Crack-Crack!

Bullets whizzed by. One ka-chingged off the table and spat concrete.

"Stay down!" I yelled, crouching. I yanked out the .45, and fired blindly, then fired again toward an astonished shout and scrabbling footsteps. I saw the pudgy one hightailing it and clambered after him, screaming curses. I heard a car door slam and tires squeal. Cresting the hill, I saw a dark-blue Chevy fishtailing down Top of the World Drive. Gasping for breath, I shot the car a finger and huffed back to the table.

"We should scram," I said. "Someone probably called — "

Veronica looked up sobbing.

"It's okay, Ronnie. It seemed scarier than it was. Punks like that couldn't hit a barn if they were in it. Probably never even fired the gun."

"I'm *bleeding*, Pete!"

"Goddamm! Let me see!"

I dropped to my knees and pulled her fingers away from a superficial gouge in the skin of her calf. I blotted the blood with my coat sleeve and examined the wound with my pocket flash.

"It's just a scratch. Not a bullet. A little chunk of concrete, I bet. Honest. It's nothing. Peroxide will take care of it. It's okay. We'll go now. Let's go."

I lifted her and carried her to my car. Next day I remembered the radio and came back, but it was gone. Since I was there anyway, I took a permanent marker from the Blazer console, and puta'd the 12th Street *placas* on the picnic tables.

With *Mister* Pete.

CHAPTER TWENTY FOUR

Hooking suddenly across two lanes, a white, Chevy low-rider plowed into the Mini-Mart driveway and scattered the Fallen Angels like bowling pins. Rocking wildly, the car yawed to a stop beside the *placa* smeared wall.

"Change your Hanes!" brayed the driver through his open window.

Cursing and thumping the roof and hood, the boys regrouped and piled in. The runt who couldn't keep his place on the sidewalk stood pouting. The low-rider carved a donut on the wet asphalt and shot from the front drive, side-slipping on squealing, smoking tires. The Chevy honked impudently at swerving traffic and roared north.

The runt kicked at a few puddles and then stamped away, holding his arms cocked like Popeye. Maybe Popeye was his idea of a tough guy. In the darker realm beyond the mini-mart, however, his swagger vanished. Hunched over, he scampered through the rain. I ducked in the seat as he passed and slipped out the door behind him.

Keeping to shadows, I tailed him through a warehouse district. He zigzagged a few blocks, then disappeared down a narrow gap between two buildings. For *my* size the weed-choked squeeze was a rough go, and I worried I might lose him. Pushing through, I flattened against a loading dock, raked the rain from my eyes, and peered in both directions. A bolt of lightning illuminated the runt slogging beside railroad tracks toward Angel Stadium. A clap of thunder jarred loose a fresh downpour that drowned the noise I made closing the distance.

When the kid suddenly took refuge under the eave of a *placa*-covered, corrugated-tin switch-shed, I slid behind a clump of tall Oleanders and watched him cram his yellow bandana into a pocket. Striking his colors meant enemy turf. While he might have been waiting out the rain, more likely he was mustering courage for the home stretch. He cupped a lighter in his hands, bowed his head, and struggled to fire a cigarette. The wind-blown flame lined his face in orange.

Creeping closer, I felt track-bed gravel crunching under my feet, but rain peppering the tin shed drowned any noise. I nabbed the kid from behind, lifted him off the ground, and clamped my hand over his mouth. Crushed between palm and cheek, his cigarette burned us both. The kid kicked and squirmed.

"Hold still!" I snarled. Lightning flashed with a simultaneous mortar blast of thunder. "Quit kicking!"

His gasping breaths sucked against my wet palm. When he stopped wriggling, I set him down, clenched his neck in the crook of my arm and let go the grip on his mouth.

"No colors, man!" he wheezed. "No colors!"

"Tiger," I spat in his ear. "*El Tigre*. Where is he?"

He wrenched his head around. "A cop! *Tu madre*, cop."

Feeling safe with a cop, he began to flail again. I caught a wrist and twisted it up behind his back.

"*El Tigre!*"

"Fu — "

I pumped the wrist up past his shoulder and throttled his yelp with my arm.

"*Tigre!*"

I eased off so he could talk.

"With Boo ... Chaka and Ratboy. Leggo! Leggo, man!"

"Where?"

"Three days gone."

"Where?" I levered his arm for punctuation.

"12th Street action. Drugs, maybe," the kid grunted. "They

don't tell me nothin'. I'm just a kid."

"Where's the Pit?"

He started to bawl. "Don't tell me nothin'."

"Where'd the Chevy go?"

"Tagging. To *puta* the City Killers."

"Guys in the Chevy go to the Pit?"

"Just the *Dons*."

I spun the kid around, grabbed his shirtfront, and banged him into the shed.

"You *raped* a woman on the River Trail."

His eyes went wide. In *his* world punishment for the rapist of a sister, a mother, a wife was more than death. I think it hit him that – cop or not – I was off the clock and rules might not save him. He began to shake, bad shakes that rattled the corrugated metal against his back. He yelled to make himself heard over the storm.

"Not me, mister. I swear. Look at me! I'm ... I'm just a *kid*. They don't even let me ride. I heard the Dons talking shit, but the rest of us was in school. I swear, mister. Swear on the virgin!"

His chest heaved against my grip.

"I'm ... just a ... kid," he sobbed. "A little ... kid."

I felt like a bully. He *was* a kid. A scared little kid, all of thirteen, fourteen, maybe. I yanked him off the wall and shoved him away.

"Get outta here!"

He shuffled backwards, feet slipping in the loose gravel. He held up his hands.

"Don't hurt me, mister. Please, don't hurt me."

Wind and rain whipped away his words.

"Beat it," I shouted.

Out of reach, the kid tugged a pistol from his pocket, pointed, and fired. Pop! Pop! Pop! Not a hint of hesitation.

Crouching, I lunged at him. Scrambling backwards, he fired again. A slug drilled into my left side. Hands straight out as if to catch the next one, I sank to a knee. Rain streamed down my forehead, stung my eyes. I blinked and squinted, focusing on the gun.

"*Estupido* cop!" the kid screamed. "*Me cago en la leche de tu puta madre!*"

Another bullet pinged the track shed behind me.

"Wait! Wait a minute!" I shouted, hoping to keep him talking. I shrugged my shoulder forward to open my jacket over the .45.

"Fuck you, cop!" the kid whooped, hopping excitedly from foot to foot. "They call me *caguetas*, say I got no balls! Well, I'm gonna cut your — " A peal of thunder drowned his boasts. "... and show *Don Tigre*. Show 'em all, man. Show 'em I'm a *life-taker! Now* they'll listen! *Now* they'll let me ride."

Runt-no-more, the kid was at last a *Mister*, a shot-caller. Howling over the bellowing storm, enveloped in a white glare diffused by rain and mist, he jerked like a shadow puppet, a tiny, pistol-waving silhouette outlined from behind in a pulsing light. I knew he would savor his first taste of power, so I gave him his moment, one so dizzily delicious that he overlooked his feet between the rails until a shrill, last-moment shriek of air horns yanked his head around. Piercing the blinding rain, an oscillating headlight beam swept across his open-mouthed face, but the tortured moan of horns, the scream of impotent brakes, the bang-bang-banging crash of cars slamming against couplings, all drowned Mister Runt's squeal as he splatted against the locomotive as inconsequentially as a single little raindrop.

CHAPTER TWENTY FIVE

A blast of air rocked me backwards. Train wheels screaked and sparked. Windows flickered past like a strobe. A red beacon over the rear car faded in the rain as the Amtrak San Diegan shuddered to a stop a quarter mile down track.

Pullman doors banged open. Flashlights bobbed through the downpour. Clutching my side, I hobbled away unnoticed and circled back to the Blazer to take stock.

A pencil-sized hole pierced my sport coat just above the left side pocket. No blood had seeped through the jacket, but a dumbbell-shaped blot stained the shirt. Electricity shot through my flank as I tugged out my shirttail and peeled back the sticky cloth. About an inch above my hip bone, a tiny, dimpled wound oozed blood. Groping where I couldn't see, I felt another puckered spot, an exit wound, about four inches back. An exit wound was good news. I pinched the meat separating the two holes between my thumb and fingers. Better yet! A simple flesh wound – as benign as a bullet gets. I shook my head and snorted. Shot in the love handle, about as silly as getting shot in the ass, *not* one for the resume.

Although I knew a medic who had developed an aversion to paperwork after he lost his license, I chose to try for home. Compressing my side through the jacket, I made my way to the Five and headed south. The ever-present construction delays were further snarled by rain, creating miles of brake lights. Blood began to soak through the cloth of the coat.

Past the Costa Mesa Freeway, lanes opened and traffic

started to flow. I gunned the car to eighty because I was light-headed and wanted to get home before I fainted. Goofy logic was the best I could do. Thoughts splattered and disappeared in my mind like the rain designs on my windshield.

Exiting at Alton Parkway, I whizzed past new corporate buildings surrounded by die-hard, but not-forever, strawberry fields. Protective plastic sheeting, covering the fields, reflected the lighted buildings like the surface of a flood. On my left, dark and derelict, stretched the scuttled El Toro Marine Corps Air Station. I hurried toward high ground – Saddleback Mountain – black, obscure, and permanent.

Swinging over to El Toro Road, I continued east past tombstone rows of orange tile roofs blanched gray by the night. At Live Oak Canyon, the muddy parking lot of Cook's Corner sat jammed with Harley's and pick-ups. A red neon sign winked *Live Country Music Night,* just as it did *every* night. Turning, I wound beneath arched, scraggly branches along a twisted two-lane road until I reached my nameless cutoff. Bumping up washboard switchbacks, I rumbled finally over rickety planks that bridged a runoff ditch and came to rest between my trees in my yard.

Home.

The one-bedroom cabin nestled against Saddleback in a half-acre notch. The blazing interior lights were extravagant, but I disliked coming home to darkness. I crawled from the Blazer, sloshed across soggy grass, and stepped onto a roofed, wooden porch. Beside the front door sat an outsized, weather-beaten Morris chair. In daylight, ensconced in the chair in a cool, breezy shade, I could see trees, the road, the mountain, and not another house or person at all.

Inside the cabin the furnace hummed. I kept the thermostat high since – out from under the smog blanket that warmed much of the county like smudge pot smoke – nights could be cold. Some winter mornings I woke to ice-etched windows, a frosted yard, and, far above me, the twin peaks of Saddleback streaked white. I plopped onto the sofa to catch my breath and jarred the coffee table, toppling several empty Sapporo bottles. One of the bottles rolled onto the floor, but I was too tired to play fetch. Besides, I reminded myself, I had *important* things to do, things I *would* do, tired or not!

In just a moment.

The heater droned. The cabin was deliciously warm. Despite wet clothes, I sweated. I was drowning in sweat ...

Drowning!

My eyes snapped open. Hand splinting my side, I lurched to the bathroom and shed my clothes into the claw-foot, enameled-iron bathtub. Hearing a tiny clink, I pawed through the pile and found a mushroomed .25 slug shaken loose from the jacket lining. I held the slug to the light and turned it in my fingers as if it posed a riddle. Shrugging, I dropped the souvenir into a vanity drawer and peered over my shoulder at the medicine cabinet mirror. The wounds had stopped bleeding.

Fetching a hand mirror and a bottle of hydrogen peroxide, I lay sideways on the floor and craned my neck to the mirror. I dribbled peroxide over both wounds, letting pink froth bubble up and subside between douses. Emptying the bottle, I mashed a clean towel against my side to stanch a fresh trickle of blood, then dressed the wounds with leftover tape and gauze squares from the last time I was shot.

I crawled to my feet and rummaged through the medicine cabinet, spilling contents onto the vanity. One of the brown, plastic bottles read 'KEFLEX. ONE CAPSULE FOUR TIMES DAILY. TAKE UNTIL GONE.' I pried off the cap and shook four remaining green and white capsules into my hand. For all I knew, Keflex was poison for gunshot wounds, but when my thumb was chomped in a fight, the antibiotic had cured an infection. Maybe it could prevent one, too. Regardless, doing *anything* felt better than doing nothing. I tossed the capsules into the back of my throat and slurped water from my palm.

Grinning smugly, I padded naked to the fridge for a Sapporo. I popped the cap and rushed back to my sofa command center to plan my next move. I eased my good side onto the soft cushions and tipped back the beer bottle. The icy Sapporo cooled my parched throat, but not the burn that gripped my waist like hot pincers. I tried to think, but my thoughts were slow thoughts, soft, siesta thoughts, warm, languid thoughts, tropic thoughts, liquid thoughts, thoughts like water, thoughts like sweat. The luxurious cabin heat engulfed me like steam in a sauna, bathed me like water in a sweltering hot tub, but, strangely, my teeth chattered and I began to shake.

* * * * *

I opened my eyes on bars of sunshine – yellow-white stripes that seemed oddly bright, as if some extraordinary pressure had squeezed the sunlight between my drawn blind slats. I had dreamed of *her* again. A lucid dream. A lingering dream. A tinted dream, its images suffused with the honeyed light of a solar eclipse.

I frowned. Dreams were alien. Dreams disquieted my dreamless, melancholic heart. But what could I do? Dreams could no more be checked than the golden sparks of dust I saw dancing in sunbeams that penetrated the blinds. And besides – I rarely thought of her while awake.

The nightstand clock read six a.m., its alarm set for seven. Disgruntled, I kicked aside the blanket and stood. Dreamless and melancholic, I was also a night-person by nature. Yet suddenly it was as if jetlag had perturbed my rhythms and some new locale demanded accommodation. But where had I gone?

Dismissing the thought, I yanked the blind cord and became ensnared in warm sunshine. *She's* the early riser, I insisted. Already awake, she's sitting in her kitchen with that same morning sunlight reflected in *her* eyes. I imagined the aroma of her cinnamon toast and coffee, the rustle of newsprint, the lilt of her laughter as she read the comics page.

I shook my head as if erasing an Etch-a-sketch. Daydreams were even more unlike me. I was a private cop, for heaven's sake. A former combat Marine. A realist! A feet-on-the ground, dreamless, melancholic, night-person who refused to indulge in fantasy spawned by some odd jetlag and a nagging dream.

Commuting, I disciplined myself by concentrating only on the balky traffic to San Dismas, ignoring the surprising number of cars that looked like hers. Nor did I think of her at my office. Certainly not as I had the two weeks I spent at Olivewood when we met … what? … three months ago already. At Olivewood her ever-presence had captured my thoughts like gravity — how her eyes seemed to reach out and encompass things she perceived like a child grasping a toy — how words and laughter spilled from her gaily like water over stones — how her face could change like a field swept by cloud shadows. I remembered a squabble over children and the court system. How her face had darkened, how her eyes had flashed. How her voice had cracked like thunder — *When did you last sit holding the hand of an abused child!* — And the rainbow smile that suddenly broke like sunshine. And how fresh the air had smelled. Like ozone.

I recalled other thoughts from those two weeks; earthier thoughts, moments when – merely watching her stand, walk, bend, sit, cross her legs – I felt an eerie awareness of her body, a kind of sympathetic vibration in the way my own face and limbs microscopically mirrored her movements. I remembered one of our lunchtime jogs on the trail that ran behind Olivewood and how – pausing to catch her breath – she had knelt to free a struggling moth trapped in a spider's web. Unable to tear my eyes from the drooping neckline of her tee-shirt, from breasts glistening with diamond beads of sweat, I contemplated time stopping at a perfect moment, but lost the thought in my eagerness that she stoop lower.

Yet that was then, I insisted. Mere propinquity! Having escaped her gravity, my thoughts were free to explore a universe of women – Bernie's Amazon secretary (too humorless), the gypsy-eyed stranger in the elevator (too tall), the big-busted clerk at the courthouse (too slow), the amorous, afternoon barkeep at Blake's (too blonde). Securely unfettered, I chose not to phone her till lunch.

Moreover, since our date was Saturday, *that* call was purely administrative. Schedules and such. Funny … two Orange County natives, pushing middle age, who had never visited Knott's Berry Farm. Considering Saturday, I recalled another Saturday, but scarcely dwelled on a slow dance in her living room that became a long, swaying kiss, a voluptuous spiral to the floor, and me lying above her, my weight on my elbows. Or how – lulled by the sinuous trace of her finger over the muscles of my arms and her throaty *'You won't crush me, you know?'* — I relaxed to embrace her, only to hear an impishly grunted "ooof!" And how, wrestling and rolling, we had laughed like children until sweet laughter, distilling, became a syrupy silence that ...

Quickly diverting my thoughts from her, I succumbed only briefly to how she touched me as if the touch pleased *her*; how she gazed at me as if looking gave her joy; how she flattered my eyes until I felt ... (Could I use such a word?) ... pretty.

At the cabin that evening, I called again and left a funny message on her machine to make her smile. Later, I drank Sapporos and read a tough-guy detective novel. Now and then I looked up and fancied her sprawled in the opposite chair, also reading, also glancing occasionally at me. Such thoughts went almost unnoticed — beneath awareness yet beyond any question — like my heartbeat.

Low in the purple sky, a faint, magenta glow lingered like a memory of day. Yawning, I closed the book, shed my clothes, switched out the light, and crawled naked beneath a sheet. How perplexing was this curious syncopation in our rhythms, I mused — a dreamless, melancholic, feet-on-the-ground, night-person retiring as early as she! I am just not myself, I thought, curling on my side, aware that she too was curled sideways between gradually warming, cold sheets.

My lament echoed.

Just not myself ... just not myself ...

Through open blinds, a full moon washed the cabin with pale, silver light. I closed my eyes. My breathing slowed. My thoughts wandered.

Not just myself ... not just myself ...

And since it was almost Friday (the day before I would see her; naturally a day I would think of her constantly), I allowed myself to imagine her skin against mine, her breath on my face, her mouth – sultry and luscious – opening to my kiss. Reverie seemed safe now, because, come to think of it, I rarely thought of her at all.

CHAPTER TWENTY SIX

The radio alarm was an icy splash. I sat with a start, but doubled in pain. Sinking to the floor, I curled like a pill bug and retched. Six hours later, when I woke again, the radio was still blaring.

Pushing away the bile covered throw rug, I struggled to my feet and hammered the radio to stop the din. I faltered to the bathroom and stared into the mirror. Beads of perspiration dotted my forehead. My eyes were bloodshot, my hair wet and matted. A white-hot fire seared my lungs and belly. I doused my face with cold water, rinsed my mouth, and braced my wobbly arms against the sink to rest.

Gathering strength, I yanked off the bandages. The first looked clean, but the second bore a brown, inkblot stain. Angling the hand mirror, I examined the crusted pucker of the exit wound. A fiery red hue diffused through the surrounding skin. I prodded the scab and expressed a yellow ooze.

Infected.

So much for Keflex.

I slurped water from my palm again and strained to squelch the heaves that came from swallowing.

Get a grip, I scolded myself. *It's like a hangover. A **bad** hangover for sure, but not the worst you've weathered. You can function with a hangover. You've had practice.* I brushed my teeth slowly, spritzed deodorant under my arms and dressed.

Sal, the day man, answered when I dialed Blake's.

"Seen Jesus, Sal?"

"Ya don' sound so good, Pete."

"Flu or something."

"Yeah, it's goin' round. Tony Giacomo ... you know Tony, right? ... he was down two whole — "

"Jesus, Sal? Seen Jesus?"

"Naw, ain't seen him all day."

I looked at my watch.

ALWAYS THERE.

"See him, give him a beer. I'll be in around four."

I stepped outside, locked the door, and stood for a moment on the sheltered porch watching the cold drizzle. The plank bridge was awash. Crawling into the Blazer, I keyed the ignition, backed onto the road, and lurched forward. The car pitched and yawed in ruts like a raft in rapids, pounding my insides. I caught my breath at the Live Oak stop sign and plowed in again toward San Dismas.

Pavement was a godsend, but the smooth ride highlighted how slowed I felt – as if my limbs were moving through water. Water filled my head, too – water that bent, refracted, blurred, and commingled images, ideas and sensations, all of which ran together like liquid colors.

Something was wrong. Worse than hangover wrong. *Bad* wrong.

I cursed the dead little bastard who shot me.

At Blake's the lunchtime crowd was gone, the evening regulars still at work. I said hello to Sal and spotted Jesus nursing a Corona at his usual table. I eased into the opposite chair.

"God damn, Pete! You look like a train hit you, man."

"No I don't."

He studied me for a moment. It was early yet, so his good pupil was the same size as the glass eye pupil. He leaned in and lowered his voice.

"What?"

"Took a slug. Thought it was clean, but ... "

"Damn, *amigo*, let's get you a corpsman."

I shook my head.

"Lenny keeps his mouth shut."

"Maybe after. Look, I need some help."

He sat back. "Like what?"

"Legwork."

"'It's legs I ain't got!'"

"A place to go with names, Jesus. That's all."

"That's *all*? You're bleeding already and ... and I ain't quick like I was, man! I ... Ohh, what names?"

"*El Tigre.*"

"The Fallen Angels honcho. Yeah, he's the one I heard about. Definitely bad news."

"Plus Boo, Ratboy, and Chaka."

"Ratboy is another Angel, and from what I hear, too Goddamm rotten to live much longer. The others *could* be Angels, but the tags are blue-label. Half the homies in San Dismas jump if you yell Chaka or Boo."

"I need to know where they are."

"Try the Mini-Mart on Main."

"I did," I said, touching my side. "Bought me a Slurpee. But those four are scarce right now. Some drug deal with 12th Street."

"Going Hollywood."

"They're hunkered down at a hideout called the Pit. It has to be near the Angel "A" and the River Trail. Poke around."

He shook a cigarette from a package on the table. "Poking at 12th Street gets me stung."

"Just a location."

"Sure. Nobody'd hurt a cripple."

"I'm not asking you to stick your neck out."

"Right."

He flicked an old, chrome Zippo emblazoned with an eagle, globe, and anchor insignia. He lit his cigarette and sat rubbing the insignia with his thumb. The gold luster had long ago worn off the globe.

"Did you get it?" I said.

Looking around, Jesus withdrew a paper sandwich bag from the pocket of his wheelchair and pushed it across the table. I peeked in the bag and saw a tear-off strip of disposable syringes and a small, yellow and black box labeled 'Morphine Sulfate Injection, U.S.P.'

I removed the box from the bag. The packaging looked legit, but phony medicine was easier to make than passable boxes and labels. Counterfeiters often switched the contents of real packages, resealing cellophane wrappers with a hot iron. The iron sometimes left a scorched odor.

"Has to be good, Jesus," I said, sniffing the box.

He pouted.

"Don't get huffy. You found it pretty fast."

"In San Dismas? Dope is nothing. Get you anything here. Get you a monkey's paw from a *curandero*."

"And a wish?" I said.

It didn't matter if he knew what I meant, since we both knew enough. Something sad and heavy came over him. He barked at Sal for another Corona.

"Ain't no wishes, Pete," he said, flicking at ashes that had dropped on his useless legs. "None, *amigo* ... I know."

CHAPTER TWENTY SEVEN

"Wish this rain would stop," said Leticia. "Be some sunshine to wake to, maybe she would."

I stroked a strand of hair from Veronica's forehead. Her cheek quivered, but her eyes remained closed.

"Don't you think?" said Leticia.

Concentration had become a boulder I was shouldering uphill. I roused myself to focus on the watcher's chair beside the bed. Leticia pondered my baffled stare.

"The rain," she said. "Wish it would stop."

I swiveled my head to gape through the gray window. Sheets of rain washed across the pane in distorting bands like water in a diving mask.

"Mr. Pinel? You all right?"

I gripped the side rail of Ronnie's bed. The sharp corner of the morphine box jabbed my chest through my coat pocket.

"What's the matter?" said Leticia.

I lugged my attention back to the nurse.

"If you need a break, now's a good time. I'll be here a while. Go ahead."

She fished the last Tootsie roll from a crumpled cellophane bag and dog-eared her book page.

"I do have to visit the ladies room," she said. "And a coffee would hit the spot. Looks like you could use a pick-me-up, too."

"Sure. Coffee's good.

"Cream and sugar?"

"Whatever ... Yeah, cream's fine. Thanks."

She waddled to the door and closed it behind her.

I leaned over the bed rail. "Veronica?"

Nothing. Breathing. My breathing.

"Ronnie?"

A weak, cough escaped. Pink froth bubbled in the corners of her lips. When I wiped away the froth with my thumb, her eyes snapped open. Her mouth formed a continuing, whispered scream not yet finished.

"It's me. It's Pete. I'm here."

She flailed against my grip with her good arm, kicking and crawling toward the surface.

"Ronnie, it's me. Pete."

Her eyes found mine. Exhausted, she clutched my arm and panted.

"Here ... before?"

I knew what she meant. I remembered how memory and dream and wish and experience all co-mingled in that murky limbo beneath consciousness.

"Yesterday."

"Do it ... Do it!"

Her eyelids shut and she sank again. The room seemed to circle like water around a drain. I fumbled at my pocket for the morphine.

CHAPTER TWENTY EIGHT

The door burst open. A flock of white-coated doctors, Hurley among them, fluttered in and surrounded the bed.

"Visitors must leave!" commanded a gangly figure entering last.

"Been a while, Doctor Hiatt," I said weakly.

Hiatt whirled. As always, the swirl of his long, unbuttoned, lab coat reminded me of a cape.

"Regard, doctors, the infamous Private Investigator, Peter Pinel, whose bullet-riddled bacon I, personally, snatched from the fires of Hell."

Hiatt wasn't big on confidentiality rules or *any* rules he didn't write himself.

"Arise! Perambulate that these minions may view my handiwork. Observe, if you will, the symmetrical functioning of the parts, the perfect — "

He cocked his head and frowned.

"Continue rounds, Doctor Calley. *You*, Pinel, follow me."

Striding from the room, Hiatt bore down the hallway on a collision course with Leticia who jumped aside. Hiatt *expected* deference and got it – not because he was a doctor, but because he was *Hiatt*. He presupposed and got obedience for the same reason and never looked back to see if I was following.

"Assume the position," he said, commandeering a vacant treatment room.

Fighting dizziness, I inched up onto the paper covered exam table. "Warranty's expired, hasn't it, Doc? Been more than a year."

"My work endures." He grabbed my chin and studied my face. "Pale and sweaty." He swiveled my head back and forth. "Nystagmus. The room is spinning, isn't it?"

"A little."

"You're abusing the protoplasm I hold a lien on."

"I could use a look-see, Doc. Off the record."

He planted his fists on his hips. "Another Goddamm bullet after all the work I put into you?"

"Just tell me if I'm going to croak."

"We're *all* going to croak. Hie thee to the emergency room, buddy. Make it official and I'll fix you as good as new."

"Not a viable option, Doc."

"Refusal might not be a *viable* option. Get my drift?"

I shrugged.

"Patients! Arrogant, high-handed patients! Never a thought for the poor doctor's feelings."

He shoved me down onto the table. I yelped and drew my knees to my chest.

"Gutshot!" he groused. "Have you any idea how hard it is to re-open an area? You have adhesions in there, Pinel. The layout is all bollixed. Try getting shot in the ass next time."

He yanked the foot-rest from the table and straightened my legs. He loosened my pants, unbuttoned my shirt, and ripped off the gauze squares.

"It's ... it's just a flesh wound, but I think it's — "

"Harvard or Hopkins, Pinel? Where did you train? Roll onto your side."

He wrenched open and banged shut cabinets and drawers until he found a blue-cloth wrapped bundle bound with a band of masking tape stamped STERILIZED. Dropping the bundle on a wheeled table, he assembled a squeeze bottle of dark-red antiseptic, a stack of sterile gauze squares, and a white, paper package of rubber gloves. He sliced his thumb through the masking tape and carefully turned back the corners of the blue cloth, revealing a stainless steel cup and a small armory of sharp, shiny weapons.

"Hey, uh, Doc ... is, uh ... " My mouth was too dry to swallow. "Is this going to hurt?"

"I'll be fine," he said, squirting a stream of red antiseptic into the cup.

One-by-one he held aloft packages of four-by-four gauze, peeled apart the paper wrappers, and allowed the pads to tumble untouched onto the sterile cloth. He split open the glove wrapper and tugged the gloves over his hands, fingering only the rolled cuffs. He seated each glove with a yank on the cuff that popped the latex against his wrist. The gesture had panache. I vowed to use it myself the next time I went burgling. When he dipped a gauze square into the cup of antiseptic, I winced.

"I haven't laid a finger on you," he said.

"But you're going to," I grunted through clenched teeth.

Circling outward from the bullet holes, he scrubbed my belly with the sopping gauze, soaking a fresh square for each pass. The scrubbing seemed to stir a bed of hot coals inside me. He stoked the coals to flame when he poked at the wounds with his fingers. Dark, mustard-colored pus oozed from the front wound. I couldn't see the back one.

"Infected, right?"

"The boon of general anesthesia is that patients cannot speak."

Hiatt blotted pus and sniffed at the stained gauze. He chose a steel probe from the instrument tray and stirred up a blood-streaked, yellow discharge in the front hole. I continued to wince and grunt as he probed the wound I couldn't see, but after a while the probing hurt less than the scrubbing, so he scrubbed again. He opened a brown jar labeled Iodoform gauze, snipped off yard-long strands of yellow, cheesecloth, and ram-rodded the strands into each hole as if he were charging a musket. He bandaged me, popped off his gloves, and pushed away the table like a man surfeited.

"What's the verdict?" I said.

Shushing me with a thermometer in my mouth, he took my

blood pressure and listened to my belly with a stethoscope. I disliked the way he kept shaking his head. He removed the thermometer, studied it, and shook his head.

"Quit that, damn it!"

"Irritability is a symptom."

"Symptom of what?"

"Fever. 102. And your pressure is shocky. This can go south fast, Pinel. I'm admitting you."

"No hospital, Doc. Things to do."

"Pig-headedness is another symptom, although yours was pre-morbid. Listen to me. In a few hours breathing might be a *major* accomplishment."

"Can you do something?"

"I can always do something," he huffed. "Antibiotics. Fluids. Open you up if you start to rot."

"Go with the antibiotics."

He gave me his rounds scowl. "Where does the script say you babble and I compromise? Here's the skinny, made succinct for your fevered brain. It *wasn't* a simple flesh wound. Bullet nicked the belly wall. You have an intra-abdominal abscess."

"That's bad?"

"*Real* bad. But the bullet missed your colon. If not, you'd be in full-blown peritonitis by now. Remember peritonitis, Pinel?"

I remembered.

"The abscess is small and localized. It sealed itself off, whence you're still kicking."

"So we're good?"

"That's pushing it. I drained the abscess through the wounds and packed them to keep channels open to the outside. With antibiotics, things should resolve, although you *might* develop a fistula."

"I don't *want* a fistula. What is it?"

"A fistula, my friend, is a new asshole – an accidental one emptying out the side."

"A BAG!"

"Not with a simple repair I'd let a resident dirty *his* hands on. But listen to me, Pinel. Rupture that abscess and you could proceed to the terminal event without further ado."

"Die?"

"Permanently. You can't be jostling your insides around. You need bed-rest."

I eased my legs off the edge of the table and sat up slowly.

"Okay. I have a bed. And you said antibiotics. I took a handful of Keflex."

"Stupid move, but lucky. It's probably helping. I'll give you something better."

"Great!"

"As soon as you're admitted."

"You're a hard case, Doc. How about the name and dose. I'll get it myself."

"That's illegal."

I ignored the irony, tucked my shirt in my pants and fumbled at the buttons.

"Is any of this getting through? You have a partial ileus now. That means your bowels are half asleep. Antibiotics may not stay down. Or fluids. If that partial progresses to full obstruction, believe me, you'll *beg* to be admitted."

I slid off the table. The two inch drop felt like a parachute landing.

"Look at you," Hiatt glowered.

"Things to do, Doc."

"Why worry about a fistula when you're 100% asshole already?" He grabbed the telephone and pinched the receiver between his ear and shoulder. He riffled pages in a pocket notebook and dialed. Waiting through the ring, he glanced at his watch, a Timex, and muttered, "Rounds. No telling *what* mischief they're into by now ... Hello, pharmacist? Telephone prescription. Dr. Anderson, A-N-D-E-R-S-O-N. Frank. San Dismas Med Center. 555-5744. Pete Pinel. P-I-N-E-L. Cipro tabs. 500 mg. One B.I.D. Number 30. Refill times one. AA-

5367834. Patient will be right over."

He hung up.

"Who's Anderson?" I asked.

"Chief of Urology. Pharmacist won't verify an antibiotic."

"How do I take it?"

"Two capsules immediately then one every night and one every morning."

"Do I take one tonight?"

"Stay with me here, Pinel. Two *now*, then one *every* night and one *every* morning. If you get worse, call 9-1-1. Otherwise see me in three days. If you're still alive, you should be better."

He moved to the sink, rinsed the glove powder from his hands, and dried with a paper towel. I noticed his watch, a Timex.

"You teach here full time, don't you?" I said.

"Pretty much."

"How come you're not doing tummy tucks and titty jobs."

"I'm a fistula."

"No, really. I've talked to people. I've seen the *Newsweek* lists. You're one of the best docs around."

He nodded. "That's true."

"So why not some kind of Newport practice? Fashion Island trophy wives? How come you're not rich?"

"I do all right."

"But you're not *rich*. Not around San Dismas. Uninsured immigrants. MediCal. Guys like me with huge deductibles they pay off over years."

He hook-shot the crumpled toweling into a wastebasket and grinned.

"What would you have me do? Like a creeping vine on a tall tree crawl upward, where I cannot stand alone? No, *thank* you! ... That's from Cyrano."

"Too proud to be a parasite," I added.

"Oh, that's right. The cop who reads on stakeouts."

"Better than donuts. Cyrano is my hero. *You,* too."

"Excellent choices. Now remember ... *bed-rest.* You have someone to watch over you?"

I shook my head.

"Me neither. Well ... do the best you can then. Take the antibiotics. No solid food, but force liquids. As much as you can stomach. Try to change the dressings twice a day, but leave the wicks alone until you see me."

"Which drug store?"

"Sav-Aide. Across the street in the mall."

Hiatt moved to the door. Watching me shuffle behind, he shook his head. "What a piece of work."

"Is man?"

"Is MINE! You patients sabotage my best efforts!"

I smiled. "Thanks for this, Doc."

"You'll get a bill," he said. "A *big* bill. You convinced me. I'm moving up."

"Sure. By the way, what time is it, Doc?"

He looked at the Timex.

"Five-thirteen. Why?"

"Nothing, nothing," I said with a smirk.

Hiatt opened the door, but stopped to scribble across a business card.

"Here's my home number. Call if you need to. *Okay?*"

I tapped the card with my finger. "Last name and two initials," I said. "That always seemed strange to me."

"I'll bet a *lot* seems strange to you."

"Just initials? On *everything*? Even your diplomas? C'mon, it's weird."

"Everyone knows my name."

"Yeah? Well in all this time, all I ever heard was Hiatt. What's your first name?"

"*Doctor.*"

"Thought so," I said.

CHAPTER TWENTY NINE

Hiatt marched down the hallway to muster his troops. I dragged myself in the opposite direction past a dividing row of *Caution: Wet Floor* cones. Waxed and polished, the whole floor looked wet, so the dry side was a toss-up and it wasn't my day. My boot heel skidded and I sat. *Hard.*

The smoldering thing in my gut collapsed. Red-hot embers scattered across my belly while firefly sparks rose into my chest. Groaning dirty words, I slumped to my side, hugging myself to quash the fire inside.

A nurse came running, the one I had called Cookie.

"Don't move!" she chided, kneeling. "You may be injured."

"Does pride count?" I grunted.

She poked at me and wiggled my arms and legs. I cursed some more.

"Did you hit your head?"

"Not unless it was in my ass. Just help me — "

"Absolutely not! You have to be cleared."

"I don't want to be cleared. I want to be *up*."

"A gurney is on the way. You *must* be cleared!"

"It isn't medically necessary," I said.

Glaring, she looked around, saw no witnesses and growled, "Personally, dipshit, you can croak right now, but you're fucking with my job, so get with the program."

Her sincerity was beguiling, but I couldn't risk flunking my clearance when some Samaritan found a bellyful of bullet holes and a pocketful of morphine. I hooked her shoulder and struggled to my feet. Every movement stoked the fire inside, stirred the embers, raised the sparks.

Cookie grabbed my arm. I shrugged away her hand. She sprinted to the nursing station and yammered into a telephone. I hobbled to Ronnie's room, saw from the hallway that she was still unconscious, and hurriedly barged between closing elevator doors. Bailing out the nearest first-floor exit to elude any clearance goons, I backtracked to my car. Hiding the morphine and syringes in the console in case I was stopped, I scooted across San Dismas Drive to the drug store.

When I asked for the prescription, the pharmacist eyed me over his glasses."You were seen in emergency?"

"Yeah. Why?"

"You, uh ... look *sick*. They sent you home?"

"No insurance."

He nodded knowingly. "Well, listen ... I'm working on it now, but before I waste my time, it'll cost about fifty bucks. Can you make it?"

"If I look sick, I guess I better."

He seemed fascinated by the sweat running into my eyes. "I'd say you better."

I drew a wadded clump of bills from my pocket, dropped it beside the register, and leaned woozily against a rack of condoms. Waiting, I watched the pharmacist pour capsules onto a counting tray. Using a blade, he separated the correct number, nudged the counted pile off the tray into one trough, and raked the rest into an opposite trough. He upended *my* pills into a small vial and dumped the remainder back into the stock bottle.

Emblazoned over the pharmacy counter was an outsized Sav-Aide logo. My fogged brain was slow to make the connection, but when it did, I blurted, "Hey, those aren't counterfeit, are they?"

"Stop with the jokes!" the pharmacist hissed, glancing at nearby aisles. "You'll frighten people."

"No one here but me and I'm scared already."

"Hold on a second." He finished his work and hurried to the counter.

"All genuine," he whispered, shaking the bottle like a baby rattle. "Are you a reporter?"

"Do I look like a reporter?"

"Yes, frankly, you do," he said crossly. "Like that CBS guy. Sarvino."

"He's dead," I said. "Oh ... I get it. You're a *comedian*, too."

"We double checked the inventory last night. The police are still making arrests, so they've kept it quiet. How'd you hear?"

"Big story on Eyewitness News," I lied, feeling a little *comedic* myself. "Saw it in the E.R. Everyone's talking."

"Oh, cripes. I took stock in lieu of salary."

"You look sick," I said.

"Tell me about it."

He rang the sale morosely and slid me a few coins in change.

"Any water?"

"In the cooler. Every brand."

"Generic is fine."

"It would be," he grumbled. "Try the fountain. Beside the front door."

Slurping from the fountain, I noticed that swallowing had become unnatural. I had to *will* the capsules down. Making my way back to the Blazer, I discovered that walking, too, was becoming unnatural. The ground seemed to be moving – not with the familiar shake and roll of an earthquake, but rather the lethargic rotation of a merry-go-round. I found myself marching at angles to compensate. The sensation was almost pleasant at first, a little like a beer buzz. Bobbing lollingly at the periphery of a giant, lazy whirlpool, I crawled into the Blazer and sped south on the Five.

After twice veering onto the shoulder, I concluded that bobbing and lolling at 70 miles per hour was foolhardy. Doing it at my cabin where police or Ramon or Kuntsler or Frankie

Mendez could find me was plain boneheaded. Conjuring an alternative – a place I knew to be vacant – I swerved onto the Laguna Canyon Road off-ramp.

The road was awash in spots and so was I. Consciousness was quickly becoming as unnatural as walking and swallowing. No longer could I simply *float* in my cosmic whirlpool, I had to tread water or sink. Sleep swamped me in half-second dunkings.

I made it through the canyon into town, beat traffic signals near the empty Art Festival grounds, but caught a long red light at Pacific Coast Highway. Fighting to stay afloat, I focused on two die-hard, Main Beach B-ball fans playing one-on-one in the rain to a who-gives-a-damn audience of homeless people huddled under tarps. Getting the green, I headed south, turned into an ocean-side cul-de-sac, and pulled up at a faded FOR SALE sign affixed to Veronica's cottage – my *home* for a while.

I pawed through the glove compartment and clicked my old garage door opener. It worked. I drove inside and lowered the clattering roll-up door. The shelves, hooks and cabinets – once cluttered with the vigorous odds and ends of two lives – were all empty. My own belongings were long gone, of course, and no doubt Ronnie's had accompanied her to Sharfstein's welcoming Newport mansion. I hadn't pictured the place vacant, however, and the sight jarred me. I eased down from the Blazer and wobbled drunkenly to a door. My house key – never surrendered – let me in.

Professionally, I would have advised Ronnie to change her locks, especially after the loony phone calls I made for a while. I was glad she hadn't, however. Perhaps it was too sad a symbol and, maybe, despite my lunacy, she trusted me. It was nice to think so, anyway.

I staggered across the kitchen, dark and stale. The breakfast set was gone, replaced by a folding table scattered with real estate agents' cards. I stumbled into the living room, cold and silent, empty save for a few cheap throw rugs and a second-hand couch.

Flailing against the spinning room, I was seized by an epiphany. The relentless whirlpool, I realized, was merely the wheel-within-a-wheel tip of a galactic vortex through which everything, literally *everything,* was spiraling down into a universe-eating black hole whose event horizon was *that very couch!*

Resistance was futile! Circling, thrashing, drawn closer-faster-closer, I kicked off my boots and tore away my encumbering clothes. I bumped up the thermostat, forced down another pill, and swaddled myself in a throw rug. Hoping for something *beyond* the horizon, I surrendered to the couch's irresistible gravity and let the black hole swallow me.

CHAPTER THIRTY

Sleep hid.

Sleep was a dark quarry I pursued through a morphing cyclorama. I heard sleep's tappa-tappa feet over the roof, a sound like my heartbeat in my ears. I heard its rapid patta-patta flutter against a window and ripped back the curtain.

The world had drowned!

All that remained was the murky, gray glow of deep water. Faint, iridescent bands swayed in the glow like northern lights. The motion warned of unseen movers, of monstrous creatures writhing just out of sight. I recoiled from the sweaty window pane. Pressure bowed the glass. Trembling, I pulled the throw rug over my head and chased sleep.

Sleep hid.

My breath was hot and wet. I felt a crushing weight of icy water, but knew I was safe in my throw rug bubble, safe and hot, very hot... hot like fire ... hot as hell. But where was sleep?

A pounding shook the front door, a hollow, insistent pounding like my heartbeat in my ears. Was it sleep?

I flung open the door. The sun blazed white. The earth lay parched. Cactuses rose as black silhouettes. Shadows – black and razor sharp – slashed the baked, alkali soil. Among the shadows stood a cadaverous black preacher draped loosely in a black suit, white shirt, black tie. Bony wrists and sapless fingers drooped from cavernous sleeves. His leather face stretched like a drumhead over skeletal knots of cheekbones and chin. He spoke of Hell. He spoke of burning. He spoke of fire. His words were hot. His voice boomed with a hollow, repetitive pounding like my heartbeat in my ears.

Where was sleep?

I saw the bathroom door at the end of a 100-yard long hallway. Clutching the pill bottle, I stumbled toward the distant goal as if pursued. Staggering between the doorposts, I hunched over the sink and swilled water from the faucet. A bleacher-stomping cheer pounded in my ears like heartbeats. Rejoicing I curled on the cool, tile floor and waited in my hunter's blind for sleep.

Sometimes it was light. Other times dark. I swallowed pills when it was light. Swallowed more pills when it grew dark. And when I thought the light had returned, I swallowed pills again.

Between dark and light in that twilight zone where sleep hid, I was alone. Manny said I merely liked to *think* of myself as alone, but what did he know of numberless days alone in crowds; cold evenings alone on Saddleback; sweltering nights alone in the Nam; long, dark, hot-cold-wet-dry childhood dawns alone in a closed room waiting for sleep.

Alone.

Hell, we're all alone and some of us know it.

I *knew*.

Yet there in that forsaken house – *right there!* – alone became more than something I knew or something I felt. For the first time, alone was something I *was*. Entombed in the marble bathroom where Ronnie and I played together in the roman tub, collapsed in the lifeless living room where we first made love, crumpled in the vacant dining room where we skewered Chinese food from take-out boxes, slumped in the empty library where we camped to read, curled at last on the unfaded square of carpet that our absent bed had shielded from the sun, *there* in that void that once had been a home, where for a time I had *not* been alone, *there* somewhere between dark and light with my eyes open, my breathing a plea, my heartbeat in my ears, *there!* – I *was* alone. Alone in my head, my heart, my body. Alone completely. Beyond salvation. Insusceptible to rescue.

Alone.

Somewhere in the deserted house, my lost pager cried forlornly, failing at last with a final, falling warble whose dead-battery after-silence left me insular and abandoned. Terror wrenched a scream from me. I screamed again when I heard no answer, not even an echo.

The jangle of a telephone jolted me. Somewhere someone *else* existed! Reanimated, but unable to rise, I flung a cushion toward the sound. The cushion arced like a flare and knocked a wall phone from its cradle. I heard what might have been a far-faraway mosquito.

"Is anyone there?" My voice was dry and feeble. "Is ... anyone ... there?"

The phone – as distant, as useless as heaven – rang no more.

One time I thought I heard the sound of a key in a lock, an opening door, and voices from another room. But it was nothing, merely my heartbeat in my ears.

Because I was alone.

I no longer had speech. I no longer had movement. Sessile, I could not find; I could only be *found*. I wished for a parent. I wished for a wife. I wished for children. I wished for a witness. I wished for a friend to watch over me. I wished for someone to hold my hand. But I was alone except for figures in dreams, dreams that would not come, because sleep hid.

CHAPTER THIRTY ONE

I heard my heartbeat in my ears – a thudding sound like pounding on a door. I moved my head on the wadded rug to make the sound go away, but it returned as ... footsteps? Shoes clumping across wooden floors?

ANYONE!

I opened crusted eyes on a looming figure. The woozy form came into focus.

Sharfstein.

"My God! Pinel! What ... what are you doing?"

Naked on the unfaded square of bedroom carpet, I rolled entangled in a throw rug. Through cracked lips my words were barks.

"*Up* ... Help ..."

"You're shot!" He dropped to his knees and poked at the wounds with his fingers. "You better not be contagious," he grumbled.

"Scaredy-cat," I croaked.

"Up yours! I pumped hearts with my bare hands in Viet Nam, but this isn't then, okay? ... Look, let's get off the floor. I have a kit in my car."

He hoisted me to my feet. Hugging like partners in a three-legged race, we lumbered to the living room where he sloughed me onto the couch.

"Don't try to stand."

"I'm not prone to argue," I giggled. I was still giggling when Sharfstein returned. "Hey, I didn't know you were in Nam,

Doc. Cool!"

He opened a white, plastic box. "Army Medical Corps."

"Army? ... Yeah, well, that's okay, too. Did you know Jesus Ramirez?"

"Who?"

"Ramirez ... Jesus Ramirez. A Marine, but maybe you patched him?"

"Unlikely. Regardless I work at *not* remembering."

"Right, right ... A lot of us do."

Sharfstein daubed the wounds with antiseptic. His touch was surprisingly painless. In fact, it made me giggle again.

"Nice watch," I said with a smirk.

"What?"

"Your watch. Veronica give it to you?"

"No."

"Keep good time?"

"It's a Rolex."

I spluttered. Sharfstein rolled his eyes and handed me a penlight to hold. He jabbed tweezers into the front wound and tugged out something long and gooey.

"JESUS FUCKING CHRIST! What the ... what's ... "

"Keep the light still. It's gauze. Packing." He dropped the gore on a throw rug. "Who did this?"

"Gauze? Goddamm!"

"Don't move the light!"

"Thought it was my *guts*!"

"Did Hiatt do this?"

"No way!" I exclaimed. "A guy I know. Used to be a Veterinarian."

"*Used* to be?"

"Sex with patients."

Sharfstein pulled packing from the exit wound. "Pretty good work for a cashiered vet."

He prodded my belly, drummed against one finger, and probed the wounds gently with a long, cotton swab. He listened to my chest and abdomen with a stethoscope, counted my pulse, and shined the flash into my eyes. Half-blinded I squinted at my Timex.

"Three o'clock? I've been out 24 hours!"

"You tell me. It's Sunday."

"What the ... *Three days?*"

Sharfstein pried the pill bottle from my fist. I hadn't noticed I was clutching it. He read the label.

"Filled three days ago."

I rechecked my watch. Sure enough the date read Sunday.

"Who's Anderson?" Sharfstein said.

"The Vet."

"Did you take these regularly?" He popped the lid and jiggled the bottle to count pills.

"I know I took them. Can't say how regular."

"Looks like you went overboard, but maybe it helped." He began to fire questions at me, those bowel questions doctors get off on. I answered to the best of my hazy recollection.

"Think you can walk?" he said.

"I *think* I can, I *think* I can!" I chanted, swinging my legs off the couch to sit. The room spun momentarily, but not like the whirlpool. I bounced up and down.

"You're giddy."

"Then giddy-ap!"

I stood, but faltered.

"I can *do* it," I growled, batting away Sharfstein's hand. I hobbled across the floor, each step easier than the one before. After a minute or two, I looked no worse than a man with bad hemorrhoids.

"There's a hand shower in the bath," Sharfstein said when he was satisfied I could solo.

"*Really!*"

"I *have* spent the night here, Pinel."

"While I was still in the hospital?"

"You don't know Veronica *at all,* do you? ... Scrub your abdomen. The wounds, too."

"Wash the holes?"

"*Scrub* them."

I must have looked skeptical.

"It's called debridement. Then squirt the hand shower right inside."

"Get outta here!"

"Listen to me. Packing kept the wounds from sealing over so they drained to the outside and closed at the bottom. They're externalized now."

"What's that?"

"Like bellybuttons. Scrub the crust off and stream the water directly into each wound. Five minutes, twice a day. They'll heal from the bottom out that way. Less chance of infection."

"I end up with two new bellybuttons?"

"That was a metaphor."

"Simile," I snipped.

"Why don't we just see who can piss farthest? It'll save time."

"Goddamm it, Sharfstein ... You *bug* me, what can I say."

"Try *nothing*." He took a deep breath. "You'll have scars, but the wounds should heal in a few weeks. Can you do this, or not?"

"You say. I do."

"Fine. Think coffee or juice will stay down?"

My stomach tensed.

"I'll try coffee."

He handed me bandage supplies from the kit. "I'll be right back."

Zigzagging through the house, I retrieved my belongings and carried the dirty clothes out to the Blazer where I kept a packed suitcase for times I couldn't get home. I pulled out a toiletry bag and a fresh outfit, went back inside, and found soap and towels in the bathroom vanity. I turned on the shower, let the water warm, then stepped into the tub and scrubbed myself until I felt clean. Squeamishly, I squirted a jet from the hand shower into the front bullet hole. It felt like washing my bellybutton. I finished, dried, gave my teeth a double brushing, and shaved. I taped gauze squares over the wounds and dressed.

In the kitchen Sharfstein stood gazing intently at something in the window. What it was I couldn't guess, since, beyond a beaded curtain of rain streaming from the roof, ocean and sky were a uniform gray. I spied a large Starbuck's cup on the card table, dropped onto a folding chair, and took an eager gulp.

"Yaak! You put a whole cup of sugar in this!"

"Cream, too. You need the nutrients and I don't have an I.V. handy."

I took a few more swallows. "Am I getting a fistula, Doc?"

Sharfstein sipped from his own cup and turned around. "Why?"

"The vet says gutshot dogs get fistulas sometimes. He puts 'em to sleep, 'cause they won't wear those damn bags."

"People are different. They adapt."

"Yeah? *Some*, maybe."

He sat. "Do the shower trick and take the antibiotics. See Hiatt when he told you to come back. With luck, you'll heal."

I could feel the caffeine working.

"So what's your stance on reporting gunshot wounds?"

"In favor, but I wasn't here, was I?"

"Why *are* you here?"

"I've been looking for you."

My breath caught.

"No. Not yet. Actually, she's awake more."

"She's *better*? You fucking clown! You said — "

"Calm down. Nothing's changed. Nothing important. Steroids finally reduced the brain swelling, so she's conscious more often, but, believe me, that's *not* better. Her heart and lungs are worse. She almost has to *will* each breath."

I stared through the window at the curtain of falling water.

"He who sleeps dies," I said to myself.

"What?"

"Nothing ... Why look here?"

"An agent trying to show the house saw the mess in the living room and called me." He swirled his cup. "That bullet wound ... from the ones who hurt her?"

"Once removed."

"Are they ...?"

"Soon."

Sharfstein made linked circles on the tabletop with the wet bottom of his cup.

"You don't know all that's happened, do you? That *Banner* reporter, the one writing those awful stories — "

"Kuntsler?"

"He disappeared three nights ago from the *Banner* lot. Next morning he and a crack house dealer were found dead on the courthouse steps. Canaries had been stuffed in their mouths."

"Old school!" I guffawed.

"Laugh, Pinel. *You* were the prime suspect. And later that day your cabin was firebombed."

I shot to my feet. "I'll rip Frankie's head off! Did he get the trees? Those trees have been there since — "

"Relax. The paper said rain limited the damage."

I sat again, but my legs were getting jouncy. "Well ... I may rip his head off anyway."

"Sure. He bugs you. What can you say?"

"Haw! Good one, Doc. You're pretty funny."

He eyed me as if the compliment were a symptom.

"If you mean Frankie *Mendez*, he was questioned, but released. Here's the latest." He slid a newspaper across the table and spread the front page. A headline read: *Landscaper Home Targeted in Drive-by*. A subhead added: *Links to Banner murder, Jogger cases.*

"The Guiterrez place in Lemon Ridge," said Sharfstein. "Wounded his son."

"Goddammit! Ramon?"

"Younger brother. An honor student. Ramon has been

missing for a week."

I tapped the paper. "Linked how?"

"After the cabin fire a tipster sent police notes from Kuntsler's computer connecting him to the Fallen Angels and the Angels to Veronica and the 12th Street Gang. You've been downgraded to a *person of interest*."

"So what's the *Banner's* spin?"

"None. They printed Kuntsler's notes verbatim with an apology on every page." He clenched his jaw. "That devil got what he deserved!"

"Winner, winner, chicken dinner!" My mood was bouncing like my legs.

"I wish I could have done it," Sharfstein said, lowering his eyes.

I felt a little sorry for the guy. "C'mon, Doc, if I tried surgery, I'd just cut myself, right?"

He looked up. "No. Not *that* ... not *just* that. I wish — When Veronica came back this time, when she came back *for good*, I hoped I could finally give her what she wanted."

"Came *back*?"

"She never talked about me?"

I shook my head. He shrugged.

"I grew up right next door."

"Wait a sec. She did mention a childhood friend one time. A doctor now. That was *you*?"

"Probably."

I scowled. "You had a few years on her, man."

"Just *five*." When I didn't say anything, he blushed. "Get your mind out of the gutter. Look, we were the *only* two kids in the neighborhood. I didn't make friends that easily. I wasn't a jock. I wasn't interested in cars."

"You could have joined the chess club."

"I don't play chess. And I don't *join* anything."

Like it or not, I saw a little of Hiatt in the guy, probably a doctor trait. Still, I couldn't help but needle him.

"So maybe it was *you*, Doc."

"Of course it was," he said matter-of-factly.

The son-of-a-bitch was about to win me over! He stood and wandered back to the window.

"I saw Veronica born, you know? Her first breath. It's true. I did. Her father was a doctor and I was a precocious, little pest. He sneaked me into the delivery room." He pondered something and suddenly shook his head hard enough to rattle it. "My parents used to say I lived *here*. Pushing her stroller became my calling. I strutted like a drum major."

I saw finally what Sharfstein had found so fascinating at the window. I watched him turn his head from side to side and study his reflection in the glass.

"Were you ever adored, Pinel?"

"You don't think Veronica loved me, pal?"

"Not just loved. *Adored*."

I thought about it. "No."

"I was. Once."

I wanted to slug him again. "Ronnie, right?"

"I saw it in her eyes. This wondrous look. It was ... alchemy! I was tall rather than spindly. Aloof, not shy. My telescope, my microscope were magic wands. My chemistry set? Secret potions. My words? Spellbinding. In *her* eyes I was Merlin!" He sighed, "Smoke and mirrors."

He turned away from the window.

"My tricks worked until, oh ... about the time I went away to college. We were still best friends. But that look? Vanished. I don't know what power over her I lost. I don't think she knows. She looked for it, though. The high school quarterback. The valedictorian. A few college professors, her doctoral advisor. An airplane manufacturer. An author. None were particularly convincing illusions. Without the blind sight of childhood hope, eyes are hard to fool. But then she seemed to find whatever it was.

"Yeah?"

"Yeah. In a private detective."

"Go figure, huh?"

"Go figure."

"Okay, Doc, you've obviously gnawed this bone. Why me?"

"I wish I knew. It might tell me why *not* me. It might explain the other curious thing."

His talking jag was giving me the fidgets, but as long as he was talking about Ronnie, especially a Ronnie I didn't know, I wanted to hear.

"What other curious thing?"

"I'll tell you." He plopped eagerly onto the chair across from me. "You've known Veronica for what? Three years? I'll bet you've never seen a dark time. Well ... probably when your marriage ended, but *otherwise*?" He shook his head. "Because Veronica's natural state is *joy*. Am I right? ... Oh, sure, she cries and hurts and worries like everyone else, but *unlike* most people, she dismisses all that. It's amazing to watch, actually. To Veronica darkness is meaningless because it's always *passing* – just a cloud shadow skimming an eternally sunny playground. I call her — " His smile collapsed. "I ... *used* to call her O.C."

"I don't get it."

He closed his eyes. What he saw brought the smile back.

"For Orange County. *Eternal sunshine*."

"Look outside, Doc."

"C'mon, Pinel! Rain? Just a blip. Sunshine is the *fabric* of this place, a part of us, the part our dreams are made on. You live here so you know that. The poor bastards stuck elsewhere? They hunker down in their winter dark and rail at our shadows. Earthquakes. Fires, floods and mudslides. The cost of living. Traffic and smog. Close your eyes, Pinel. You'll see. We have shadows because we have the sun. And it's *always there*."

I did close my eyes. What I saw was Ronnie.

"Okay, Doc. You get this one. But what's the *curious* thing?"

"Well, you see, *I've* known Veronica for a lifetime. Long enough to witness rare eclipses. Times when she *lost* the sun."

"Over what?"

He shrugged. "It might be anything. Some obvious pain. Or, then again, nothing. Nothing knowable, anyway."

"Yeah, so?"

"So in darkness she turned to *me*. *Only* me. *Always* me. I might hear nothing for *years* and then ... a three a.m. call from Kansas or New York or the phone booth on the corner. Sometimes she was crying. Sometimes all I heard was her breath. Isn't that curious?"

"What did she want?"

"As crazy as it sounds, I think it was to hear *my* breath."

"That's sounds crazy all right."

"Oh, usually she needed words. Usually time together. A few days or weeks. Why? ... I don't know. She's the psychologist, and she couldn't or wouldn't explain. But you're right. I *have* gnawed this bone. Long enough to come up with a theory and here it is. I think that adoration also addicts the adorer."

He nodded silently as if re-weighing the idea.

"Imagine having an *exalted* view of someone. I'm not saying it's the correct view. Maybe it's just a trick, but, regardless, it's there, and all you can expect in return is disdain. So what if, instead, you get special attention ... almost a world to yourselves? Wouldn't you feel a kind of kinship? Deserving, perhaps? Even ... chosen?"

"Are you shooting for created in his own image?"

"Well ... something *like* that. Wouldn't such a feeling be addicting?"

"Hold on, Doc. Let me get the players straight. So Veronica was Eve and you were ... *God?* Wow! That's a stretch even for a surgeon."

"Oh, please! Some detective. I heard you had a knack for reading things."

His reaction shocked me since I thought he was talking mainly to himself, saying things he had told himself before. But no. He wanted me to understand something.

"I'm trying to say that adoration is a drug. For *both* parties. It *hurts* to lose it."

I shrugged. "Living in *any* shadow gets chilly," I said.

"But that's just it. Adoration is *light*. Only when my tricks failed did Veronica begin to feel darkness. Not often – she was good at ignoring clouds – but sometimes it *does* rain. When it did, I think she yearned for that bright time and place *before* her eyes were opened. I think she turned to the last thing she remembered from there."

"You?"

"Certainly not the me she adored. He was gone. But me as a physical reminder, maybe ... a marker."

"Like a gravestone?"

He surprised me by merely reframing it.

"Not *exactly* ... more like a gate she passed through. And if she could still hear, still see and touch that gate, perhaps just beyond ... " He sipped his coffee to fill the ellipsis. "Oh, I don't know. *Something* like that. Don't you have a lost piece of yourself you want to think is still there? *Always* there? Some vestige of it you return to?"

I looked around the empty kitchen.

"Maybe."

"I do. It was that long-ago time *here*. Sometimes I stand outside on the sidewalk and look at the houses. They're different. And the people inside? Even the ones I knew are strangers. But a part of me still holds on. A part of me insists that everything is waiting. That *if I could* go back, I'd still feel what I once felt."

I said nothing.

"When you separated, she called me again. This time she stayed."

"Finally got it right?"

"About as right as you, Pinel. Listen, I would have done *anything* to see that look in her eyes again. I've tried! ... I remember going away to college with a single goal. To become a *real* Merlin, not just tricks. For *her*. And everything since. All of it to make her look *up* to me again, *adore* me again. All so she would *stay* the next time she called." He lowered his eyes. "Hopeless."

"She married you, didn't she?"

"Yes, she stayed. She might have stayed forever."

He upended his coffee cup, stood, and walked to the sink. He stared into the window pane again and shook his head at what he saw.

"But adoration? ... As I said, it's an illusion you have to see blindly. Open your eyes and it's lost. Innocence is bliss."

He dropped his empty cup into a trash can and turned back.

"Is all of this bullshit?" he said.

I gave him points for honesty, and I hated to give him points.

"Not *all* of it."

"Veronica thinks it is. And I know it's a lie, but ... it's *true*, too."

I stood. It was easier this time. Easier to move. It felt good to move again. Pacing, I flexed my arms, my wrists, my fingers, cracked my neck.

"Did she ask for me again?"

He nodded.

"Tell her I'll be there tonight."

"There's no guarantee she'll — "

"Then it won't matter will it. I *have* to finish this."

"It's done, man!" He grabbed the newspaper and shook it in my face. "Read! The police will —"

"When I finish my work."

"*If* you finish! That bullet wound may sour."

"When life hands me lemons — "

"Be serious. You still have a fever. Just moments ago you sounded delirious."

I touched my forehead. Hot but dry. I felt a glow in my belly like heat off a banked fire.

"Leave them," he argued. "Veronica doesn't care."

"Oh, but I do, Doc. *I* care."

I saw Sharfstein grimace and asked myself why in hell he was making faces?

All I was doing was laughing.

Laughing with tears in my eyes, laughing about to choke.

Laughing as if I couldn't stop.

CHAPTER THIRTY TWO

Roaring through Laguna Canyon toward San Dismas, I realized I was hurtling forward with no internal guidance – an artillery shell rather than a missile, a mindless arc of blurred action connecting a trigger impulse to a target: *El Tigre*. Images scudded through my mind like storm clouds. I needed to think. Think or explode senselessly on blind impact.

I thumbed the window button to lean my head into the wind stream. Rain pelted my burning face. The air smelled of wild sage and thistle until I reached the gash carved across unspoiled canyon for the new toll-road. Tunneling through the permanent shadow of two massive overpasses, I smelled only a basement odor of dank cement.

Pills?

Had I taken any that morning? What time was it now?

Time!

I looked at my watch. My eyes were arrested by the promise etched in steel — ALWAYS THERE.

Pills.

I dug the plastic bottle from my coat pocket and swallowed another tablet.

A red flash just ahead yanked my attention back to the road. A tiny Geo had slowed suddenly. Wrenching the steering wheel, I slewed the Blazer into the opposing lane where a speeding Corvette swerved and blasted its horn. I rocketed away.

Time.

Mumbling to myself like a child talking his way through a project, I labored to order my thoughts.

>*I'm on my way to San Dismas. Veronica needs me*
>*at the hospital. Wait, wait! ... First I have to take*
>*care of El Tigre and his Fallen Angels. El Tigre is*
>*... El Tigre is ... El Tigre is ... The Pit! Had Jesus*
>*found it?*

I poked Blake's number on the car phone.

"Pete? Goddamm, man!" Blake exclaimed. "Little Ricky thinks you're in deep doo. He's going nuts."

"I'm fine. Let him know, okay?"

"I will when I can. Tawny can't find him."

"Ask her to keep trying. Where's Jesus?"

"Hidey-holed at the Geronimo, bookoo scared. Something about poking your bee's nest. I figure he's trippin' again, but with you missing and the papers — "

"If you hear from him, tell him to stay put. I'm coming."

"You got it, Pete. And *watch* yourself, man."

I disconnected.

Back when Disneyland was new, the Geronimo on Mesa was a party-spot for tycoons and movie stars who fancied high-stakes poker games. The party ended, however, with a celebrity bash that included a still-unsolved rape-murder. The owner held on for decades, but died heavily in debt. Bickering heirs and assigns, interested only in the acreage, had neglected the place through ten years of court battles. It limped along as a mostly vacant, last-chance flop, next stop the street.

I turned into the entranceway of the two-story, L-shaped structure. A deteriorated portico had long ago been demolished as a safety hazard. The renowned lobby, stripped of its marble walls and gilt mirrors, had been shuttered and a cashier's window set at the Mesa end of the building. I pulled up to a flickering OFFICE sign and shouted at a speaker mounted in thick, green glass.

"Ramirez. Jesus Ramirez."

The clerk shrugged. The Geronimo was a cash joint. Real names were rare.

"Wheel chair. Long hair. Scarred eye."

"143. All the way back," scratched the tinny speaker.

Daytimes the Geronimo was residents only – luggageless, edge of the world drifters, grifters, and druggies who arrived on foot. The long parking lot was almost empty and would remain so until streetwalkers punched in and filled slots with cars hooked from evening traffic. I looped the Blazer around to the far end, doused the engine, and darted through the rain to a fingerprint-smeared door.

"It's Pete." I said, pounding.

I heard a muffled growl. "You ain't dead?"

"Open up, Jesus."

"HAY-sus, you *cabron*. HAY-sus, not GEE-sus." He cracked the door. "Thought they greased you, man. Get on in here. They're watching!"

I squeezed inside. Drawn drapes left the room in darkness except for a bare bulb burning in the windowless bathroom.

"Lock it! Use the chain!" Jesus ordered, waving a foot-long Ka-Bar.

"You'll cut yourself with that thing, man."

"They're out there. I saw 'em."

His hair was wet, his face sweaty. Wary of the knife, I forced his head back. His good pupil was as wide as a manhole.

"Leggo, man. Leggo!"

The muscles in his shoulders and arms twitched.

"You're coming down hard, Jesus."

"Fuckin-A! Blake has Sal bring this C-rat shit instead of what I *need*." He swept the Ka-Bar across a table and toppled a row of untouched fast food bags.

"You say you saw someone?"

"Watching."

I shook my head. "No one was outside."

"I *saw* 'em."

"You're probably seeing spiders and snakes, too."

"I know a Goddamm ambush, Pete. I *been* to that school. The spotter keeps moving, different places across the street. And a black car circling like some hungry buzzard."

I peeked through the curtains.

"Nothing."

"They're there, I tell you! I got myself marked nosing around for your stinkin' Pit."

"What'd you find?"

"*El Tigre* and his pals hijacked a load from 12th Street. The Pit is where they're hunkered down. I make it as two hatches. One's right on the River Trail beneath the Angel sign."

I pictured the spot and shook my head. "Nothing there, Jesus."

"That's the word, man."

"Not on the Trail."

"Service shed? Pump house? Go look."

"In the stadium lot maybe?"

"*On the trail.* That's the word."

"Okay, okay. How about the second hatch?"

"At the Zoo."

"That's a half-mile away!"

"I'm telling you the Zoo. Two ways in. The trail and the Zoo. Different people, same story. That's what I got."

"Well ... *where* at the Zoo?"

"Just the Zoo."

"I need *more*, Jesus!"

"People in Hell need Gatorade! If it was easy, Mendez would have it, man, and he don't."

"You think Frankie's after you?"

He shook his head. "The day Tiger's house got sprayed, two pogues wearing yellow sweat rags tipped over my chair outside the Lucky Seven. Some brothers came running and the little pukes skied. The brothers walked me here."

"Why not home?"

"They had my *name*, man! I ain't showing there 'til you

send somebody a message."

"First I need an address — Wait a minute. The Zoo!"

I had switched the contents of *El Tigre's* Olivewood file to the clean jacket when I changed clothes. I pulled out the packet, licked my fingers, and slapped at the pages.

"What's that?"

"Ronnie's file on Tiger. He was — Here it is!"

I ran my finger under the handwritten words and read aloud.

> *"Final evaluation session: Except for his superior IQ scores, Ramon disparages my findings. 'I reveal my head, but not my heart. Otherwise, you'll keep me caged like the tiger at the zoo.'"*

"Zoo!" said Jesus. "See, I told you, the Zoo."

> *"He describes watching secretly at night as the keeper taunts the tiger with his keys. (Perhaps a recurring dream? Is the keeper with keys me?) Ramon says the tiger is caged because it cannot choose to hide its heart. Choice is paramount to Ramon. The vexing choice to hide his heart allows him more satisfying choices."*

Jesus grimaced and massaged his stomach.

> *"When I ask for examples, he relates that on a night of his choosing, a time when he feels a particular love for the tiger, he will kill it slowly and watch it suffer. Asked why, he replies 'to prove that I can choose.' When I note that, actually, he is revealing his tiger heart to me, he laughs. 'Hidden in plain sight, because Lambs do not believe in Tigers … until they feel the teeth.' I reassured him that adolescent fantasies of destructive omnipotence are common; that despite his ominous word play, he is not really the monster he imagines himself*

and pretends to be. Indeed, his MMPI and
Rorschach results indicate ... "

I skipped through the mumbo-jumbo, saw little else that I understood or cared about, and stuffed the pages back in my coat.

"Okay, the zoo it is. Let's say he *does* watch the tiger at night. How would he get in and — "

"Sonuvabitchin' cramps," Jesus wheezed. He held his gut and doubled over.

I checked the pulse in his neck. Too rapid to count. Sweat dripping from his face polka-dotted his pants.

"You need to detox, Jesus!"

He rocked and moaned. "Ain't going back to no stinkin' V.A."

"They'll get you past this. At least you'll have a choice."

"Shee-it!" he hissed through clenched teeth.

"I'm not arguing. Let's go."

"Ain't going back to no stinkin' V.A."

"Screw this noise. Don't make me carry you."

"Pete! C'mon, man, you can't mean that."

"Put away the Ka-Bar."

He clenched the knife handle. Surrender is something a man weighs and, despite his broken body, Jesus' heart was still a man's heart. I waited for him to choose. He released a trapped breath and stashed the fighting knife in the pocket of his chair.

"Any stuff?" I said.

He didn't bother to look.

I opened the door and maneuvered the chair over the threshold. A rattletrap car hissed by on the rain slick street.

"The key, man!" Jesus said suddenly. "Got a fiver on the key."

"Where?"

"On the nightstand."

I stepped back inside.

"Don't see it," I shouted.

"Check the table."

I pawed through the food bags.

"Nothing here, Jesus."

Silence.

"Jesus?"

Through the doorway I saw him hustling down the long parking lot. His arms pumped the chair wheels with a desperate flapping motion as if he were trying to fly. He had a lead on me, but where could he go anymore that I couldn't catch him? Running was a lousy, *lousy* choice, yet I could see how he might prefer it.

As I stepped outside, a black Camaro screeched to a stop across the street. A hulking kid scuttled from behind a blue dumpster and dove through an open back door. Peeling away in a howling power-slide, the Camaro laid smoking tire-tracks across four lanes, bottomed against the motel driveway and bounced wildly into the rain-swept lot. Pitched from side-to-side, *El Tigre* and two others fought to level barrels through open windows. Shrieked laughter punctuated pistol cracks, a shotgun boom, and a short *uuuuurp* from an Uzi. Caught in the hail of bullets, Jesus cut toward the building. I clawed free the .45, fired twice, and spider-webbed the Camaro's rear window. The car swerved violently and slewed to a stop.

I sprinted toward the Blazer for cover. A barrage from the Uzi sent bullets buzzing past me like bees. Holes marched across the Blazer's fender and exploded the driver's window. I dropped like a base runner and slid feet-first into the far-side front wheel.

Crouching, I fired blindly over the hood, broke for the rear hatch, and peeked through the glass. Shuddering in reverse, the Camaro banged into a beam supporting the balcony. The driver rammed the stick into first and floored the pedal. The car hesitated, then squealed toward Jesus who was bucketing down the lot, his arms flailing. I emptied my gun on the run and heard a scream. The car fishtailed on the slippery drive, but straightened. Glancing behind, Jesus feinted left then cut right and backtracked – broken field moves from a time you *couldn't* catch him if he got a yard or two on you. Smoking tires hydroplaning, the car skimmed by him sideways, powered through a 180, and made another run.

"STAIRWELL!" I shouted as Jesus scooted past me. The stairwell breezeway was too narrow for the car.

Planted in the Camaro's path, I dumped my empty magazine, jammed in a reload, and pocked the windshield with desperate snap shots. Ducking, the driver lost control. The swinging car knocked me ass-over-elbows and spiraled to a stop. Jesus disappeared through the breezeway to safety.

The driver revved his engine as if pawing dirt. Struggling to my feet before he charged, I heard an Apache war whoop and saw Jesus shoot from the stairwell to rush the car. I fired my last round and pounded forward.

Startled by the blitz, the driver wavered. Jesus whooped again as if to draw fire. Tires smoking, the car lunged at him. I saw the handle of the Ka-Bar jutting from the wheelchair pocket and read the play.

"YEAH, MAN! YEAH!" I screamed. "CUT THE FUCKING DRIVER! CUT HIS FUCKING HEAD OFF!"

Jesus flogged his wheels, jinked left then right. The driver over-steered, gunned the engine to correct, and threw the car into another cocked slide across the puddled asphalt. Gauging the car's trajectory, Jesus halted, wrenched his chair backward a foot, and grabbed the fighting knife. Tractionless tires spraying rooster tails of water, the Camaro arced toward Jesus' raised arm like a rushing bull positioned perfectly for the *estocada*.

Afterwards I realized that the parking lot was uneven, somewhat crooked, not on the level. The builder had left at least one small patch of asphalt mounded minutely above the rest. Perhaps he was just a garden variety bungler. After all, an engineering degree doesn't mean that you're always paying attention or that you're perfect. Or perhaps, despite good intentions, he was simply as vulnerable as the next guy to some inescapable randomness in things. Of course, the irregularity could also have been the builder's choice – a necessity of his design that I didn't understand or, for that matter, even a whim.

Regardless, as the slip-sliding Camaro crossed that invisibly higher, but, consequently, *drier* patch, the banshee wheels miraculously found traction. The thundering car yawed, slammed nose-down into the wheelchair and crushed Jesus against a balcony support.

I caught up to the car and yanked at a locked door handle. I smashed the side window with the empty .45 and pistol-whipped the cringing driver. The front seat passenger drew dead-bang on my head and click-click-clicked the trigger of his spent revolver. Fending me off with one battered arm, the driver jammed the floor shift into reverse. The car rattled backwards.

"Get outta here! Get outta here!" Ramon screeched from the rear seat, wriggling to free himself from a blood-spattered body.

"Can't get the —"

"NOW!"

Grinding gears as he fumbled for first, the driver found third. The car lurched forward, almost stalled, then jerkily began to accelerate. Gripping the door handle, I ran alongside, pounding at the driver's shoulder and arm until, unable to keep up, my feet slipped. Dragged a dozen yards, I finally let go and rolled. The car dropped into second, spit water from the tires, and tore away. A wild shotgun blast boomed as the car swung around the corner and I heard the Angels crow.

Jesus lay twisted and motionless. I crawled to my feet, wiped rain from my eyes, and staggered over to his crumpled chair. Runoff from the balcony drummed against the stiff fabric of his open field jacket. His shirt was blood-soaked as if beneath the cloth his heart had burst. I felt for a pulse, knowing I would feel nothing.

Although I heard sirens, I stole a few seconds to free Jesus from his chair, carry him to shelter through the balcony uprights and place him on the dry stairs. I raked his long, black, Apache hair away from his face, squeezed a hard-callused hand, and scrabbled to the Blazer. Rocketing away, I looked in the rear view mirror and saw Jesus framed between the two uprights.

"See you, GEE-sus," I said.

But I heard no reply.

* * * * *

The Newport Art Museum's cinema series had featured a film-noir night: *Double Indemnity* and *The Postman Always Rings Twice*. Neither was our kind of movie, but Veronica was eager for a chance to "examine dark minds under an expert's black light." Her remark was deliberately ironic, of course, and the conversation was fun. Heading back to her place, we babbled about choice and fate, duty and betrayal, men with women. Eager to keep it going, we stopped for coffee and pie at Ruby's Diner on Coast Highway.

We were having a good time. I liked Ronnie a lot and they were all good times. The moment seemed right for my surprise.

I handed her an Orange County Performing Arts Center envelope. She swallowed a last bite of apple pie, dabbed her lips with a napkin, and ran a finger under the envelope flap. Removing two tickets, she beamed.

"Eurydice!"

"Great seats, too."

"Great? Impossible! *Eurydice* was sold out day one. How did you even get these?"

"Broke a few thumbs."

"Why do I believe you?" she chuckled, but looking at the tickets again, she frowned.

"What?"

"Oh, Pete! This is Saturday. I'm sorry. Really, I am, but … I can't go." She spread the tickets on the table. "Saturday is my group night. It's at my place this time."

"Your *group*?"

"My women's support group. We get together once a month."

"Why?"

"You know what friends are, don't you, Pete?"

"Sure. You're my friend."

She smiled. "And you're my friend, too. More than a friend, I think."

"So let's see the play."

"Pee..ete ... I do have *other* friends, you know."

I studied the gutted pie crust on my plate. I only ate pie for the filling. I jabbed at the dry crust a few times and dropped the fork.

"Don't *you* have other friends?" she said.

"A few," I said. "Just a few."

CHAPTER THIRTY THREE

A half-mile ahead was the San Dismas Zoo. A half-mile farther was the Angel A. Somewhere between was the Pit. Pulling to the curb for flashing blue lights racing toward me, I thumbed the eject button on the .45 and let the empty magazine drop into the console. I withdrew three loaded magazines, slammed one home and pocketed the spares along with a few loose rounds. I waited for the caravan of cruisers to wail past and roared away.

I was burning like a falling star. Burning hot, hot as fire, hot as hell. I looked in the mirror. My face was red. I touched my forehead. Hot. My cheeks. Hot. I wrenched at the steering wheel, careened through traffic, passed cars right and left.

A colder part of me warned that I was giving Ramon an out; that I was hotfooting it straight to jail or to a hospital; that I needed to be hot *and* cold. I leaned through the shattered side window and let the rush of cold drizzle temper me.

Joining the parade of Main Street traffic, I glanced right and left down side streets, passed the closed Zoo entrance, and turned at the intersection. The tall, razor-wire topped perimeter fence looked secure. At the corner behind the zoo – a street of Sunday-dark commercial buildings – I turned again and spied the sign of a Guiterrez Nursery warehouse. Racking the .45, I stormed into the parking lot and targeted the only car. Stamping the brake just before I rammed, I yanked the wheel and screaked sideways to a stop.

The Camaro sat abandoned. Steam spewed from its crumpled grill. Across the rear seat sprawled a body. Rain through the open door had washed most of the streaked blood from the upturned face, but neither rain nor Hell fire could expunge the puffy, fresh tattoo: a *boastful* teardrop.

I was glad it wasn't *El Tigre*. Ratboy? Boo? ... A big guy, probably Chaka, but who gave a damn. Let God sort them out.

If there were a God.

Who made *life-takers*.

At the rear of the lot, animal enclosures rose just beyond the zoo perimeter wall. I spilled from the Blazer, crouched behind the door, and scoped the lot for ambush points.

Some must choose.

Clenching my teeth, I eased into the open.

Nothing.

I scurried to the wall and found no shoe scuffs, ladder scrapes, no breaks in the razor wire. Turning in a slow circle, I looked down and noticed a manhole cover missing its retaining bolts.

Of course! A pit would be in the *ground!*

I lowered the hammer to half-cock and holstered my gun. Stooping to grab two hand-holds, I hefted the iron plate aside. I switched on my pocket flash and dropped down a laddered shaft to a four-foot wide storm drain.

A stream of refuse-strewn water coursed noisily through the drain toward the San Dismas River. Bent double, I slogged about fifty yards. Vertical openings showered me from above while lateral inlets gushed against my sides. The water began to reek of manure. Fighting heaves, I felt a strong, draft, and clambered through falling water to the top of another short vertical shaft. I found myself looking though a wide, curbside grate inside the zoo.

Leaning forward to gulp fresh air, I grabbed two grate bars and almost slipped when the bars came loose in my hands. I examined the iron rods in the beam of my flash. The hack-sawed ends were rusted. *Old* cuts. Minus the bars the grate was wide enough to crawl through, but the bars would be impossible to reposition from outside. Ramon and company were still somewhere below. I dropped the bars, took a last clean breath, but froze when I heard a clatter on the pavement.

Passing just in front of my face, a khaki-uniformed zookeeper pushed a wobbly-wheeled metal cart over to a dark, barred enclosure. Unlocking a low barrier fence, he lifted a stainless steel tray from the cart and shoved the tray through a waist-high floor-slot in the bars. He seemed to be talking, although rain and streaming water drowned his words. His belly shook with laugher. He waggled his heavy key ring.

Deep in the enclosure, black shadows wavered vaguely like a shimmery dark mirage, like movement without a mover. Dissatisfied, the keeper flapped his arms and raked the key ring across the cage door. As if conjured, the hidden mover – an enormous tiger – exploded into the light with a silence so startling I almost lost my footing again. Cool and cocky, the keeper held his ground, betting *everything* on his case-ace of steel bars.

I watched him taunt the animal. Capricious gestures, postures, faces, rattled keys. Noiseless, patient, seemingly impassive, the tiger merely measured the width of his cage in padded, clockwork steps. The rippling of his slow, thick haunches recalled the surface of a pool disturbed from below.

The keeper grew bored. Done with his game, he re-locked the barrier gate and moved on. The game, however, was not done. Ignoring fresh meat in the tray, the tiger appeared to consider a choice. His fixed, burning eyes never wavered from the man's neck.

Feverish nightmare images gushed from my unconscious – pursuing monsters impervious to pity or reason. I touched my gun as I might a lucky piece and almost shouted a warning. After all, the keeper was human. Unlike the soulless machine in the cage, he was *human.*

Oblivious to terrors that *might* have been, the keeper

vanished around a corner. The tiger waited, muscles coiled, eyes like red coals. Bound by perception, however, the tiger was unable to conceive a relentless course, as could a man. Tossing his massive head as if to discard the zookeeper's useless, fading image, the 600 pound animal sprang at the steel tray and lighted as soundlessly as the angel of death would light. Finger-long fangs ripped through slabs of dripping, red meat pinned by claw-studded paws. With a rumbled purr the tiger slashed at the meat, gnawed it, nuzzled it.

The eyes!

In the tiger's smoldering eyes my fevered mind saw luminous phantasms like the evanescent truths that sometimes appear in the hearts of flames. I saw Lemon Tom's eyes as he prepared to shoot me; the runt's eyes as he savored his triumph; *El Tigre's* eyes in the newsreel tape. I saw in those eyes a nature appalling – one for which meat given was never so satisfying as meat *taken*.

I saw, as if through Ramon's covetous eyes, Ronnie holding her keys to the ward door. I imagined her naïve *I don't believe you're the monster you pretend* piercing him like the jangling of those keys.

Because he *was* a monster.

Bitterly in hiding.

Lusting to be seen.

A monster and more!

The tiger would covet the keeper anew each day, yet bend to natural order and *present* need. *El Tigre* was free to choose *yesterday* to kill *tomorrow*. He killed by *design*.

What was the Zen phrase? All things, even tigers, are Buddha things, all a part of that eternal story written before we were born?

But a man is *not* a tiger.

A man *edits* what was written before.

And I knew, then, whose awful hand or eye framed

monsters that were men.

Knew for certain.

Knew with the truth I saw in the all the human eyes I had envisioned in the tiger's eyes; knew with the truth I saw in eyes that stared back from my mirror.

Perhaps ... *perhaps* God made tigers.

But *El Tigre* had made *himself.*

I climbed down the ladder and sloshed forward another hundred yards, halting where the drain emptied into a larger shaft from which branched a hopeless labyrinth. Cursing, I poked the flashlight into dark tunnels looking for telltales. Fever-addled, I almost plunged blindly into the nearest opening before a colder, thinking part of me remembered Kuntsler's notes and Jesus' insistence on *two* hatches – one at the Zoo and one on the River Trail. Fire damped by reason, I waded back through the sewer, and climbed out.

Steam from the abandoned Camaro had dissipated. In the back seat what remained of Chaka was undoubtedly a little colder, too. I climbed into the Blazer and stared down at the body. Facial muscles, constricting in death, had drawn Chaka's mouth into a grin – *risus sardonicus* – the morgue boys called it. He looked like he knew a secret.

"Burn in Hell," I said as I fired the engine.

Chaka kept grinning.

CHAPTER THIRTY FOUR

Crossing the wide San Dismas River channel on the Orangewood bridge, I pulled to the railing. Ahead stretched a vast, deserted parking lot. Partially shrouded in sheeting rain, Angel Stadium loomed over the lot like a derelict ship on an empty sea. Immediately to my right rose the dark, Angel "A." To my left were the hospital, Juvenile Justice, and Olivewood, all murky specters save for the blue glow of the medical center sign. On a *sunny* day, however, I could have seen Ronnie's office.

But no ...

She never got that window, did she?

The Zoo, Juvenile Hall, the hospital, Olivewood, The River Trail, Veronica Lamb, *El Tigre*, a place called the Pit, and me – points on lines drawn to intersect where the Angels sometimes played.

Lines drawn by ... ?

I had told Hurley that *'just us'* was less scary.

It is.

I continued across the bridge, found well-padlocked gates securing the stadium parking lot, swung a hard left, and rocked up the driveway of a two-story office building. I killed the engine, slid down from the Blazer, and angled back over a grassy embankment to a narrow ramp that led down from the street to the River Trail. Beside the ramp stood a large wooden sign proclaiming trail rules. Black spray-painted FxAx's had puta'd the rules.

I massaged my stomach. The pain was gone, but heat remained. I sloshed down the ramp to the trail and cut back under the overpass toward the Angel "A."

The River Trail was an asphalt lane for bicyclists and joggers that wound beside the San Dismas River Channel. The Channel – two-hundred yards wide in places – was a mountain-to-sea sump gouged across the San Dismas flood plain to drain the low-lying flatland through an underground maze of sewers, culverts, and cisterns layered like ant tunnels beneath the valley. For most of the year the Channel remained a dry gully. Steep, 30-foot high banks of boulders or smooth cement flanked a floor of sand, cracked mud, and tumbleweeds. During the rainy season, however, storm drains carried run-off from nearby hills and distant mountains through the underground maze and spewed it into the channel from thousands of concrete mouths. Thirty miles of dry gully became the San Dismas River – a churning, grime-frothed, near-overflowing torrent coursing to the sea.

I trudged along the trail directly behind Angel Stadium. My thoughts remained fever thoughts, racing and scattered. A yowling wind lashed my face with raindrops blown horizontal. Beside me, inches from the top of the bank, the river rushed and groaned. Every year a kid or two chose to challenge the vicious current and drowned. Spaced along the bank like sentries were graffiti pocked signposts warning DO NOT ENTER THE WATER.

I found the spot where the *Banner* said it happened – a small grove of eucalyptus trees growing in the shadow of the giant, haloed "A." I knew the place. I remembered a dozen, summer days when two winded joggers had stood listening to sighing breezes and murmurs from the stadium when the Angels were home.

A pleasant place.

A shady rest for a runner to catch her breath.

I looked down. Beer bottles, cigarette butts, and broken crack vials littered the ground.

A gathering place.

A shadowed spot for Fallen Angeles to loiter concealed.

Did God make the trees?

Branches dipped, swayed, and creaked. The wind wailed. Rain-bruised leaves reeked of eucalyptus – a medicinal, hospital room smell.

My eyes swept the slope behind the grove. Like chalk dust revealing a fingerprint, runoff had exposed a faint path trodden through the brush and ground cover. I scrambled up the wet slope hand over fist, painting my face with mud as I wiped rain from my eyes. Jutting from the earth was an ivy-shrouded, cement manhole. I muscled aside the boltless cover and gazed into a black, bottomless pit.

Looking back at the stand of weeping trees, I pictured the scene on a sunny day. I saw Fallen Angels rising from darkness, emerging from the cement tube like young spiders spilling from an egg sack. I saw Fallen Angels creeping down the slope, disappearing into the shadows of the trees. And there, approaching – a jogger.

Crossroads.

Are they but chance intersections in a mindless universe?

Or set pieces designed by a savage God?

I saw Fallen Angels waiting noiseless and patient in a web of verdant camouflage. I saw Veronica, beckoned to catch her breath by a shady, fragrant garden.

Like a little Eden.

* * * * *

Jouncing down the steps of the Olivewood Administration Building, I heard my name called.

"Mr. Pinell!"

I looked around.

"Over here."

I spotted Veronica doing warm-up stretches against the staircase. She was wearing an exercise outfit – white-satin shorts and tee-shirt, anklets and running shoes. Her legs looked great in the skimpy shorts. I liked the tight tee-shirt, too. Of course, she had also looked terrific in a dress the day before.

"Hi, Ms. Lamb!" The eagerness in my voice surprised me.

She stood straight and bounced a few times on her toes. She raised her arms over her head, swiveled, and bent from side to side. All that bending and bouncing had to be good exercise because I was working up a sweat myself! And no doubt, she knew it.

"See? I told you we'd meet again," she said.

"Lucky guess?"

"Woman's intuition."

"You mean I was pretty obvious yesterday. Look, second meeting and all, why don't you call me Pete."

"Ronnie."

"Ronnie! I *like* that! That's what Archie called *his* Veronica. You remind me of her."

She stopped stretching.

"Who?"

"You know, in the Archie comics? Veronica. The brunette."

She tossed her hair and laughed. The sound evoked images of wind chimes and water over stones.

"I pay Fashion Island rates to resemble a cartoon? I'm changing conditioners."

"Not just the black hair. More the eyes. Cathedral window eyes with a look of joyous wonderment."

"Why, you big flirt! Joyous wonderment? You did *not* just make that up."

I grinned.

"A time was, I thought a lot about Veronica."

"And you're not even wearing glasses!" She smiled like someone who liked to play. "But, as I remember, the blonde one ... what was the blonde's name?"

"Betty."

"Betty was the sweet one, right? Veronica was, well, a bit of a bitch."

"Merely eager for life on her own terms."

"Exactly. A bitch."

A breeze stirred her hair. The black strands broke the golden sunlight.

"Only dinks went for Betty," I said. "Real men? Veronica men."

"Then you're a *real* man?"

"Sure."

She grinned. "Cock-sure ... So have you cased the joint yet? Nailed that computer mob?"

"You sound like a gun moll ... schweethaart."

"Well ... I *do* pack a .38," she said with a sidelong glance. " ... Now spill it gumshoe. Did you bust the dirtbags?"

"In one day? Even *real* men gather clues. Ratiocinate."

"My! What *big words* you have!"

"The better to *impress* you, my dear."

"A man's reach should exceed his grasp."

I tried to keep a poker face. "You really are a bit eager for life on your own terms."

She laughed. "Now *that* was impressive."

I almost blushed. "The word means — "

"I know what it means," she said smugly. "To reason. Think logically. Poe used the word in *Murders in the Rue Morgue*. Oh ... and by the way ... I think he was the *last* to use it until today."

"Wow! You *gotta* go on *Jeopardy.*"

"Veronica's Dad was rich, right? Mansions have libraries. Maybe Veronica reads."

"No one reads anymore. I read all the time!"

"When you're not ratiocinating."

"Truth is, I'm more a hunch player."

She rolled her eyes. "Tell me something I *don't* know."

"Okay ... what else do you know then?" I said.

"I know that two unrepentant readers could swap stories about books."

"Perfect! I'll be working here for a few weeks."

"As what? Private *eye candy?*"

"Hardly. Meet your new Assistant Director."

"Ooooo ... undercover work!" Her smile sparkled. "And a head man to boot."

I leaned in and lowered my voice. "The bunch who swiped your computers last week have hit other county offices. The M.O. points to employees. Any ideas?"

"*Cherchez la femme,*" she whispered coarsely through one side of her mouth.

I glanced at my watch, noticed I was late for an appointment, and leaned back against the staircase.

"So ... shorts and sneaks," I said. "Going for a run?"

"You saw my windowless, sheepfold of an office. Lunch time I get *out*. And jogging's healthier than fried pork fat at T.G.I.F."

"Not if you're jogging on San Dismas Drive."

"That's for sure. Too many intersections. But the River Trail is just behind the building here. Out the back fence."

"You run a lot?"

"Trying something new. I'm sick of aerobics classes."

"Probably a Spandex allergy."

She stuck out her tongue. "Jogging, I get some air and I can do it at work."

"So listen. I run too. I could join you?"

"I don't know. Assistant Director? ... I'd hate to put you in a *compromised* position."

"Aren't they the best ones?"

She chuckled. "You're on then. I doubt I can keep up with you, though."

"How far do you go?"

"All the way with the improper encouragement." She tried to look coquettish, but lost it to a giggle. "Actually, I'm up to four miles already. Slow though. No more than a trot."

"Four miles it is then. You set the pace."

"What if I can't make it?" Her eyes twinkled. "I bet a real man would carry me?"

"How about if I stop and wait for you to catch your breath?"

She laughed. "It's not Hollywood, but it'll do. Bring your gear tomorrow and meet me here at noon. Bye!"

She turned to leave but I caught her wrist.

"Wait!"

She smiled as if she knew something I didn't. Veronica smiled that way at Archie. I dropped her arm.

"Hey, uh ... so tell me, why do you exercise, anyway? Women hate to get all tired and sweaty."

"You read that in *Ms. Magazine*, did you?"

I felt awkward. I wasn't used to feeling awkward. "No, but ... I mean ... well, you don't need to watch your weight or anything."

"Maybe I want to live forever," she said sprightly.

"Right! We'll probably both have heart attacks running."

"No. Absolutely *not*. Life can't be that unfair."

"Yes it can," I said.

"But if you try and all, don't you get about what you deserve? In the long run, at least ... Don't you think?"

"The race is not always to the swiftest."

A shadow flitted across her face and disappeared. "But it *is* the way to bet, isn't it? See ya!"

She spun and jogged off around the building toward the River Trail. Although she was gone, she lingered like perfume. The music of her voice, the sunlight of her smile, that look of joyous wonderment.

Her zest for play.

That distinct edge of eagerness for life on her own terms.

I felt a stirring inside me like something awakening.

A warm thing deep in my chest.

About where my heart was.

* * * * *

I lowered my legs through the manhole onto a rung of bent rebar sunk into the cement access shaft. If *design* governed, what came next was out of my hands. I grabbed a rung and descended.

CHAPTER THIRTY FIVE

Within a span of ten feet, I passed from meager daylight through deepening twilight into darkness. I felt smooth ladder rungs supplant the gritty rebar and groped for the wall, but the shaft had vanished.

"Tiger!" I howled above a roar of rushing water. My fever still raged despite sodden clothes that clung like cold, wet sheets. "Tiiigggerrr!"

The shout reverberated.

Hooking the ladder with my forearm, I switched on my pocket flash. The beam revealed a 30-foot diameter cement chamber that flared out from the manhole shaft. Continuous with the rebar handholds of the shaft, the ladder dropped an arm's length from the chamber wall. At six foot intervals narrow catwalks encircled the chamber, allowing access to large and small radiating tunnels, one of which probably led from the Zoo. Tunnels on the first two levels were dry or trickling. Most of the lower tunnels poured or gushed, but some merely dribbled. I lowered myself through a dank exhalation and paused to examine the passable openings. At each level the flow of water increased until spoke-like geysers shot from every tunnel and splashed together in an explosive hub. Aiming my flash through a rising mist toward the bottom of the chamber, I saw a seething, near-capacity culvert that probably drained the channel's overflow.

"Tiger! Tiiigggeeerrrr!"

No answer.

"TIGER MAN!"

Nothing.

Working upward again, I replayed the light over dry tunnels. As my eyes accommodated to the feeble, black-and-white world of the beam, I spied an overlooked marking, and swung around the ladder onto a catwalk. Clutching a safety-chain, I hitched along the grating to a small tunnel and kneeled. Scratched into the cement was a *placa* – FxAx. I drew the .45, cocked the hammer, and wormed into the tube.

Tunnel rats in Nam had boasted that few people could hack the job – that most flat-out refused, regardless of consequence, and those who tried generally froze or went bugfuck crazy. Bugfuck crazy was *easily* understandable – I already felt it nibbling at me. Still, if something *had* been done, I usually figured I could do it, too. Flash in one hand, .45 in the other – just like a tunnel rat – I wormed forward.

Tough from the start, it got worse *fast*. With every movement I banged and scraped my head, elbows, knees. My eyes blurred from tears as well as sweat. I was fighting an uphill slope, too. Muscles burning, I had to keep stopping to stretch out cramps. I wondered how far I had crawled, but my watch said minutes not hours. With no room to turn around and a head full of horror stories about tunnel rats having to *back* out, I asked myself the *real* question: how far did I *have* to go.

Faint squeals, screams, and snatches of demonic laughter whispered my answer. *El Tigre* was *somewhere* ahead. I had to go *that* far.

It was time – past time – to douse the light, but the thought of blinding myself pushed me closer to bugfucked. Only by imagining the ring of light in front of me from the *other* direction – as a target with me at the bulls-eye – could I choose.

When I killed the flash, however, the blackness that engulfed me was worse than I feared, far worse than the darkness of my descent from the manhole into the chamber. Compressed by the coffin-like tube, this blackness filled my nose and lungs like a cold, inky liquid. Suffocating, I flailed, shredding clothes and skin against cement.

Jutting into a cold dribble, my hand recoiled as if burned. Fantasy turned every invisible sensation into some monstrous possibility, but to halt was unthinkable. Either I pressed forward or scrabbled backwards in panic. Probing the tunnel wall, I found the source of the dribble, a narrow-bore, vertical opening, probably a vent to the surface. Wriggling past, I craned to look up, felt a fresh-air draft against my cheek, and saw a gray, nickel-sized circle of sky. Wrenching my face from heaven, I writhed toward the Pit.

My heart galloped from exertion, but equally from a need to see. The urgency mounted like pressure to breathe when the breath is held. Moments from mindlessly risking the flash again, I caught faint silhouettes of my hands against an erratic glimmer. Clawing forward, I tumbled into a larger space. *A lighted space!*

The light was flickering and faint, but sufficient to sketch my surroundings – a wide, steeply-sloped, corrugated-steel pipe. My crawl-tunnel pierced a cement wall that closed the bottom of the pipe. Light emanated from a bend at the top. Unfolding, I found I could stand with my head bowed. Stifling groans, I worked out cramps and kinks.

Nearby voices and squealed laughter reverberated in the pipe and echoed in my head, making me giddy again. I itched to shout names, but sniggered quietly instead like some practical jokester saving surprise for a special treat.

Almost there, El Tigre. Are you ready for me?

I fingered my way up the corrugated incline and halted. Around the bend glowed an opening. Reflected light enveloped me like a wavering flame. I raised the .45, flicked the thumb safety, and savored the clear-cut click of a final, freed restraint. I crept forward and peered down into the Pit.

CHAPTER THIRTY SIX

The Pit was an egg-shell colored, cylindrical cistern, 35 feet deep and 60 feet across. Dead reckoning put it somewhere under the stadium grounds, probably part of a drainage system designed to keep the Angel's field playable. The bend of the corrugated pipe opened onto a grated steel catwalk that ringed the cement cistern near the roof. A hissing Coleman lantern hung from the top cable of the catwalk railing. Bolted to the roof was a large electrical box. Beside the box was a hatchway that looked sealed – no hinges or latch. A corroded metal ladder dropped from the hatchway through a hole in the catwalk to the Pit floor. Two five-foot wide openings at floor-level I took for inlet and outlet pipes since, several feet inside, I saw what looked like the riveted bottoms of closed valve plates. Judging by wrist-thick conduits that ran from the electrical box and pierced the cistern above each pipe, huge motors opened and closed the valves. Despite the rain, the cistern was bone-dry, however. I suspected that it had outlived its usefulness.

On the floor below, three boys cavorted around a makeshift table hammered together from narrow planks. Surrounding the table, four sleeping bags lay crumpled on cardboard pallets. Atop and beneath the table were a second hissing lantern, a camp stove, cookers, drying tins, glass pipes, duct-taped bricks, and several, gallon cans. Two red cans I recognized as kerosene for the stove and lanterns. An unmistakable drug-lab stink suggested that other cans held ether.

From the sealed hatchway and jerry-rigged table, I gathered that everything below – paraphernalia, planks for the table, tools, clothes, blankets, and a truck-load of refuse – had been muscled through the crawl-pipe. If so, the Fallen Angels had occupied the Pit undisturbed for quite some time. Except for narrow clearings around the table and sleeping bags, the cistern floor was strewn ankle-deep with fast food trash, grocery bags, newspapers, stacks of magazines, and wads of toilet tissue.

Squealing, reveling, reeling, the boys pranced through the litter like kids through fallen leaves. The lanterns and candle flames cast monstrous shadows against the cistern wall. The twisted shadows gyrated, merged, and parted as the boys caroused.

"Ratboy. Ratboy," giggled one boy insanely. "You drive like shit, man."

Ratboy pointed a revolver. "You *are* shit, Boo. And I got your Charmin, right here, *cabron*."

Both cackled.

"You see that *hijo de puta, Tigre*?" squealed Ratboy. "Squished his ass!"

"You drive like shit," said Boo.

"Squished his ass, man."

"Drive like shit."

"*Me cago en la leche* – "

"Drive like shit."

El Tigre moved to the table, heated a glass pipe in a candle flame, and inhaled the white fog that bloomed in the glass. Howling satisfaction, he stretched out his arms and began to twirl.

"*Tigre?* Hey, *Tigre*?" said Boo, suddenly serious. "*Listen*! I been thinking, man."

"Are you sure?"

"No, really, listen. What happens when they find the car?"

"You mean the car with Chaka's body in it? The one with

our fingerprints all over?"

Ratboy stopped prancing. "*A la chingada!* It'll bring the cops on us!"

El Tigre laughed. "You think?"

"Yeah, but ... but listen," Boo persisted. "What I'm thinking is, we're still juvies, right?"

"Damn straight!" Ratboy said, scurrying to the table. "Still juvies."

"Worst we get is a few years at that camp in the hills. I hear they got baseball there and ... and *everything*. Just juvies, right? Right, *Tigre*?"

"Wouldn't count on a juvie trial," Tiger chortled, spinning again. He stopped and swayed drunkenly. "Besides, Mendez has us marked. Even if we make it to a lock-up, the shot-callers around here are all Twelfth Street. I wouldn't count on a trial at all."

"*Leche!*" said Ratboy. "Then ... then like *what, Tigre*?"

"Ask Boo. He's doing the thinking."

"Okay, okay, so check this!" Boo said. "We do like a witness protection deal! I saw it on T.V."

"Sure, Boo. We get immunity to testify against *ourselves*. In return for the conviction, the cops set us free. Give us a little money, a house. Maybe even find Ratboy some pussy."

"Mierda!" Boo moaned.

"Wipe your ass! No one finds us here, man. No one finds us till I *choose*."

"We can't *live* in this stink-hole," Ratboy beefed.

"Why would we? We have *choices*," Tiger said, brandishing the Uzi slung over his shoulder. "We'll take the drugs and go."

"When?"

"Whenever I choose."

"I'm down with *soon*, man. Where to?"

"I choose ... *Vegas*! Live like kings."

"Hey, *Tigre? Tigre!*" Boo cautioned. "Vegas *cholos*. They might — "

"Fuck those *maricons*!" snarled *El Tigre*.

"Those *maricons* got *choices*, too. You ain't God, you know."

"*Me cago en Dios.*"

Boo frowned and crossed himself. Ratboy cackled, unzipped his fly, and began to piss where he stood.

"Por Dios!" Ratboy roared.

"Hey! Piss somewhere else!" barked Tiger.

"I got to go, man!"

"Piss somewhere else!" He pointed the Uzi.

"*Chupame la verga!*"

El Tigre loosed a short burst of rounds at the ceiling. Ratboy ducked as ricochets whined off the cement. He looked up perturbed.

"*Que punetas!* I pissed on my shoe!"

"You were pissing on my bag, you *animal*. You don't piss on the bags."

Boo giggled. "We can piss on Chaka's bag!"

"That big *pendejo. Don Idiota,*" laughed Ratboy.

"*Don Mierda!*" chorused Boo.

Boo undid his own pants and urinated directly on a sleeping bag. Holding himself, Ratboy shuffled beside, stood over the bag, and urged out a few last drops.

"You got no *pito*," Boo sniggered.

Ratboy hastily zipped his fly. "Got enough, *cabron*."

"Got no dick."

"It gets the job done."

Kicking the bag into the mounded trash, Ratboy scampered back to the table.

"Hey, Tigre, if we gotta rot in this hole, how about we get some pussy, man? And, like, we bring her here, see? *Here.* Do her for days."

"We're leaving for Vegas."

"We ain't going tonight, are we? Ain't going till you fucking make up your mind and who knows when that is."

Tigre prepared another hit. "I'm not dragging some

pendona through the tunnel. Hard enough dragging all this crap through."

"She'll crawl. One in front, one behind. No problem."

"We might need this place again, Ratboy. Can't leave her here to rot."

Boo shivered. "For sure I ain't coming back to *that* nasty shit, man."

"So we go easy," Ratboy argued, fidgeting. "That's the beauty! If we don't bust her up, she'll crawl out, too."

Boo nodded as if weighing the idea. "Yeah, that's good. She *crawls* out. I'm *liking* it!"

"She's thinking, like, fuck, man! What a God-damned day, but now it's Miller Time. Only ... when we get to the big drain ... " Ratboy chortled and made a shoving gesture. "We flush her! Picture that face, man! All like, wow! So fucking *unfair!* C'mon, *Tigre*. We flush her, it's like she never was. What's the problem? C'mon."

"It's raining."

"C'mon!"

El Tigre paused to heat the glass tube, sucked in, and held his breath. "Tomorrow ... if it isn't ... raining," he wheezed between coughs.

"Now, man!" Ratboy wheedled. "We jack a parked car, then snatch some *puta* off the street."

"A blonde!" exclaimed Boo.

"Bald for all I care," said Ratboy.

Tiger scoffed. "Off the street? On a rainy Sunday night? Great plan, geniuses. We'll bag us a unicorn, too."

Ratboy gnawed his lip and suddenly beamed.

"Crystal Cathedral, *genius*. People always come late."

"Hey, that's *perfect*," said Boo.

"No cops and it's *close*, Tigre. Time enough to tap the bitch's ATM on the way back."

"Primo!" chimed Boo. "Like two birds, right? We're back here before we get wet and then we're all doing her till we're fucking *sore*, man. Till we leave. Only we can't bust her up like the *santarona, Tigre*. Why'd you bust her up like that anyway?"

"To prove a point."

"So, it's proved," said Ratboy. "So this time we go easy. C'mon. C'mon, let's do it."

El Tigre chuckled. "Do what, Ratboy? *Watch*? Boo says you have no dick."

Boo bent double with laughter.

"*Jodete!* I was *Don Fuck,* man! You saw."

"*Don* Fuck? ... *Don Cherry!* Your only time, man."

"*No me chingues!*"

"You can't count your mother, *guey. She* did you."

"More than once, *guey*. And that *panocha hedionda* ain't all who wanted more."

Ratboy stamped through the trash to a section of wall plastered with centerfolds. He tugged down a white triangle that crumpled easily in his hands like a pennant. "You saw, *Tigre*. You heard." Rocking his hips back and forth, he buried his face in the cloth and crowed, "*Both* of you saw. *Don Fuck!*"

Instantly some protective iris of my mind slammed shut, shielding me at first from the enormity of Ratboy's pantomime. But when he lifted the cloth like a veil, a scorching, elemental evil radiated from his face. I felt hard-charred. Petrified.

"Oh, God. Please, God! NO! Oh, God. Please!" he aped. "You both saw. I had the *santarona* praying, man!"

Bursting into a giggle fit, he rooted at Ronnie's panties again and snuffled like a pig.

The rage inside me erupted. Hurled forward, my hand pointed the .45 like a damning finger. The cistern flared with the crack of a thunderbolt.

CHAPTER THIRTY SEVEN

Blasting through the wadded cloth, the slug split Ratboy's head and splayed him backwards into the splattered cement. A convulsive, arched-back extension pinned him upright long enough for me to dart onto the catwalk and shoot him twice more for the hell of it. Boo and Tiger scrambled for the two large pipes.

"Shoot him! Shoot him, *Tigre*."

The Uzi burped and a pistol fired. Bullets and ricochet fragments whizzed around me.

"TIIGGEERRRR! I've come for you." I fired down into the Pit, pumping slugs into the pipe mouths, hoping for a bank shot. Bullets clanged against the valve plates.

"He's there! GET HIM!"

"Fuck you, *Tigre*! You try."

"I'M HERE TIGER BOY! TIME TO CHOOSE!"

Barking, growling, frothing in the corners of my mouth, I scurried back and forth on the catwalk looking for a shot, taking wild shots. BAM. BAM. BAM. BAM. BAM. Firing, firing, changing magazines, firing.

"I see him, *Tigre*! There! THERE! Kill his ass."

Tiger chose. He peeked from the pipe. Rounds from the Uzi whirred over my head and pitted the cistern wall. I dove onto the catwalk, snapped a shot over the edge, and hit the table lantern. The pressurized tank exploded, raining burning fuel like napalm over drifts of paper trash, cardboard pallets, sleeping bags, clothes. Instantly the floor was ablaze. Tiger ducked back into his pipe. I took a free shot at a gallon can that I hoped contained ether. WHOOM! A seething, blue fireball filled the Pit.

Boo broke for the ladder. My .45 boomed. Yelping, he clutched his thigh and tumbled against the table. WHOOM! Another can of ether blossomed into a swirling mass of blue flames.

"*Tigre! Tigre!*" Boo squealed, engulfed

Lurching through the fiery debris, Boo reeled like a dog chasing its tail. He ripped at his burning shirt, raked at his smoldering hair, scratched at blackening skin. The surrounding inferno splashed his shadow against the cistern from every angle. The walls and ceiling were a crush of tortured figures writhing in a lake of fire.

Flaming arms outstretched as if to embrace, Boo staggered into Tiger's pipe.

"Get away, dumb ass. Get away!"

A kick sent Boo stumbling backwards. Charred fingers clawing the air, he toppled stiffly like a tree and wailed as the fire consumed him. The wailing took a good, long time.

Thick smoke stung my eyes and lungs. Hunkered inside his pipe, Tiger coughed and wheezed. WHOOM. A can of kerosene burst and then a second. WHOOM. Burning fuel splattered Tiger's hidey-hole. He bolted, emptying the Uzi blindly as he zigzagged through flaming mounds. A whirligig line of slugs dotted the roof and the large, conduit fed electrical box. The box exploded in a skyrocket shower of blue sparks.

I felt a shudder in the catwalk frame. Metal screeched against metal. Through the grating I saw a tremendous gush of water from the inlet pipe. Tiger covered his head and tried to scream.

CHAPTER THIRTY EIGHT

A thundering wave swept the burning garbage across the floor and quenched the hellish flames. Crashing into the cistern wall, the water began to spiral. Saved from darkness by the lantern hanging from the catwalk railing, I saw Tiger tumbling in the whirlpool. He seized the bobbing table, but floundered against the current and lost his grip. His mouth moved, but the maelstrom drowned his shouts. I holstered my .45 and craned over the railing for a better view. The lantern threw my black shadow across the roiling pit.

"Try to breathe water, *Don Mierda*," I bellowed.

Goaded by the sight of my laughter, he flailed toward the wall. As the whirlpool churned him past, he hooked the ladder and jackknifed to plant his feet on a rung.

"No Goddamm way!" I yelled as he began to climb. "You're Goddamm drowning!"

Scurrying down the ladder, I stamped Tiger's fingers until he let go. The vortex sucked him away, but circled him back. He smashed full-body into the ladder and started climbing on the opposite side. With water over my knees, I couldn't land a snap kick. When I stepped up a rung and swung around an upright, Tiger caught my free leg in his arms. Trying to shake him off, I lost my footing and splashed into the water.

I still had hold of the uprights, but the current battering two of us forced me to use both hands. Tiger clawed up my leg, grabbed my pocket, my belt, and fistfuls of jacket. He snaked onto my back and locked one arm around my neck. I twisted and shrugged and butted my head backwards into his face, but he managed to grapple the rung above me. Releasing one hand, I yanked his shirt and broke his grip. Lunging for the ladder again, he plunged my head underwater. I felt him slithering over my shoulders.

No way in hell!

I opened my fist and let the deluge carry us away.

CHAPTER THIRTY NINE

We tumbled together submerged. Tiger was a scratching hellcat about to drown us both. I wrenched an elbow into his jaw and felt teeth snap. A second elbow knocked him loose. I surfaced and saw him paddling outward to hook the ladder. With a few hard strokes I swooped over his back and pushed him underwater. I grabbed for a fistful of hair, felt the halo headband, and tugged it over his face to his neck. Trying to fend me off, he kicked and wind-milled his arms, but I simply twisted the knotted cloth in my fist and throttled him like a bad dog in a choke collar.

The cistern seemed to revolve around us. Towing *El Tigre* at arm's length, I side-stroked through the whirlpool. The ladder whirled by once, but on the second pass, I snagged it with my forearm. Squirming to plant my feet, I found a rung. With one arm hooked around the ladder upright, I boosted myself into position.

The water was less than ten feet from the catwalk. So close to deliverance, Tiger bucked again. I locked my arm to keep the ladder out of reach and let him thrash. Water flushed over his face and nose and drained through gaps of broken teeth. I craned toward his ear.

"Ramon. *El Tigre* ... **Don Tigre**, right? Can you hear me Tiger? You have to listen. I want you to hear me."

His eyes registered the words. I shinnied up a rung as the water rose to my chest.

"I want you to know ... why you're dying," I gasped.

Holding two bodies against the current again was draining me. "Plenty of good reasons ... for you to die. *Those* reasons ... another day, another way. *One* reason you die now. Only *one*. Veronica."

"Please! ... Please!" Water squirted from his mouth with each word.

I tightened my grip on the band around his neck.

"Veronica Lamb Sharfstein," I shouted, climbing another step. "I know you know who I mean."

"The doctor."

"Not what she did. Who she *was*. Her *name*. SAY IT!"

I torqued the headband, choking out the sounds.

"Veronica ... Lamb ... Sharfstein!"

"She's drowning, too. Any day, any minute, but not before you."

Water splashed across his face.

"Didn't ... know," he sputtered, "Didn't know ... she was yours!"

"She wasn't *mine*. She was *hers*. Her life was **hers**. You took it."

The whirlpool swirled around and over us, threatening to drag me away again. I set my forearm higher on the ladder and heaved upward another rung.

"Please, man! Please! I *liked* her. She was — "

I straight-armed his head beneath the water to wash the words from his mouth. I let him struggle, then jerked him back to the surface.

"Nothing but her *name*, Tiger. *Nothing* else."

I forced him under again for punctuation.

"Veronica! Veronica ... Lamb ... Sharfstein," he coughed when I hauled him up. His eyes were reeling.

"I called her Ronnie. She had weird tastes in food. Cottage cheese with gefilte fish. Yogurt on cinnamon toast. Goddamm *unnatural* stuff! ... She liked slow dancing. She liked American movies with plots and sunny endings. She loved *life*, Tiger. *Life* is good. Life is GOOD! Who do I mean?"

"Veronica Lamb Sharfstein."

"Everything she was. Everything she would be. Her life was irreplaceable. *Sacred.* You took it."

"I ... I couldn't help myself."

"No, you *chose.* You chose to take her life and *waste* it. Now it's gone. Like holy water spilled in dirt. You can't give it back. You can't atone. But you *can* die. That won't put it right, but it's as close as we'll get. It's justice. Who am I talking about?"

"Veronica! Veronica!"

"She told me about drowning once. Here's how it'll go. First you'll hold your breath until you can't and then you'll scream and scream until all your air is gone. You'll want to pass out, but you won't. You'll refuse to breathe water, but you will. And when you do, you'll hurt. *Hurt bad!* But you won't die right away. You'll *want* to, but you won't. You'll be trapped in a hell of pain and fear that goes on and on."

I dunked him, let him wiggle, then lifted. He coughed and huffed.

"SAY HER NAME!"

"Veronica ... Lamb ... Sharfstein. Please! I'm just ... a juvie! I'm just a *kid.*"

I laughed and dunked him again. When I hoisted him up, his face was round-eyed, incredulous.

"You're no kid, Tiger. And you're no animal. You're a man. The both of us, we're *men.* We choose."

I clenched the knotted headband tighter. My knuckles pressed into his throat. He felt it coming.

"Veronica! Please ... Veronica Lamb Sharfstein! I'm saying it! Veronica Lamb Sharfstein! Please, I'm saying it! VERONICA LAMB SHARF — "

With her name on his lips, I stiff-armed him beneath the water as if I were baptizing him. He writhed and clawed. I leaned away from the ladder, pressing straight down with my weight to keep him under.

He held in that last, irreplaceable breath longer than I thought possible. But then I felt him spill it, felt the shuddering vibrations of bubbles through my knuckles gripping the headband around his throat. Maybe he was saying her name as a final bargain or, more likely, merely screaming. When the bubbles stopped, I felt him fight the irresistible impulse, felt his body stiffen until his limbs shook. Inevitably, he sucked water into his air-starved chest. I felt lung-ripping spasms heave water in and out of his mouth and nose. His body arched in a convulsive, back-breaking rigor that jarred my arm like a jackhammer. And then, anticlimactically, he simply went limp. I chose to hold him a while, chose to watch his arms wave passively in the current. He seemed lighter, as if whatever was burdensome in him had washed away. Satisfied, I released the halo headband and flexed my cramped fingers. *El Tigre* – wide-eyed, looking astonished – bobbed upward and foundered as the water took him. Hauling myself through the catwalk opening, I collapsed face up on the grating. Gulping air to extinguish the fire in my lungs, I saw patches of light – reflections off the spiraling water – circle the roof like indolent ghosts.

CHAPTER FORTY

Something brushed my back through the grating. I jerked upright and looked down. The choppy water was already lapping at the catwalk. I pushed to my feet, fetched the hissing lantern from the railing, and stumbled back to the bottom of the steel pipe. Dropping to my knees, I poked my head into the crawl-tunnel, but froze at a noise behind me. I turned, raised the lantern, and saw a gurgling stream of water cascade down the corrugated slope.

Normally, I guessed, the inlet would have closed or the outlet opened, but bullets through the switchbox weren't normal. The backup system was obvious, however, even to me. I had neglected enough running sinks and tubs to recognize an overflow drain.

Water swirled around my knees into the black maw of my exit. Some must choose.

No fucking way!

I scrambled back to the cistern. Ankles awash, I waded onto the catwalk, hooked the lantern over the railing, and scaled the ladder to the hatchway. I pounded the cover. My fists made dull thuds. Heaving against the steel plate with my shoulders, I merely bent the ladder rung. I was trying to lift Angel Stadium.

I splashed down onto the catwalk. Water rushed around my calves. Yowling a curse, I drew the .45 and emptied the magazine into the electrical box.

Nothing.

I holstered the gun and snatched the lantern. Floating debris, log-jammed against the railing, gathered in the eddy where water spilled into the tunnel. The makeshift table, swinging in the current, thumped against the walkway.

A *solid* thump!

I hooked the lantern on the railing and bent to wrestle the table from the water. I rapped the top – sturdy planks fastened together securely. As I pumped the legs like jack handles to free the nails, *El Tigre* bobbed up. Open-eyed he swayed in the eddy. His head flopped from side to side as if to say no.

"Kiss my ass!" I snarled, hoisting the tabletop under one arm. I grabbed the lantern and slogged around the bend.

The corrugated slope had become a roiling spillway. The narrow drain tunnel was nearly submerged. I hoped that by positioning myself in front of the tunnel with the tabletop against my back, I could worm inside and let the planks dam the water long enough for me to get clear. The crawl had only *seemed* forever the first time and the return trip was downhill. All I needed was a few minutes. After that, if the water came, I could hold my breath for two minutes, maybe three. It was *doable*.

I told myself.

The wet, steel slope was impossible to maneuver upright, so I sat. Holding the lantern clear of the torrent rushing against my back, I wedged my feet against the corrugations and prepared to scoot down when Tiger's corpse, spilling from the cistern, tackled me from behind. Sent sliding, I lost the table, but desperately held the lantern. In the reeling lantern light, Tiger's staring eyes, clenched teeth, and water-beaded face coruscated as if some fiery core were burning through. His floppy limbs seemed to clutch at me. Entangled, we crashed into the tunnel wall. The lantern shattered, plunging me back into darkness.

Blindly I wrestled invisible arms and legs. *El Tigre* was a furious puppet worked by the raging, waist-deep water.

Crouching beneath the surface, I jammed my neck into his stomach, sprang up, and hurled him sideways over my shoulder. The current pinned him to the flat wall long enough for me to paw for the tabletop, raise it like a barbell, and sidestep toward the slurping drain. When I felt water rushing directly past my legs, I lowered the tabletop behind my back in an overhead triceps curl, guzzled air, and squatted beneath the water.

My plan was screwed!

The flood-battered planks threatened to dislocate my shoulders and attempts to crane my head into the tunnel were futile. When I re-surfaced, the water was at my neck.

I remembered an astronaut saying that with ten seconds of air left, he'd *think* for nine seconds and then *act*. The general prescription was dead-on, but I never expected to face that *specific* problem. Water at my mouth, I rose on tiptoes and gulped breaths. Going head first was out. The planks would catch my legs. I pictured all the tunnel rats I had ever known laughing at the only option.

Seven ... eight ... nine!

Bug-fucked backwards!

Gripping the tabletop through gaps between the planks, I lifted it from the water and inched around to face the current. Something bumped me in the dark.

"Choice is a bitch, isn't it, Tiger?"

Positioning body parts I wished to keep (such as my head!) directly behind the planks, I stiff armed the tabletop in front of me, kneeled into the water, and lifted my feet. The planks caught the rushing flow, ram-rodded me into the tunnel and slammed like a hatch cover over the opening. My fingers broke free and I felt myself spilling down a cataract.

CHAPTER FORTY ONE

Engulfed in a deafening torrent, I plunged blindly, feet first, belly down. Cement flayed clothing and skin. My head drummed the wall. Brilliant, purple flashbulbs exploded in the blackness.

How long?

My lungs cried for air. Air or water. *Anything* to extinguish the fire inside.

How long?

Abruptly I grated to a stop. Air? AIR! The tabletop had worked, but the stream still coursing past meant that water was leaking around and through the planks. As the mass of water dammed by the planks increased, the table would give way or wash aside allowing a solid bolt of water to rifle through the tunnel and finish me. Chest heaving, I shoved against my palms and wriggled backwards, hydroplaning the rushing stream like water on a water-slide. My hands, my knees, my elbows, my gut, my lungs smoldered.

Hearing the boom of a faraway burp, I stretched out and trapped a breath. I felt a blast of air against my face and a crushing wave that shot me through the tunnel like a bullet through a barrel. Battered to the brink of coma, I held a single thought – *remain rigid*. A leg snagging the tunnel wall would snap backward and fold under. The gusher would crumple me like a spit ball.

Unexpectedly I skidded to another halt. Water washed past in stops and starts. Glancing over my shoulder, I saw a fuzzy, circular patch one shade lighter than the surrounding blackness. With breaths granted by whatever had re-plugged the drain, I squirmed toward salvation.

Spilling out onto the narrow catwalk of the access chamber, I heard a rumbling crescendo. I managed to grab the side chain, but could barely haul myself aside. Water sputtered, surged, dribbled and spurted from the tunnel mouth until, at last, a thunderous geyser flushed out the obstruction. Catching for an instant on the chain, *El Tigre's* spit-balled body flipped and plummeted in the gushing water.

Immobile, except for the huffing bellows of my chest, I took inventory. My long bones seemed intact, but both knees were hideously ballooned. I noted some ribs and a collarbone as *possibly* broken, and *everything* else as sprained and in spasm.

I suspected concussion, too. My head had drummed the tunnel wall with the rhythm of a speed bag, and while I *believed* I had dodged a KO, I knew that I had taken some eight counts. Testing myself, I handled some mental arithmetic and seemed to know the date and the president, but my *thinking* was haywire. Thoughts seemed to waft through my head and pop like soap bubbles. I couldn't quite … the word that drifted by was – *(pop!)* – ratiocinate. I hoped whimsy was a good sign in concussion.

Dopily I listened to the roaring jet that spewed from the crawl tunnel. Something in the arc of water crashing into the far side of the chamber set adrift another bubble. I waited as it floated closer to consciousness. I sensed that it contained … formulas for calculating volume?

What the hell was that about?

Suddenly I was ratiocinating at redline and struggling to sit. The Pit and the access chamber were both cylinders whose volume varied by the *square* of the radius. And while that obsessive, old prick of a 10th grade geometry teacher, Mr. Monticelli, would have failed my answer, it sufficed. The Pit held a helluva lot more water than the access chamber and the gusher showed no sign of abating.

I peered over the catwalk. Earlier the culvert at the bottom of the chamber had looked near capacity. With no flashlight, what I saw was ambiguous, but what I *heard* was a singular command.

Go!

Since my swollen knees vetoed walking *or* crawling, going meant snaking along on my belly and pulling myself arm-over-arm. My left collarbone went immediately from the *possibly broken* to the *definitely broken* column of my inventory. Progress was glacial. Eons seemed to pass. I pictured Eloi lolling about on the surface. Reaching the ladder, I chinned myself upright, but – *waaay* overdrawn – that was it. Climbing was impossible. I clutched the ladder, unable even to *sit* again.

From the roar of the rising water, I gathered I was almost out of time. *Do this thing* I ordered myself, pushing against the ladder rung. My leg buckled. *Goddamm it! If I only had a little more time!*

A scuffing noise drew my attention to a figure eclipsing the gray disk of the manhole. All I could conjure was another Fallen Angel descending the ladder. Bone-weary I wrestled the spring clip of the shoulder holster for possession of the empty .45. Sure to lose my grip if I pawed my clothes for a lose round, I pointed the useless gun and banked on charisma.

"One more rung and you're dead!" I bellowed, thumbing back the hammer. "Toss the gun! *Now*, ass-hat! NOW!"

A flash spilled over me. I squinted at the light.

"Pete?"

"Manny?"

"Put the gun away. You might shoot me."

I heard a shout from the top of the shaft. "Pete? You okay, Dude? You okay?"

"Relax, already, I got him," Manny called.

"How did ... ?"

"Will you *please* holster that fucking cannon! And start

climbing, man. You're about to take a bath."

"I ... I can't make it. Get a rope."

"Sure thing. Maybe Home Depot's open." He scrambled down until our feet shared the rung. He took the .45, lowered the hammer, and jammed it into my holster.

"How'd you find me, Manny?"

"The kid. You told him to look for the pit, so he kept dicking with Kuntsler's computer and finally cut a deal with the Feds to use some hardware. Showed 'em ... I think he called it *molecular surface mapping.* Gotta be something only Ricky and God can do, because the blue-suits soiled themselves. Damned if he wasn't pestering me with the route to this place when the call came in about Jesus and the stiff at the nursery."

"Hey, dudes. Talk to me," Ricky shouted. "Zup?"

"Chill, dude! We're coming," Manny yelled. He looked down. I noticed that he didn't look down again. "It's time to book, Pete."

"Yeah? How?" I said.

"How else? And I'll need *both* arms and *both* legs to piggyback your big ass up this ladder. Can you hang onto me?"

"I can try."

"No mulligans, man. Let go and your next stop is Catalina." Pondering it a moment, he yanked off his belt, ran the end through the buckle, and slipped the noose loosely around my right wrist.

"What are you doing?"

"Improving the odds."

He ducked under my arm and shimmied up between me and the ladder. Gripping the ladder with one hand, he reached around and grabbed my pants in back with the other.

"I'll steady you so you can let go. Right hand first. Drop your arm over my shoulder. Then bring the left one up under my armpit. Slip that wrist through the noose, too, and lock your fingers together."

"Wait a minute — "

"I'll have to let go of your pants, so be ready. I'll use my free hand to loop the belt around your wrists a few times and cinch it. Clear?"

"Listen, Manny, you're making us Siamese twins. I can't bail and you can't shrug me off. You're *all in*."

"Well, in *that* case ... "

"Take a look. That's a *lot* of ladder."

"Would you just hurry-the-fuck up!"

I did.

Manny grunted and strained upward. As my feet slipped free of the ladder, I sagged down his back. Although Manny was a weightlifter, squatting a floppy, six foot-four, 220 pound backpack was not among his sets. Each rung was a shuddering effort. Each rung was a bigger shudder, a slower rise, a longer rest. The math was simple. Given enough rungs, one would have our names on it.

"Are we there yet?" I said.

No answer. Just heaving breaths and perfect concentration, broken at intervals by single grunted words. No doubt the words were linked in sequence, but I preferred to think of them as separate, since the faraway period of a sentence might loom as unreachable.

Ladder ...

    ... Is ...

        ... Filthy ...

            ... Owe ...

                ... Me ...

                    ... A ...

                        ... Suit ...

With the final word our heads poked through the manhole. Ricky grabbed my arms to drag me off Manny's back, but, until he undid the loops, the belt binding my clenched, blue hands constrained me to a half-sprawl over the lip of the access shaft. When he freed me, I oozed over the concrete lip, flopped to the ground, and slid in the mud to the base of the ice plant covered hill. Unwilling to wallow, Manny remained standing in the manhole to gather strength for a decorous exit. His head and shoulders bobbed as he gasped for breath.

I turned to stare upward. Cold rain pelted my face. Muddy rivulets ran against my back. Tall eucalyptus trees rose above me in converging lines. Continuing the lines, the giant "A" marking the Angel's playground towered above the trees like a soaring steeple. My sense of perspective was acute. With my back against the earth, everything seemed to rise in vertical lines aimed like arrows toward a vanishing point shielded by the overarching, unbroken heavens – a massive gray vault like an impermeable containment vessel.

Like a cement bell-jar.

CHAPTER FORTY TWO

Ricky hovered while Manny gave me a field-medic once-over and volunteered that I might live for a while. He said I owed him a truckload of answers and alibis in addition to the new suit, but all of it could keep.

"You need to get to the hospital, Pete."

"Thought you said I'd make it."

"Not for you," he said.

Buttressed on either side, I faltered up the trail ramp. Each step was torture I couldn't hide.

"You can't drive this way," Manny said when we reached the Blazer.

Although the trek had worked some movement back into my knees and I could stand without support, he was right.

"No sweat," Ricky chirped, climbing behind the wheel. "I've had a license since I was eleven."

Manny boosted me into the passenger seat. "I'll hoof it to my car," he said. "Get going."

As Ricky sped toward the hospital, I lowered the visor and gaped in the vanity mirror. My hair was blood-matted and tangled. My face was a quilt of meaty, red scrapes. One eye, mostly shut, was a purple plum. I pried open my mouth. A pain in my jaw hurt worse than all the other pains. In the mirror I spied a broken tooth. A wisdom tooth.

Probing the jagged crevice of the broken tooth with my tongue, I pecked out the hospital number on my car phone. As I waited for Sharfstein to answer his page, I opened the box of morphine from the console and slipped the vial and a syringe into my jacket. A thump-screech-thump-screech racket made thinking impossible, but my thoughts were already so jumbled, it took a moment to realize what it was.

The rain had stopped.

"Ditch the wipers, Ricky."

"Oh, yeah," he said sheepishly.

The page operator connected me to Sharfstein. "Pinel? ... Are you there? Pinel?"

I sucked at my aching tooth.

"Are you all right?"

I eyed the oozing scrapes showing through the tatters of my clothes. I lifted my shirt. Blood trickled from the hole in my side, but blood beat the alternatives.

"Are you all right?"

I *thought* I was, but the question was a tough one. Lemon Tom, Kuntsler, maybe even *El Tigre* ... we all tend to think we're all right. It's a *very* tough question.

Sharfstein must have heard my breathing, because he waited for me to choose.

"I'm all right, Doc, right enough anyway, but, listen, I'm pretty banged up."

"Is it — "

"Yeah. It's over. All over."

"Good," he said and wisely left it at that.

"Can you meet me at the emergency room door in two minutes?"

"Do you need help? I mean, uh, medical help. For *you*, I mean."

"I need a white coat to run interference."

"No problem. Listen, uh ... your friend? The fellow here with you last year?"

"Jesus," I said. "He's dead."

"Hiatt tried everything. He wanted you to know that."

"I do. He's Hiatt." I took a couple of deep breaths. "Is he still there?"

"Hiatt?"

"Jesus."

"No ... no, I'm sorry. Police cases go immediately to the county morgue."

"I'll figure something out."

"If it helps, Hiatt listed you as next of kin. Is that true?"

"Yeah ... we were brothers. I'm pulling in now, Doc."

"On my way."

The phone clicked.

I asked Ricky to drop me at the ER ramp before he stashed the car. When he pulled over, I told him I owed him a lot more than an Angel's game. Looking embarrassed, he grabbed my forearm and held on for a moment with a grip that said things men don't say.

I crawled from the seat and rested against the door until the pain ebbed. All around me, orange streetlights were flickering on. Somewhere in the west, the day had died behind a gray shroud of clouds too thick to make a sunset.

Leaning heavily on the handrail – my body threatening mutiny at each command – I struggled up the ER ramp. Sharfstein rushed outside with a commandeered wheelchair and hurried down the incline.

"My God, man! You *do* need help."

"Not now." I plopped into the chair.

"Your abdomen?"

"Who knows? Other parts hurt worse. Maybe it held together. Who knows."

He pushed me up the ramp. When the doors whooshed open I felt a wave of warm air and realized that all my own heat had dissipated. I was cold again.

"No fever," Sharfstein mumbled, touching my forehead as he jockeyed me across the waiting room. He tried to check my pulse, but I shook his hand away.

"Not now. Not yet. Just get me past these cops."

The waiting room was spattered with uniforms – Orange County Sheriff green, Highway Patrol brown, San Dismas blue – a rainbow sprinkling of tired cops who stood and waited. They waited for sobbing victims, moaning casualties, shackled inmates, and grumbling drunks. They waited for abused children, beaten wives, car wrecks, OD's, botched suicides, attempted murders. Waiting, they chewed gum or took turns grabbing quick smokes. They downed cardboard-flavored, coin machine coffee and sneaked peeks at cop shows on the waiting room TV.

The scene was all too familiar, but something caught my eye. Around each waiting cop I saw a kind of aura. Concussion was an explanation, of course, but the auras weren't the shimmery colored halos that go with brain damage or insanity. Instead, they were curious zones of *relative* clarity, spaces a little less blurred by chaos. I think it was real enough, what I saw. The gleaming stars and badges were tiny night lights in the dark war of all against all – flickers of peace, sparks of certainty, glimmers of hope for pain amid pandemonium for which design was unthinkable.

Waiting cops

Their waiting served.

"It's just us," I whispered.

"What?" Sharfstein said.

"Nothing ... talking to myself."

"Witnesses at the motel got your plate. Hiatt says — "

"Stick to Veronica."

He looked down at his hands. "Suffering."

Sharfstein shoved the wheelchair into an empty elevator. The car groaned upward. My sopping clothes puddled the floor. When the doors rattled open, he jostled me past round-eyed nurses and visitors. At Veronica's doorway, I pushed myself out of the chair and hobbled inside.

"Merciful Jesus!" Leticia exclaimed.

"An accident," I said. "Just a scratch."

"Miss ... uh, nurse," Sharfstein said. "Bring me a set of surgical scrubs and clogs. Also a bottle of Betadyne, a box of 4X4's, and tape."

Shaking her head, Leticia said to me, "Honey, it's all this rain. Can't blame a soul for what happens on those streets."

"An act of God," I said.

My tone must have signaled blasphemy because she glowered and waddled away muttering.

"Use the bathroom shower," Sharfstein said. "Tend to those wounds and change."

My eyes shot to Veronica.

"I can stay that long. She's not conscious now anyway. Go ahead."

Closing the bathroom door, I unzipped what was left of my jacket and dropped it on the floor. I removed my shoulder holster, draped it over the sink, and cranked the shower handle to parboil. As steam began to billow in the green tile room, I gingerly separated ragged clothes from oozing skin, peeled off the clothes, and let them fall onto the jacket. Grateful for the seat and safety rails in the shower stall, I stepped inside and drew the plastic curtain. The hot, needle spray burned my scrapes and cuts like iodine, but I let it cleanse and thaw me until the water around the drain turned from red to pink to clear again.

When I tugged back the curtain, I saw stacked on the sink counter towels; a green surgical outfit; white, plastic, shower clogs; and first aid supplies. Taking frequent breaks, I dried, painted wounds with antiseptic, and taped myself together as best I could. I pulled on the surgical garb, slipped my feet into the clogs, and dug through the wreckage of my clothes to pocket any surviving effects along with the syringe and morphine. Blaming training and habit – nothing is more useless than an unloaded or jammed gun – I stripped, cleaned, and dried the .45, checked the action, and reloaded it with two loose rounds I had found in my pants. Unable to think of *another* dodge, I piled everything onto my jacket and tied the sleeves to make a bundle. I stared into the fogged mirror, cleared a circle with my hand, and combed my fingers across my wet hair. The shower head dripped with a tick-tick-tick sound. I glanced at my watch – ALWAYS THERE – hoisted my bundle, and opened the door.

Devices cluttering the room thwarted Sharfstein's long back and forth strides. I watched his eyes leap from the heart monitor to Veronica's face to his watch to the open hallway door. He halted when he saw me.

"I'll take care of her now," I said, plopping my belongings beside the bed.

Sharfstein turned to Leticia.

"You can go home, miss ... uh, nurse. You'll be paid for the entire shift, of course."

Leticia dog-eared a page in her Danielle Steel novel. "Didn't finish it," she said, closing the book. "You won't need a night person, will you?"

Sharfstein looked at me. I shook my head.

She gathered her things into her large, brightly-embroidered straw bag. The words *Puerto Vallarta* rose above an empty, tree-lined beach where seabirds soared across a golden sun. I wondered if she had actually been there or had simply chosen the bag to persuade herself such places were possible. The large, black lady stood beside the bed and touched Veronica's good hand – not the wrist where she counted heartbeats, but the palm. Her thick fingers rested as lightly as a butterfly. She whispered a word or two, then looked around as if to inventory the room and take with her what mattered. Settling the strap of her heavy bag, she lumbered away.

CHAPTER FORTY THREE

Veronica coughed – a choked run of weak, wet coughs. Her eyes fluttered.

"John!"

Sharfstein sprang to her side. He cradled her wrist in his hand.

"John! John!"

"Your pulse is thready. I ... I'll get Hiatt. The isoproterenol is —"

"No! Don't go ... pl...please."

Sharfstein dropped her wrist. He gazed at his empty hands and stood stiffly. "I ... I don't know what more I can do, Veronica."

She stared. He reached across her body to adjust the IV machine.

"Find ... Pete," she said finally.

"He's here! Look, right here."

He yanked me *Presto* from the shadowed corner, yielded his place beside the bed, and began to pace again. I squeezed Veronica's fingers. She eyed my scraped and swollen hands.

"You ... did your work," she said.

"It was — "

"Should I care?"

"Ronnie! I did it for *you.*"

She looked away. Her silence was leaden. The flashing monitor tallied beats.

"You *had* to know, Ronnie," I said finally. "I wanted you to know."

She turned back. Her breaths were tiny, rapid wisps.

"*You* wanted."

Sharfstein elbowed me aside.

"They've paged me repeatedly, Veronica."

"Stay."

"I can't."

"Stay."

The room held but one chair, Leticia's chair near the head of the bed. The *watcher's* chair. You could sit in the low chair face to face with the dying and hold a dying hand through the side rail bars. You could watch the bubbling oxygen in the jar on the wall, watch the dripping drops from the suspended IV bags, watch the summed beats on the high monitor. You could watch, but *not* control. From the watcher's chair, all controls were beyond reach. No switch, no valve, no button, no plug — nothing within reach but the dying hand. Sharfstein, I knew, had never occupied that chair.

"*Stay.*"

Something in the way she said the word cut the deck I had so carefully stacked. No matter how much I yearned to see things that way, my hunch that Ronnie had spurned Sharfstein because he wanted more than mere Eden was dead wrong.

Ronnie was too selfish for that. Sure, she could be jealous, even possessive, but needy? Never. After all, she turned heads and she understood why. Not just because her looks put a catch in your breath or because you saw right off she was a brain. It was also the way she burned with ideas and wit and enthusiasm, with a kind of mad fire that people were drawn to even if it scorched them. In a lackluster sky Ronnie was a brilliant light who *knew* it. She *respected* herself and that made her not just self-sufficient, but downright cocky about it.

I looked at the inscription on my Timex. In the way that something ever-present can snap suddenly like an optical illusion into an entirely different perspective, I realized that,

just like me, Ronnie would *recoil* from someone always there –
someone who encumbered her as his everything or only thing,
whose always there offered the tedium of a Sunday sitting
room.

Ronnie's world was too wide for narrow people. She
populated it with rare birds who displayed their values like
peacocks' tails. Among her own values was fidelity. A lover
would be faithful not just to her, his *highest* value, but by
degree to *all* his values. While *always there* was something he
would never be, *she* would be a constant in *his* every equation,
a context for his every thought and action, a *consideration* in
his every choice. Wherever he went, he would carry her heart.
She was always there.

"*Stay.*"

With each repetition I thought I saw in her eyes a spark of
blind hope. Sharfstein had called adoration an illusion you
see blindly, so perhaps Ronnie's long-lost look was still within
reach. I imagined a single choice transporting them both back
to that place where Ronnie adored him, and – because he
needed adoration like breath – she *was* his highest value. I
suspected that Eden's gate would swing open if Sharfstein
surrendered all that he had become *without* Ronnie for the
moments remaining *with* her – if he took the watcher's chair.

Some must choose.

"I ... I ..."

He stared again at his empty, trembling hands.

"I can't! I *can't*! ... I can't do this, Veronica." His eyes
pleaded. "I can't just wait. I can't just ... *be here*."

Mastery of craft is intrinsic to a man's becoming. I knew
the struggle and I knew how insidiously those works and days
can become an undoing. Sharfstein's gaze floundered in the
equipment laden room – the oxygen regulator, the chest tube
box, the IVAC, the breathing alarm, the relentless,
remorseless monitor.

"This isn't me, Veronica. I have to *do* something." His eyes seized a device, discarded it, then grasped for the next. His hands opened and closed on nothing. "What can I *do*?"

Convinced that the adoration in Veronica's eyes was a trick whose continued success required ever greater legerdemain, Sharfstein had set out to become a *real* Merlin. Transmuted into an illusion of devices, distraction, and sleight of hand, however, the real Sharfstein disappeared. The magician *became* his magic.

"I can't," he begged. "I can't."

Veronica looked to me then back to Sharfstein.

"Close ... the door."

He leaned over the bedrail.

"Veronica, I ... I do love you. You know that, don't you? I ... I always have. You do know that, don't you?"

"I've *always* ... loved ... " She closed her eyes, perhaps to see him better. "... You."

Hesitating at the threshold, Sharfstein looked back, then nudged the door to release the hold. The door eased shut with a soft, expiring sigh.

CHAPTER FORTY FOUR

The bubbling oxygen bottle gurgled. The monitor cast its eerie, undulating glow. I removed the syringe and vial of morphine from my pocket.

"Do it," she said, looking away.

I heard breathing.

My breathing.

Some must choose.

"No."

She turned back.

"I thought I could, Ronnie. Until this second I thought I *would*."

"You *promised*. Don't leave me ... like this."

"That's what I'd tell myself. That you begged me. That I promised. That I did it for *you* because you wanted it."

"Don't leave me ... like John to — "

"I won't leave you at all." I looked at the words engraved on my watch. "Funny. I had your inscription wrong the whole time, but I get it now. And the thing is, Ronnie ... you *were* always there. From the moment I met you. Even *before* I met you, if you can understand that. You were *always* there in the thoughts and feelings that guided my every choice. I guess it didn't show. Or maybe you missed it. And I can see how the Four to Four was hard for you to reconcile, but ... " I shrugged. "You *were* always there. And you're with me now. *Here*. I'll wait."

She groped for the syringe, fumbled at it.

"I understand. More than you know. If *you* can't wait, make the choice. I'll *still* be here."

"Can't ... fill it. Can't reach — "

I swept up the vial. "This drowns you *faster, but you* drown. If you really want an end, make a sunset."

I stooped to untie my bundle of wet clothes, buried the syringe and morphine in an intact jacket pocket, and removed the .45. I pumped the slide to chamber the first round. If the trigger were pulled, the last was automatic.

"Here's *fire*, Ronnie. Fire and darkness together. I'll stay with you whatever you choose. But *you* have to choose. It's the only way to know."

I placed the gun backwards in her good hand, molding her fingers around the handle to disengage the grip safety. Arm quivering against the weight of the pistol, she raised it to her pillow.

"You won't ... save me?"

"I can't."

"I'm drowning!"

"I know."

"You said — "

"I know."

She faced the barrel – a black hole that would swallow the universe.

"What ... do I do?"

"Choose."

Her thumb found the trigger. I stood as rigidly upright as a stacked domino. The monitor was a flicker in her eyes. My pounding heart paced the flicker.

Pounding in my ears!

Pounding!

"No!" she gasped, releasing the trigger. " ...No ...No ... "
She began to weep. "Life ... is ... good."

I leaned forward, lowered the hammer to half-cock against my thumb, slipped the gun from her open fingers and stuffed it back in my bundle. I sat, took her hand through the side rail bars, and waited in the watcher's chair.

"I'm … afraid, Pete. I don't … want — " She clutched my hand with all her remaining strength. "I don't want to be *alone*."

I enclosed her hand with my other hand and held on through a bleak caesura I *thought* said everything until – in the way a single, penetrating sunbeam refutes the lies of clouds – the wispy trace of her chuckle pierced the dismal silence.

"What a … God-damned … drama queen … " she snorted. "Dying wish? … An *audience*."

I closed my eyes to see her look of joyous wonderment, her greedy, laughing cathedral window eyes through which poured eternal sunshine.

Something gripped my throat until it seemed the pressure would burst my heart.

"I'm here," I said. "I'll wait with you while you catch your breath."

CHAPTER FORTY FIVE

I held her hand and waited. Sharfstein returned two hours later.

"I'm waiting," I said to his unasked question. "We can both wait, you know. She wants you here more than me."

I stood to offer him the watcher's chair.

Sharfstein shook his head – more a shudder, really – and busied himself with his devices.

"Can we lose the noisy ones?" I said.

He flipped several switches. The monitor screen went blank.

"Thanks," I said, turning, but he had vanished.

Nurses came and went. They asked me to go when they changed her bedding, but I didn't, and no one pushed it. When Veronica could, we talked. Mostly *I* talked, but sometimes she replied with a look, a whispered word, a frail squeeze of my fingers. Between the lucid moments stretched fitful intervals of something like sleep. The intervals grew longer like shadows near sunset, but, toward morning, she woke and together we watched the dawn.

In the eastern sky sunrise gilded billowing white clouds and painted a rainbow above Saddleback. The western horizon was perfectly blue, washed clean of haze – as clear as pure water. Jutting in crystalline relief from its sparkling perimeter of ocean, looking close enough to touch, Santa Catalina Island seemed verdant and unsullied, like a sunlit paradise, like some protected garden you want to believe is fresh and evergreen.

Faithfully around seven, Hurley made his rounds. He peered into Veronica's half-open eyelids with a pencil flash and sighed.

"She's gone," he said solemnly.

I gazed through the window at the illusion outside. Catalina was, in reality, a faraway, craggy, desert place – mostly barren hills spotted with dry sage. The warm, surface sparkle of the Pacific belied a dark, icy abyss. And blue sky? ... For a heartbeat, perhaps, because hidden below the horizon were legions of leaden clouds advancing rank on rank. It was only November. The rainy season had just begun.

"She's gone, Mr. Pinel," Hurley repeated.

"Yes," I said, still holding her hand. "Yes ... I know."

* * * * *

Passing through the Olivewood lobby, I heard someone laugh. It was an eager, greedy, self-indulgent laugh unencumbered by guilt or fear or pain – deadweight feelings I knew *far* too well. The sound tickled me. Laughing a little myself, I stopped and looked around.

Behind the lobby carrousel, the Olivewood receptionist – a vacant, joyless, blue-eyed blonde – popped her gum and studied a *People* magazine. From nearby offices spilled the empty jabber of clerks, a sound as meaningless to me as Greek. Outside the building a clattering jackhammer gnawed away at something old and once thought permanent.

I heard the laugh again and traced it to a bright, open door at the end of a short, dark hallway. A pint-sized brunette sat lounging back in a swivel chair. Hands behind her head, she hugged a telephone receiver between her ear and shoulder. Her nylon-stockinged feet, crossed at the ankles, were propped atop the desk. The hem of her white, silk skirt had worked its way up her thighs. *Nice* thighs. She noticed me watching from the doorway and wiggled her toes.

"There's a man ogling me, Karen. Should I see what he wants?"

She laughed at the reply, cradled the phone, and insolently resumed her pose.

"What *large* eyes, Grandma!" she said.

"The better to see you with."

"*I'm* up here, big guy," she said, pointing at her face. "So *you* must be a leg man."

"Feet," I said. "I'm into feet. You know, shoe catalogs and stuff. Yessiree! Feet are the ticket, especially really *large* feet."

"Interesting ..." she chuckled. "First time at a new playground and our boy jumps right up on the scary see-saw. *Rara avis.*"

"That's me alright – one rare bird."

"It's also translated as *strange* bird, sweetie." She dropped her feet to the floor. "So, what can I do for you ... Pinel's the name, isn't it?"

"*Pete* Pinel."

"Veronica Lamb."

"Hello, Veronica."

Her eyes twinkled. "Hello ... MR. Pinel."

She was playing with me. I liked to play.

"Quick," I said. "And a scrapper. *Ring* material."

"Proposing so soon?"

I laughed. "Different kind of ring."

She placed a hand on her waist. "Is *this* the body of a boxer?"

"Well ... I was thinking Sumo."

"That's it!" she said, reaching for the phone. "I'm calling security and you WILL be Maced."

"I'm blinded already," I said.

We both laughed.

"How'd you know my name? We haven't met. I'd remember."

"Why belabor the obvious?" she said. "Actually I was eavesdropping at the coffee pot a few minutes ago and someone mentioned a new guy named Pinel who looked sort of... " She milked a pause. " ... *Rara*. I also knew the Director was talking to a P.I. about our stolen computers. Voila! ... You wuz made, shamus!"

"Nice Sam Spade impression," I said grinning. "Or have you done time?"

"Nine to five. A little off for bad behavior."

My grin seemed to be stuck in drive, but I slammed on the brakes.

"Damn! This case was starting to interest me."

"Relax Pimpernel. Your secret identity is safe. Most people lack my nose for clues."

"*You're* a detective, too?"

"A psychologist. But that makes me a keen judge of ..." I caught that little glint in her eyes again. "...*Characters.*" She bent to retrieve her shoes from the knee well of the desk. "So. Will you find 'em?"

"The computers?"

"The *bad guys.* Isn't that what it's all about — good guys and bad guys?"

"Pretty much."

"And the good guys always win, right?"

"Maybe. Maybe not ... Depends on what you count as winning."

"This little visit here ... " She slipped into the expensive black and white heels. "Do I need a lawyer? Are you interrogating me?"

I watched her point her toes and make a show of straightening her stockings.

"Hah! *I* might need the lawyer. *You're* interrogating me, and I'd say you always get your man."

"Maybe. Maybe not," she said. "Depends on what you count as getting."

We laughed again.

"Fact is, I was passing by and heard that laugh of yours. I was curious."

"About the snorting? Everyone mentions the snorting."

"Well, of course, *that!*"

She chuckled. Sure enough I heard a little snort.

"Nooo ... the **joy!**" I exclaimed. I mulled it for a moment and shrugged. "Funny ... I guess I just needed to see *someone* who could laugh like that."

"... Needed? ..."

When our eyes met – almost as if I could see it reflected in her gaze – I realized just how much her sound of joy had meant to me.

"Okay ... *needed,*" I said. "As in thirsty, okay? See? I'm confessing already."

"What? Confessing what?"

"Too much."

She knew. She grinned.

"Well, anyway ... thanks for the laugh," I said.

"Anytime. How about a Memorex to take with you?"

I tapped my head. "Made one."

"So ... until we meet again?"

Another time or place I might have turned somersaults for her, or walked a fence or balanced a straw on my nose. But clever was good, too, so I tried to sound clever. "No one knows what was written before we were born," I said.

"Dee..p!" she drawled. "You've watched *every* Charlie Chan movie, haven't you?"

My own laugh – saddled with a foolish weight I accorded sorrow – lacked her joyous lilt, but with her example, it was closer ... close enough perhaps to sustain a dry man in a bad land.

Her phone rang. She cocked her head and gave a little pout.

"Well ... if I *don't* see you again, Pete Pinel, good-bye."

I seized one last, long look at her before I turned back to my affairs.

"Good-bye, Veronica Lamb."